WINE AND ROSES

Penniless and alone in the world, Coriander knows that life must have more to offer than drudgery in a Cornish orphanage and fending off the unwelcome advances of unscrupulous Ezra Follett. As though in answer to her prayers, Ralph Beringer, newly returned from the Napoleonic Wars, brings news that his father's wine business now belongs in part to Corrie. Under the terms of his father's will, whoever makes the most profit from their inheritance in a year will win control of the company. The battle commences—but is there more than money at stake?

WINE AND ROSES

WINE AND ROSES

by
Freda Lightfoot

Magna Large Print Books
Long Preston, North Yorkshire,
England.

British Library Cataloguing in Publication Data.

Lightfoot, Freda
  Wine and roses.

  A catalogue record for this book is
  available from the British Library

  ISBN 0-7505-1400-0

First published in Great Britain by Severn House Publishers
Ltd., 1998

Magna Large Print is an imprint of
Library Magna Books Ltd.
Printed and bound in Great Britain by
T.J. International Ltd., Cornwall, PL28 8RW.

HISTORICAL NOTE

While this is a work of fiction, all the facts given about Napoleon Bonaparte are as correct as I can make them. On 22nd August, 1815, bound for exile to St Helena aboard the British ship, *HMS Northumberland,* Napoleon called into Funchal Bay on the island of Madeira. Facing a grim prospect ahead of him, he asked for books, fruit and wine. The British Consul, Henry Veitch, sent him a cask of the 1792 and payment was made in gold coins which were later laid within the foundations of the English church. Napoleon never managed to escape from exile, and after his death in 1822 the wine was returned unconsumed, probably due to his gastric ailments. It had naturally improved with keeping and was bottled and sold for a good price. The Beringer family and wine company in this story bear no relation to any family or company, alive or dead, in Madeira.

CHAPTER ONE

The rider sat pensively listening upon the bay horse, knuckles clenched overtightly upon the reins. Violet eyes behind the velvet mask narrowed with concentration on the country lane blending into darkness below.

The horse nickered, shifting its feet and tossing its head with sudden restlessness. As the sound of approaching hoofbeats reached the rider's ears too, the wide mouth lifted into an impulsive smile of satisfaction.

'So we are to strike lucky after all, Pye.' An answering quiver rippled through the horse's flanks, revealing it had read the signals of excitement in its rider and was eager to be away. 'Stand, boy. Hold till I say.' The kid-gloved fingers curled firmly upon the reins, shortening them still further to hold the animal in check.

Stars winked in the clear April sky, while trees like swaying ghosts poked black bony fingers up into the deep blue canopy. Rider and horse waited as one, completely motionless.

Vibrations from the oncoming hoofs now

registered with every other night creature and all seemed to grow still. Even the night breeze rifling through the new grasses held its breath. The only movement was that of a tiny shrew blindly scurrying homeward perilously close to the waiting animal's great feet.

'Timing is all important, Pye.' Move too soon and the unsuspecting victim would be warned. Delay too long and an easy escape could be affected. One fine-boned hand slid silkily over the glossy coat, soothing, gentling. 'Not yet. Not yet.'

The hoofbeats were growing louder, vying with the creak and clack of carriage wheel and spring. Yes, a small vehicle indeed. As expected. The sickle moon hanging low in the sky lent insufficient light to identify the vehicle as yet, nor those that lay in wait for it, praise be. But the smile widened with anticipation. It was he. No doubt of it. Bowling self-righteously along, fat pocketed and skinny-hearted. The night's adventure would not then be wasted.

'This will be the best caper yet. We'll set him in his place at last, and do ourselves some good at the same time.'

The carriage was almost upon them. Booted heels dug into the glistening flanks and the horse sprang forward, clattering out on to the open lane directly into the path of the oncoming vehicle. The very air seemed charged with excitement.

'Stop.' The voice rang out clear in the still night. 'Hold, or I empty my pistol into your head.'

Brakes screamed, harness jangled, and two perfectly matched greys skittered to a lathering halt, snorting their furious protest to the heavens. Contrary to plan, the highwayman was compelled to retreat a pace or two as the flying vehicle lurched sideways, its momentum carrying the huge yellow wheels right off the road and into the muddy ditch.

'By the oath, what is this?'

With a click of the tongue the highwayman's horse was urged forward. 'Hand me your purse and watch.'

'I do not carry a watch.' The reply came in a low growl and for a second the pistol quavered the slightest degree.

You are not he. The words almost popped out of their own volition but some instinct, survival perhaps, held them back. The single occupant of the doomed curricle, though by no means the gentleman he appeared if the oath he now emitted was anything to go by, was as unlike the intended victim as he could possibly be. Even so, it was too late now to retreat. The deed must be concluded, for good or ill.

'Your purse, then.' The gloved hand stretched out, flicking impatient fingers. 'Make haste, I have not all night.' Eagerly the highwayman leaned across the spinning wheel, anxious to get the business done with.

'And if I refuse?'

Violet eyes widened in astonishment. What uncommon bad luck that this fierce-eyed stranger should happen along this particular private road at this precise moment. He seemed almost too large for the low sporting vehicle. Poised on the edge of the leather seat, he looked for all the world like some wild animal about to pounce. The grip upon the stalwart weapon tightened.

'You are either brave or a fool to challenge the pistol, sir.'

'Or perhaps both,' came the deceptively soft reply.

As the weight of a satisfactory purse filled the ready palm, the highwayman breathed again. Perhaps too much pity should not be lavished upon this unsuspecting victim after all. He might well be another such as Ezra Follett who fed himself like a carrion crow from the mouths of babes. Experience had proved that riches usually went hand in hand with dishonour.

A stray cloud blotted out the moon,

and the world went black. And in that instant a band of steel fastened itself inexorably around the vulnerable wrist, pulling it relentlessly forward. But almost as swiftly, the long nose of the pistol was brought into direct contact with one lean cheek, imprinting its violent promise just below the prominent cheekbone.

'Pull me from my horse, sir, and I'll take your jawbone with me.'

The grip at once loosed its hold, likewise the errant cloud mimicked the action by abandoning lady moon. Then one large hand snaked out and the velvet mask was whipped from its place, leaving violet eyes gazing mesmerised and unprotected into swirling green, dark with anger.

'By all the saints!'

Then the hat followed the mask to be trodden into the mud as slithering hoofs turned to flee.

Raul Beringer watched in open-mouthed astonishment as the silver halo of hair vanished into the rising night mists. Had he indeed witnessed a spectre, or was it an altogether different creature who had lightened his pocket this night?

Letitia Larken's hand froze on its journey for a second slice of buttered tea-bread as she gazed in dismay at her handsome visitor.

'Coriander May? An inheritance? Can you be serious?'

'Never more so. Though there are conditions attached,' he said grimly.

'Well, what a surprise. We thought there was no ...' Letitia cleared her throat then gave a little laugh. 'Whatever will Mr Follett say? She is not an easy child, you see. There is a sweetness to her nature, do not mistake me. But to be perfectly honest with you, Mr Beringer, she disguises it most artfully. There is a certain wildness to her character. Mr Follett, I fear, claims she is nothing but a trouble-maker.'

Raul Beringer leaned back in the hard chair with a sigh and regarded the small fluttery woman opposite with patient interest. 'If she is indeed trouble I should have thought the trustees would be glad to be rid of her.'

Childlike eyes stretched wide, unfolding the soft creases in the round face, surprising him by revealing a hint of once pretty features.

'Oh, but she is so useful. With the younger ones, you know.' A small frown dimpled the brow between forget-me-not eyes. 'And staff are so unreliable that Mr Follett is in sore need of the older girls to help. We are but a charity. Our funds are low.' She smiled at him, hoping he would take the hint, for he seemed to be

14

a very well-placed kind of gentleman. A donation would be useful and it might help considerably to placate Ezra.

'I have no wish to deprive Mr Follett of what is rightfully his, but tell me, Mrs Larken, what form does Coriander May's "trouble" take?'

Letitia firmed her lips with a downturn of disapproval. 'I am afraid she can be a wilful, rebellious girl, Mr Beringer. We have had her since she was a babe-in-arms, so none knows her better. Prone to tantrums as a child, now that she is a young woman she is independent to a fault. If she is requested to do one thing, she does the precise opposite. Sometimes I quite despair.'

'I see.'

Letitia looked vaguely anxious. 'She would very much have benefited from a normal family upbringing. Besides which, she and Mr Follett do not get on. A clash of personalities, I suppose. But I like to think that she looks upon me as a friend.'

'I am glad to hear it. Everyone needs a friend.'

The blue eyes grew inquisitive. 'And you did not know of her existence until now, until your poor dear father's death?' Her voice was breathless with wonder and curiosity.

'That is of no consequence.' She could

15

hear his teeth grinding together, and, knowing he lied, sensed a mystery and her avid curiosity quickened.

'Are you certain that it is she?'

Raul Beringer stirred restlessly on the too low chair, not quite knowing where to comfortably place his long legs. He was beginning to suspect the silly woman of prevarication. Nothing at the moment was going to plan. He had intended to have the matter settled by now and be on his way again. That he, who had fought in the long Napoleonic war, should be routed by a chit of a highwayman and now blocked by a stubborn, chatterbox of a woman was trying his patience to the utmost.

'If, as you say, she was brought to you by a Captain Benson after surviving a shipwreck in the South Atlantic, it could be none other. My father was clearly convinced of her authenticity.'

'Rather too much excitement for one so young,' prattled Letitia.

'A tragedy, indeed. Did you never think to enquire about her parents?'

A crumb lodged in Letitia's throat. It was some moments before she could speak. 'Her parents were assumed drowned.'

'And the rest of her family?'

Letitia nibbled thoughtfully upon her lower lip. A nervous gesture Raul did not fail to observe. 'I believe Captain Benson made an effort to trace them, but failed. Do try a piece of the angel cake, will you not? It simply melts in the mouth.' She would try a sliver herself. It had only been fish for supper, after all. And she was not feeling at all herself.

Raul Beringer ignored her offer. 'I should very much like to see her.'

'Oh, I do not think that is possible. It is very late,' she flustered. 'Besides, I can do nothing without Mr Follett's express permission. He is most pernickety about such matters.' Letitia enunciated each consonant with special emphasis for she felt suddenly beset by panic. Ezra could make things most uncomfortable if she did not defer to him in all things. 'And for some reason he has not yet arrived this evening, which is most unusual,' she apologised.

Raul gave a wintry smile. 'Perhaps he too has been waylaid by our friend in the velvet mask.'

Her hand flew to her mouth. 'Oh, my, oh, dear. Do you think so? You did not tell me the whole story of your hold-up. Was it the most terrifying experience imaginable?'

Raul cleared his throat noisily. 'It was inconvenient. I shall be forced to prey upon your good nature for a day or two while the axle is replaced.'

Letitia's hands flew up in the air in a way which would have been becoming in a younger woman but in her seemed false and strangely agitated. 'We shall be delighted, delighted to have you.'

'At least it will allow me time to speak with Coriander and make the necessary arrangements.'

She nodded anxiously. 'Indeed, indeed.' This visitor was most disturbing, coming along so late at night with his strange tales of a hold-up, and of an inheritance. 'What a worrying day it has been. First the children choose to be more vexingly naughty than usual, then you are accosted by a highwayman when none has been seen in these parts for years, not since before that awful little Napoleon started the dreadful war which I am sure we are all most thankful to see the back of. Why, you might have been killed.'

Raul Beringer sighed. 'You need not concern yourself, Mrs Larken, on that score, for you see me here before you perfectly well.'

'You must understand, I am only the warden in this orphanage, Mr Beringer. As chairman of the trustees, Mr Follett holds the real power. It is to him you should direct your questions.' She jiggled forward in her seat. 'Though if you should care to confide the nature of this—ahem—this

18

inheritance and how you plan to administer it, I would be delighted to advise you how best to approach Mr Follett. He can be a mite unpredictable, you see, on first acquaintance.' She raised a pair of plucked brows in expectant invitation.

She reeled slightly before the grim, green-eyed glare and glanced nervously at her best china cup held so tightly within that great tanned fist; she was certain it was about to be crushed to pieces. Had she gone too far? She gave a slight cough and a flicker of a smile. 'More tea, Mr Beringer?'

A long moment's pause and then the sudden fierceness seemed to evaporate as if it had never been and the cup was held out to her, the brilliance of those same eyes now melting her with their glowing charm. 'You are most kind. If you look after your residents half so well as you do your guests, I doubt the young Miss May will wish to leave.'

Letitia Larken simpered girlishly. What a strikingly handsome man he was with his sun-bronzed complexion and hair so black, though perhaps a little overlong for true fashion. But such a face. Noble and aristocratic, yet clearly one which had experienced life.

She sought refuge from her embarrassment by thrusting a plate of griddle scones beneath his chin, asking in tremulous tones if he should care to try one since they were freshly made that morning, or did he perhaps require anything else?

Setting aside the fragile cup untouched, Raul got to his feet, uncoiling with an athletic grace which mesmerised her. What a magnificent figure of a man. She gazed up at him transfixed, taking in the broad shoulders, the lean waist, the powerful magnetic quality of his smile which was clearly meant to dazzle. She gave a small, shivering sigh. If she were but twenty years younger.

'Perhaps it would be best if we were to continue this discussion in the morning, when all the relevant parties are present.'

'Relevant ...?'

'Parties. Coriander herself and, of course, Mr Follett.' Again the dazzling smile showing a soul-destroying display of white teeth. Even dear Ezra did not own such an asset. Letitia snapped her wandering thoughts to attention.

'Oh, but of course. An excellent notion. Why did I not think of it myself? Mr Follett will know best how to explain matters to you. We could not think of letting Coriander go.' She slanted a cautiously wicked glance in Raul's direction. 'And with a strange gentleman. We could never allow such an impropriety.'

Raul Beringer drew in a deep breath

20

and gave a small inclination of his head. 'I welcome your caution, Mrs Larken. It shows that my father's ward has been kept in safe hands all these years. But I trust that on the morrow I shall be well able to reassure you of my credentials and that I am a more than trustworthy person to take over your role of guardian to this child. Though I can see, I shall have great difficulty in emulating your gentle care.' Painfully aware of his unaccustomed and inadequate attempts at flattery, he was astounded to find it meeting its mark as Letitia Larken flushed to the roots of her frizzled hair like a young girl. 'In the meantime, I wonder if I might call it a day and retire to my room?'

She jumped to her feet, scattering a shower of crumbs on to the carpet. 'Indeed, yes. I shall see to it at once. You must have had an even more trying day than myself, which I do not hesitate to confess has been more than usually vexing.'

Raul was not unaware of the generosity of such an unselfish thought. 'You are most kind.'

'We always keep one or two rooms ready for unexpected guests. This was my parents' house once, you know, and Mama was always most particular about such matters.' Letitia issued a sad smile. 'They are long departed now, of course, and the world is not what it was or I would not be forced to earn a living in such a manner. But there, we can at least keep our standards high, can we not, Mr Beringer?'

He inclined his head in agreement, but weariness robbed the gesture of much of its graciousness.

Letitia rushed to the door in a hustle of skirts. 'I directed Molly to air the bed in the blue room, and to light a fire for you. It will be ready by now so I shall take you there myself.'

With a heartfelt sigh of relief, Raul followed his hostess from the room.

'Was it a real pistol, Coriander?'

'Of course it was real. It was one of the pair kept on the wall of the office. I borrowed it.'

'But how did you know how to use it?'

'Easy.' Coriander obligingly demonstrated her stance, though she had long since replaced Sammy's borrowed breeches for her cotton nightgown. She stood now upon the hard mattress, giving a good likeness of her former self for the benefit of her pop-eyed audience. 'What's more, I captured a gentleman.'

'Oh!' Cries of astonishment and round-eyed glee.

'Did you overpower him?'

'Don't be foolish, Pearl. Hasn't Corrie just explained how she carried a pistol? Besides, how could Coriander, five feet nothing in her stockinged feet, overpower a great man?' The luckless Pearl was given a heartless pillow-battering by her nearest comrades till Coriander put out a hand to stop them.

'Enough. Leave Pearl alone. If she needs to ask a question, let her. We are not all born with your sharp wits, Sally Moffatt.'

'Or yours, Corrie,' whispered Pearl, with adoration shining in her brown, doelike eyes.

Coriander bent and kissed the child's cheek with real affection, thinking worriedly how it seemed to grow ever thinner no matter what she did to improve her meagre diet. 'Not so, my sweet. It is simply that what I lack in brains and education I make up for with daring and what Mrs Larken would call wanton stubbornness.' She laughed gaily and rocked the child in her arms.

'Go on with the story, Corrie. Your escapades are the only spot of excitement in this dull hole,' whispered Emma softly, creeping closer to share in the petting. She was a dark-haired child with bright blue eyes who had been found abandoned on the doorstep in a basket eight years previous.

23

Smiling mischievously, Coriander swung back her long pale blonde hair, tucking it hastily behind small earlobes. 'You should have seen his face. He was so angry. I believe he would have beaten me to a pulp were it not for the fact that his precious curricle had decanted into the ditch, leaving him with a somewhat slanted view of the world.' A gurgle of laughter bubbled irrepressibly forth and everyone joined in, rolling about in helpless mirth. But Pearl's laughter ended in a fit of coughing and Coriander waited patiently for it to abate before continuing.

'I simply took his fat purse and left him to untangle himself as best he could while I galloped off into the night.'

She made no mention of the loss of her mask and hat. It was far too dark for him to have identified her, she was sure of it. Besides, her sense of drama told her it would have taken the edge off her tale.

'Was he an old gentleman?' asked Pearl.

Coriander paused before answering, letting her mind picture the scene in the half-light. She could remember exactly how he looked. She could see even now the latent strength in his coiled body. Most of all she could recall his eyes: green as a cat's, glittering with danger. Not an old man's eyes in any way. Nor an old man's body. She could not restrain a shiver of unexpected excitement at the memory.

'He was not at all old,' she told them, clearing the gruffness that suddenly fuddled her normally clear tones. 'He was young, and strong, quite athletic in fact. I am certain he is not accustomed to being held to ransom by a lady.' She would have laughed out loud again at that, but some recollection, some fleeting image of his face held her in check. Angular, noble even, made up straight and true like a perfect statue fashioned in bronze and blazing mysteriously to life with a secret, potent power. She had been held in its thrall for several heart-stopping, risky moments before stirring herself to flight.

'Can you imagine it? Our own Corrie, a highwayman?' Fresh paroxysms of laughter tickled everyone at the thought till Coriander was flapping her hands at them all in desperate agitation.

'Hush, hush. Someone will hear.'

Giggles were hastily stifled, tears wiped, aching sides nursed, while several pairs of alert ears strained nervously for any sound of movement deep within the house.

'Mrs Larken will be at supper yet,' hissed Sally in a loud whisper. 'I hope it chokes her.'

Coriander settled herself more comfortably upon the bed, pulling Pearl close into the protective crook of her arm. 'Don't be too hard on her. We would not manage as well as we do were it not for her secret kindnesses. It is Ezra Follett who wields the real power. I think sometimes she fears him almost as much as we do.' Violet eyes glittered to pure gentian for a second. 'But we will eat better these next few weeks. I have seen to that. We will also buy some soothing syrup for your cough, Pearl.'

Sally winked one eye suggestively. 'Reckon she wouldn't mind being the next Mrs Follett, given 'alf a chance.'

A shudder slicked icy fingers down Coriander's spine. 'I doubt it, Sally.'

'Imagine being kissed by Ezra Follett night and morning? Ugh!' Sally made a gruesome noise in her throat as if she were about to be sick and ripples of laughter once more threatened so that Coriander had to be quite firm to calm them. The younger ones would never sleep at this rate.

'I shall marry someone kind and very handsome,' whispered Pearl sleepily from the snug security of Coriander's lap.

Coriander smiled. 'At just ten years old, you need not worry overmuch about a husband yet awhile.'

'What about you, Corrie?' asked Emma in sepulchral tones. 'You are turned eighteen now. Will a husband be found for you soon, do you think?'

There was the smallest pause while Coriander thought of something to say. Then Pearl's skinny arms tightened instinctively about her friend's slender waist. 'You will not leave us yet, will you?'

Coriander smiled reassuringly into the child's troubled gaze, though the smile in her own eyes had quite disappeared. 'No, my pet. I have no intention of marrying anyone just yet. How could I leave you all when I love you so much? Besides, you would never keep your lockers tidy without me to chivvy you every moment of the day.' She began popping kisses on each upturned face and small frowns faded into the ready smiles Coriander's caresses and teasing always provoked.

But Pearl put out a small hand to stroke a straying curl that hung over Coriander's slender shoulder. 'But you will marry one day, Corrie, we all know that, for you are so beautiful.'

Coriander pushed at the hand playfully. 'Oh, what a flatterer you are, Pearl Neilson. And who would wish to marry such a wild, independent miss with a mouth too wide and a chin too pointed? Not to mention one with criminal tendencies.'

'Another highwayman?' came Sally's quick reply, and Coriander leapt after her to a chorus of squeals of delighted fear. She chased each child one by one round and round the narrow room, bare feet padding on the wooden boards until each one was caught, heartily kissed and tickled, and tucked up firmly in bed.

'Tell us another story,' came a sorry wail as Coriander lifted the lamp and started for the door.

'I think we have had enough exciting tales for one night. You can dream of what you would like Sammy to bring from town now we are in funds.'

'A meat pie running with gravy.'

'A great crusty loaf.'

'Hot.'

'With butter.'

A sad smile played about Coriander's generous mouth as she softly closed the door behind her. Leaning back against the worn panels, she let out a tired sigh. What a responsibility they all were, depending so much upon her. Yet not for a moment had she considered the possibility of real danger when she'd devised her latest madcap scheme. Her one thought had been for the children and their empty bellies. Coriander knew well how Ezra Follett came along that quiet stretch of road every Friday at the same hour, and, since he openly bragged of the vast sums he collected in rents from his tenants, she had meant only to relieve him of a small portion of that sum. It would have been no more than their just entitlement, for didn't he dip his grasping fingers even into the paltry amounts granted by the trustees to feed and clothe the institution's unwanted and abandoned young residents?

Her stomach cringed with distaste, reminding her of her own hunger. She should be used to it by now. But it had grown worse of late, much worse. They had never been quite so ill fed before. Once there had been fresh eggs and vegetables, and fat yellow cheeses. But no longer. Not even a Sunday roast for over three months. Hardly a fit diet for growing children who Coriander knew needed fresh fruit and green vegetables if they were to grow straight and strong. Playing highwayman might feed her own appetite for adventure in her attempt to satisfy the children's more painful variety, yet she could hardly embark upon a serious life of crime as a solution.

But how much longer could she hold out? And was it fair to allow the young children to suffer so? Particularly Pearl, who did not seem to grow at all. The child reminded Coriander so much of herself in her younger days. She too had often cried long into the night, yearning to belong to someone, anyone, if only she could have a family of her own to love.

She had dreamed of a beautiful mother returning to claim her, despite knowing that her parents were feared drowned in a violent storm at sea. Yet there had been a letter once, unsigned and undated, promising a visit. She had hidden it in her secret place and waited, her bag half packed, for months before letting all hope finally die when the miracle never happened. She believed now that the letter had been sent as a cruel joke by one of the other orphans at that time. Rejection bit deep into Coriander's soul. Now she was inured against the pain of it, for she had contrived a shield of protection about herself strong enough to guard the softer sensitivity of her heart. Never again would she trust the words of love. She intended in future to expect nothing and offer nothing, then she would not be disappointed when she was given nothing in return.

If she ever afforded herself the luxury of a dream, it was to establish security, perhaps even a fortune for herself without the assistance of anyone, male or female. She tilted her chin in jaunty defiance. And she would do it, too. One day. Only then, when she was equal to all, would she consider taking a husband. Or not, as she chose. She would map out her own destiny, on her own terms. And Ezra Follett did not fit into the picture at all.

As if conjured up in response to her thoughts, the familiar heavy tread could be heard upon the stair. Coriander's heart jumped, flooding every part of her with pounding, pulsating fear. He was coming again.

Grasping the skirts of her thin nightgown, she flew on bare, light feet up the next flight of stairs. Pushing open her bedroom door, she bolted it quickly on the inside before leaping into the single bed.

She lay perfectly still in the darkness, listening to the sound of her own breathing and to her heartbeat thumping in her breast. Then she heard another sound, that of soft footsteps which stopped when they reached her door.

'Coriander. Corrie. Can you hear me? Let me in, there's a good girl. See what I've got for you, m'dear.' Ezra Follett's smooth voice crawled under the door and permeated the room like a yellow smog. Coriander could scarcely breathe.

'I know you are in your bed, but it's early enough. Open the door, see what I've brought you.'

Silence while he waited, in vain, for her reply.

'Wouldn't you fancy a nice bite o' chicken? And I've brought a bottle o' wine to go wi' it. We could have some fun, you and I. What d'you say, eh?'

A shiver rippled down the whole length of her from the top of her blonde tousled hair to the tips of her small toes. Her eyes dilated, growing accustomed to the gloom as fearfully she watched the door-handle turn, heard it rattle with impatience. 'Coriander? You know others will pay for your obstinacy. Open this dratted door and put an end to this misery.' The tone had developed an undercurrent of menace, scouring away the glaze of charm.

She could hear the whistle of his laboured breathing, and every now and then the handle would again be rattled with growing irritation. But at last she heard the shuffle of his departing footsteps. Then silence. It was over for one more night.

Pulling the sheet right up to her chin, she was surprised to find her body actually shaking. Closing her eyes, she tried to relax. Somehow a solution must be found. But not now. She was too exhausted to think after the long day's work, and with another awaiting her on the morrow. She was desperate for rest. Even so, it was a long time before sleep came.

CHAPTER TWO

Ezra Follett swallowed the measure of brandy and winced. It did little to quiet the queasy rumblings of his stomach which grew ever more troublesome of late. It was all the fault of that dratted girl. She tied his guts into knots every time he thought of her, or watched her move in that unconsciously alluring way she had. What a contrast was her pale beauty with its classically perfect lines to this overpainted, overstuffed female who now smiled at him so beguilingly.

'I trust I did the right thing, my *dear* Ezra,' twittered Letitia Larken. 'He was most insistent on seeing her, but I simply refused to be hustled.'

Ezra disliked the personal emphasis she placed upon his name, but offered her a concessionary smile. 'Indeed you acted most properly, Letitia. We cannot allow strangers access to our charges without first making stringent investigations as to their character. Who is this gentleman and from where does he claim to hail?'

Ezra Follett glared at Letitia so fiercely from beneath beetled brow that she stumbled momentarily over her words. 'Some island or other. I did not quite catch the name. Oh, but he is a very fine young man, Ezra. Quite done up in the very finest blue cloth coat with white breeches. He was ...' Her blue eyes rolled slightly as, mouth pursed, she considered her choice of word. She rejected handsome as too trite, and magnetic as too fanciful, likely to cause Ezra offence.

'Well?'

'Oh, I know not how to describe him. There was a quality about him that I can only define as one of supreme confidence. A very proper young man of perhaps eight and twenty who spoke perfect English in a rich, well-modulated voice, but his appearance, his demeanour, Ezra, in fact his whole bearing showed him for a man of character, of mystery even. Do you see?'

'I can see that for someone who declares she cannot describe him, you are doing remarkably well. You seem quite smitten.'

Letitia fidgeted in her seat. 'How you do tease, but it is true he made a most marked impression.' Her eyes glazed slightly as she brought his visage to mind. 'He was most charming, yet not light-minded. He looked for all the world like some foreign adventurer who had risked untold dangers.' She prattled on, warming to her theme. 'Perhaps it was the small scar that crossed one dark brow which gave him a slightly rakish appearance. Yet I have no doubt he has the kind of inner strength which seems to be an intrinsic part of all men of great wealth and power, do you not think so?'

Ezra Follett snapped back his lids which had begun to droop with boredom, accustomed as he was to the fact that, as in everything else, Letitia talked to excess and said very little.

'Power? Wealth? You said nothing of this before. What makes you think so?'

'Why, the inheritance he spoke of. Did I not tell you?'

Ezra decided he must pay closer attention to Letitia's prattle. There had been some mention of an inheritance. The pain in his stomach must be addling his wits, for he had quite overlooked it.

'Though he offered no details as to its nature or size, he gave the impression that he intended to exercise complete control over its administration.' Nudging forward in her seat, Letitia leaned closer to whisper confidentially. 'I did not speak of our little scheme, Ezra. Nor the full tale of Coriander's history as we know it.'

Ezra started. 'I should hope not. It is none of his concern. None but ours, in point of fact,' he told her crisply.

She looked slightly uncertain about the truth of this. 'I must confess there are times when I do worry about it all. I lack your resolution of purpose. Your unfailing single-mindedness. I cannot help but look at the children sometimes and wonder if we do right.'

Stifling the twinge of irritation that twisted his features, he rubbed abstractedly at his stomach. 'How often have I told you, Letty, to leave such worrying to me? You have only to do as I say. The children are perfectly healthy. Overeating and rich food does them no good at all, nor you for that matter.'

Letitia flushed with embarrassment. 'But I have such a delicate stomach. You know the orphanage fare does not agree with it.'

At that precise moment Ezra had no wish to be reminded of weak stomachs, and hastily sought to steer the subject back to more fruitful lines.

'If this gentleman is as wealthy as you claim in your lengthy biography of him, we may well be able to manoeuvre something to our advantage out of this situation.' Ezra chewed thoughtfully upon his lower lip. So there was to be an inheritance? Well, well, and he had thought that source fully exploited.

'In what way?'

'Hard to say at this juncture, but I shall know best once I have the full tale from him. To my mind he cannot expect to waltz away with Coriander, if that is what he intends, without first offering some form of compensation.'

'Compensation?' Letitia was bemused, mesmerised yet again by the familiar glint in Ezra's eyes. He worried her most of all when he wore this look of artful deviousness. Yet she so admired his agile mind.

'Have we not given her a good home all these years?' he continued. 'We surely deserve something in return?' Ezra's mind was in fact fully engaged with the more tantalising form of recompense he had been considering for some time. Ever since Coriander had blossomed into seductive womanhood he had been obsessed by her. His mouth went dry whenever he looked into those defiant, beautiful eyes. And his fingers itched to trail through the bright cloud of hair which carried the sweet fragrance of her even in these miserable surroundings. With an effort he quelled his fantasies and regarded reality in the form of plump Letitia Larken who was most generously replenishing his brandy glass.

'You are so clever, Ezra. And so mindful for the security of our future together. It is such an exciting prospect, I can hardly wait.' The expressive cheeks betrayed her inner confusion. 'I would have lost this place, my home, everything, had it not been for you. I can never repay my gratitude enough.'

He took the brandy in a single swallow. A silly woman, he thought, but unfortunately necessary to his plans. For the moment at any rate. He rewarded her with the grimace of a smile, which showed small yellow teeth that sloped inwards, rather like a stoat's or a weasel's.

'We must keep our heads, Letty, at all times. You can safely leave the matter in my hands. But before Coriander is brought to him, see that she is more suitably dressed. Frugality is all very well in the day to day, but there are times when it is necessary to make an impression.'

'As you wish, Ezra.'

The brandy was taking effect now, warming and soothing away the soreness of his stomach. News of the stranger's arrival had unnerved him for a while, but his confidence was returning in a surge of good will. Even Coriander's obstinate rejection of him seemed merely a temporary state of affairs. Given time and the right kind of persuasion, she would soon see the advantage of a liaison between them.

He walked over to Letitia and laid a hand upon the nape of her neck, feeling the shiver his touch elicited in her. 'Tomorrow, when we meet with him, you must check your natural inclination to frankness, Letty. It would not do for Mr Raul Beringer to know the full extent of our gratitude with regard to Coriander.'

Letitia gazed up at him anxiously. 'How patient you are with my prattling tongue, Ezra dear. I shall do as you say.' She twisted in her seat so that his hand slid down her back, and she shivered again, as a giddiness beset her. 'What if he should probe? How shall I cope?'

Ezra replaced his grip upon her plump throat with a sensuous, stroking motion. '*You* will pour the tea, Letitia. It is *I* who will be asking the questions.'

The tight breathlessness in her chest threatened to overwhelm her, made worse by the constriction of her corsets. 'I shall never sleep. You will help me still my fears, will you not?' Her voice was soft, her eyes beseeching.

Ezra gazed down upon her. His loins were already pulsing with the frustration of rejection and the effects of the brandy. Letitia Larken was no real compensation for Coriander, but he was not unaware of the hold he had upon her and she was not uncomely. Nor did he think she would be entirely unwilling. One day, if necessity demanded, it might be worth investigating the possibility. But that would only be when he had given up all hope of ever having Coriander. A prospect he found hard to envisage.

Coriander counted the coins one by one into her lap. She had done this three times already, so she knew it must be right. There were exactly fifty. The enormity of her plunder astounded her, and the urge to return the purse to its rightful owner, could she find him, was strong. Only the thought of the children's constant hunger and Pearl's nagging cough served to ease her conscience.

The markings on the coins were strange to her and for a moment she wondered if their evident foreignness would mean they could not be spent. But then she remembered that Plymouth, being a port, was surely used to unusual coinage. As the rosy pink light of dawn washed over the coins she saw how they glowed guinea-bright. This, together with the weight of them in her lap, causing her nightgown to sink right down between her knees so that they rested upon the bed, convinced her. Without doubt the coinage was gold. That alone would give them ready passport.

But she must take care. This was a small fortune she had snared, enough to see them all secure for years. Should Ezra Follett discover it, or even suspect ... She let the thought lie unfinished in her head, not wishing to express her fears, even to herself. Anxious now, she dragged her nightgown free of the coins' weight and slid from the bed to push herself with difficulty beneath it. To her shame she found a film of dust covering the boards. Since no one but herself occupied the room, she made a mental note to find a spare moment in her busy work schedule that day to give the floor a good scrub.

Her fingers found at last what they sought. Close to the bedhead one of the floorboards was loose. With further poking and pushing it finally loosened sufficiently for Coriander to slip the bag of gold coins beneath, saving one, which she clasped firmly in her dusty palm.

Breathing a sigh of thankful relief, she dusted herself down and began to pour washing water from the jug into the basin. Stripping off the cotton nightgown, she shivered as she quickly slapped herself all over with the ice-cold water. Then, damping her comb, she started on the tangles in her hair, combing and smoothing till the soft tendrils sprang with ordered vigour around her fingers. When she was done, and dressed in one of her two work dresses, she could feel her skin tingling with new life.

Wrapping the single gold coin carefully in her handkerchief, she tucked it down the front of her dress. It pressed cold and heavy between her young firm breasts. She would give this one to Sammy, not mentioning the rest to him or anyone. He knew what to buy. Any nourishing food which they could eat in the secret dark of the night. Apples, carrots, cheese, currants. But this time she would also request he bring cough syrup for Pearl, and two large apple turnovers. They would celebrate their good fortune. Her mouth watered at the delightful prospect.

Coriander picked up the neatly tied bundle of Sammy's borrowed clothes, and on swift silent feet slipped down the back stairs and across the cobbled yard to the stables.

The stone buildings looked ghostly pale in the morning light, but she went confidently enough towards them. No one was ever about at this early hour, except Sammy, who had to feed the two horses and turn them out into the small paddock behind the house.

Tucking the bundle under her arm, she called his name softly as she pulled open the stable door.

'Sammy. Are you in here?' She knew he must be for the door was unlatched. 'I have the things you lent me, Sammy, and an errand for you. You'll never guess.' Eager to show him her prize, she ran into the stable, savouring the sudden rush of warm horsey smell that hit her nostrils.

'What is it that Sammy will not guess?'

Coriander came to an abrupt halt to stare up in startled surprise at the man before her. He was so tall his curly black hair almost brushed the cobwebs from the rafters. He was propped casually against the wooden stall, and in one swift, all-encompassing glance she took in the powerful physique, the bronzed lustre of his skin and the sensuous, provoking smile. All too dreadfully familiar. Even in the gloom of the stable she could see the unmistakable glint of green eyes, lighter now that they were filled with devilish mischief instead of fury. She wondered fleetingly how long that happy state of affairs would last, surely only seconds, until he recognised her. The cold golden coin burned against her breast. Taking a deep, steadying breath of courage, she found her voice.

'I beg your pardon. Your presence here startled me, for I expected to find Sammy.' She did not call him sir.

'Sammy is not here.'

'I can see that.' Did he take her for a fool?

'Your lover?' The mouth quirked with deeper amusement, and to her intense dismay she felt a hot tide of colour bathe her cheeks.

'Indeed not. Sammy is the stable-boy and but thirteen years old.'

'Ah. Then if it is not an assignation, what brings you to the stable at this ungodly hour? Surely kitchen maids do not take early morning rides?' He raised one finely shaped brow in quizzical amusement, and her quick brain utterly failed her, just when she needed it most, beneath the mesmerising effect of those bewitching eyes.

'I am no kitchen maid,' she retorted, and could have kicked herself for the fatuousness of the remark. Only an unwanted orphan, which was surely worse. Even kitchen maids had families, homes, loved ones.

'But you have spirit, whatever you are.' It was as if he had read her thoughts.

'Don't patronise me,' she snapped right back at him so sharply he was visibly startled. 'I live here and have the right to come and go as I please. It is you, the stranger, who needs to explain his presence.' She lifted her chin in brave defiance, pleased with her little speech, and the violet eyes flashed.

For a long moment he regarded her in total silence, head tilted very slightly to one side and one eye beneath a marred brow slightly narrowed as if in consideration. The moment seemed suspended between them as she ceased even to breathe. Then he smiled, pushing himself off the wooden partition to take a step closer to her. 'You can climb down from your high horse, metaphorically speaking, for I have come here, literally, to tend mine.'

For the first time she noticed that there were four animals in the stable instead of the customary two. She looked, with fast-beating heart, upon the graceful lines of the two greys. Even in the dark their beauty had been apparent. In the light of the early sun that lit shafts of dust motes in the stable, their aristocratic breeding was clear. A sickness pervaded her stomach when she thought how near she had come to injuring these beautiful creatures.

She took a step or two forward to smooth a knowledgeable hand over each glossy rump, feeling the warm, velvet-smooth coat beneath her palm.

'Fine mares,' she murmured. 'Good lines.'

He acknowledged the compliment with a slight tilt of his head. 'But in a highly nervous state at present,' he said coolly.

She turned bland questioning eyes upon him, her heart thudding loud in her breast.

'They have suffered something of a shock.' He briefly outlined his encounter with the highwayman, and all the while he talked she tried to disguise the guilt

45

she was certain must shine from her eyes. Yet try as she might she could not tear her gaze from his. Did he recognise her? Did he know that it was she? Her breath caught and held in her throat, but still she could not speak. It was he in the end who broke the hold, and the knowledge of it was clear in his dancing eyes.

'Since you are here,' he said mildly, 'you can help me to feed them. I suppose you do have some barley to spare?'

'Food is not plentiful here,' she said stiffly, anger burning suddenly within her, for she hated to be bested. 'But oats we do have and your horses are welcome to them.' Taking a bucket, she went to dip it into the feed bin.

Raul watched the swing of her hips with appreciative interest, and his lips curved instinctively upwards as she bent over to reach down into the depths of the bin with her bucket. He caught a clear view of a tempting length of shapely calf beneath the skimpy dress which, even when she was standing still, he had noticed, stopped far short of her ankles. Whatever colour the dress had possessed was long since lost with the too evident scrubbing. Its cleanliness was about the only mark in its favour, he decided. Certainly it had not grown in pace with its owner, as the straining over her full, rounded breasts

46

made only too delightfully plain. Yet the rest of her was much too thin, and the expression on the young face too knowing for someone little more than a child. Something was amiss here? Yet food had seemed plentiful enough last night.

As she swung the filled bucket up out of the bin and tipped a measured amount into each manger his eyes enjoyed every nuance of her natural grace. Despite the poverty of her clothing, and skinny hips, her skin and hair glowed with a rare vivacity. There was undoubted promise of beauty.

'Are you going to stand idly staring all day, or will you be useful and fetch water? They are your horses, after all.' Embarrassed by his undisguised scrutiny, Coriander took refuge in temper. She saw at once how the clouds gathered in the swirling depths of his eyes, glowing with a multitude of expressive emotions which she could not begin to name.

'Since when did kitchen maids give orders to their betters?' He frowned down at her, his head slightly tilted in the now familiar manner, and his expression brought a chill to her heart. Was he playing some kind of cat-and-mouse game with her? She was almost certain that was the case, yet she dared not risk challenging his bold stares.

'Was it you who served tea in Mrs

Larken's room yestereve?'

Coriander froze in the task of grooming, the dandy-brush poised in a paralysed hand. 'No. Sir,' she mumbled, pushing her face into the horse's side as she returned to her brushing with renewed vigour. She could sense his presence close behind her, see him without even looking at him. He disturbed her heartbeat just by being there, even more than the fear of discovery.

The tips of his fingers came down upon her arm and instinctively she jerked away from him.

'Don't do that. I do not like to be touched.'

He looked faintly surprised by her vehemence. 'I believe that portion is quite free of any loose hair and simply gleams from your attention. Perhaps you could move along and do the next part a little?' There was the veiled hint of sarcasm in his tone, gently proffered, but unmistakable. She could not let this confrontation continue. She had to get away from his presence.

Coriander turned abruptly to face him, one hand flying defensively to her breast as she felt the warmth of his gaze. 'I should point out that there are other, more important duties awaiting my attention. It is my job to get the children up and see they are dressed and tidied before breakfast. I have not the time to spare on tasks more usually executed by the stable-boy,' she finished pertly.

To her fury he actually laughed out loud. 'Yet you must bear some of the responsibility, must you not?' he asked, with such an oddness in his tone that her fear of him intensified, causing a sudden rush of burning heat to scald her heart.

Tightening her lips with fresh determination, she thrust the brush into his hand. 'I have told you of *my* responsibilities. Now take care of *yours.*' They were both aware of the quiver that ran through her as they touched this time.

Placing one hand on the door-post behind her head, he leaned closer. 'Why is it that you do not like to be touched, little one? What is it that you fear?'

A strange lassitude stole over Coriander as his breath stroked her face—an intoxicating blend of fear and excitement that robbed her of cohesive thought. It took a supreme effort to ignore its debilitating effects. 'You still have not told me who you are, nor why you are here.'

'I forget,' he said, and chuckled softly. 'Perhaps I have secrets I have no wish to divulge, even to a comely kitchen maid in a warm stable. Though I confess your company is infinitely more entertaining than that of any stable-boy, however worthy this young Sammy may be.'

'I know well how dalliance is the sport of the lone preying male,' Coriander tartly informed him through trembling lips.

'Do you indeed?' His lively eyes roved over her lovely face. 'Are you then a woman of experience?' He emphasised each word with lazy contempt, bringing up his other hand to capture Coriander's small face in a caressing grip. Holding her prisoner, his eyes and gentle touch explored every contour of her face. He traced the line of her brow, her neat, straight nose and the soft fullness of her lips. He felt he had known this face for a lifetime, yet he was strangely compelled to impress every feature of it upon his memory.

Coriander pressed herself back against the hard, unyielding panel, desperate to avoid his touch, shattered by its effect. For one heart-stopping moment she was sure he was about to kiss her.

But then, as she tried to express the storm of words of fury that rattled her brain, the door of the stable was flung back and a breathless, much agitated Sammy burst in upon them.

'I overslept. He'll skelp me. And he's shouting for you, too, Corrie. Everything's late this morning.'

In one swift movement, Coriander

ducked beneath the muscled forearm, tossed the bundle of clothing to Sammy and fled from the stable on wings of an altogether different kind of fear, making that she had experienced with the stranger seem almost pleasurable. At least Sammy's intrusion had put a stop upon his dalliance. But as she ran to urge the children from their beds she could not help wondering what his kiss would have been like, and feeling very slightly cheated.

It was late in the morning before Coriander was able to return to her room with bucket and scrubbing brushes in hand. She still hadn't managed to hand over the gold coin to Sammy. Perhaps there would be an opportunity this evening after supper when he brought the horses in from the paddock. Surely the stranger and his lovely greys would be gone by then. Ever since her encounter with him that morning she had kept herself fully occupied, carefully out of the way, hoping to avoid any possibility of running into him again. And all the time she had wrestled with her conscience. If he had recognised her as the highwayman who had deprived him of his purse, why had he not challenged her, demanded the return of his fortune? And if he had not, why then had he teased and baited her in that knowing way?

51

She should go to him. She knew that. She should go at once and confess to her great sin. And she should return his gold. Even the children would not wish her to place herself in mortal danger for them.

Pulling the bed away from the wall, she stared down, unseeing, at the dusty floorboards. It had never been her intention to steal from a stranger, only to make Ezra Follett suffer for his meanness and take from him what was rightfully theirs in the first place. Could she explain all that to the green-eyed stranger, without making further trouble for herself? There was no doubt in her mind. She had to try.

Coriander could see his face, his eyes, as they had looked into hers, telling her all too clearly that he knew, and was merely biding his time before he revealed his knowledge. On that first night he had reminded her of a wild animal, and as such he would stalk her, play games with her, and then he would pounce. A terrible fit of trembling gripped her. What did they do to people who stole? Would she be transported? Whipped? Hanged?

With fevered fingers she clawed and tugged at the loose floorboard. Dragging out the bag of coins from its dusty cavern, she set it to one side with a lingering sigh of reluctance. As soon as she had finished her cleaning, she would take it to him. It was the only thing to be done.

Dipping the brush in the bucket of hot water, she started scrubbing the floor with excessive vigour. Hot tears welled up in her eyes and plopped on to the floorboards, making small clean circles in the dirty foam. She did not cry out of self-pity, but from a burning frustration that ate into the heart of her. There was no way out, no escape from their miserable life, not for herself, nor the half-starved children who were her friends. Yet she could not stay at Larken's Farm forever. She had hoped to better the children's lot before she went out into the world to earn a living. Now that dream along with all the rest, was washed away like the dust on these floorboards.

So busy was she, concentrating on her work and on her miserable thoughts, that she did not hear the door open. Coriander was unaware she was no longer alone until a voice spoke above her head, and for all its quiet tones she started as if she'd been stabbed.

'Sneaking time off from your duties, Corrie? Naughty, naughty. I thought you had been sent to cut bread for dinner?' Ezra Follett slid through the narrow opening and closed the door softly behind him. His malevolent presence seemed to stifle

Coriander in the tiny room and she berated herself with a kind of fierce panic for having forgotten to lock her door, something she always took good care to do.

Sitting back upon her heels, she looked him full in the face. It would never do to show how he affected her. 'My room has to be cleaned and it will hardly take a moment to prepare dinner, will it?' There was a strong hint of sarcasm in her voice which she failed utterly to suppress.

He gave her a sidelong look, the small eyes narrowing as they roved over her, the narrow bed behind her, and the room itself. Instinctively she leapt to her feet when he took a further step towards her, knocking the bucket with her foot as she backed away so that it rocked recklessly back and forth for a moment, slopping soapy water over its wooden sides.

'I would prefer it if you did not enter my private room without permission,' she said, heart pounding with fear but holding desperately on to her dignity.

He was not listening to her. He was no longer even looking at her. His eyes were fastened avidly to the bag, which lay revealingly half open behind her, its glittering contents spilling out on to the damp wooden boards.

CHAPTER THREE

'I didn't mean to take it.' Almost as soon as the words had popped from her lips, Coriander recognised her mistake.

Ezra Follett strolled across the narrow space that separated them and, picking up the pouch of gold, weighed it in his hand then peeled his lips back into the parody of a smile. She saw how his dark eyes gleamed.

'What was it you meant, Corrie?' The question was mildly spoken, almost kindly in its tone. Coriander was not deceived. 'Who was it you stole it from, girl?'

'I didn't say I stole it.'

'But that was the way of it, eh? Bags o' gold don't drop out the sky, do they? Overstepped the mark a bit this time, wouldn't y' say?'

Coriander fell silent, despair sweeping over her. In all her dealings with Follett she had always held on to some kind of status. Pride, independence—however it might be termed, it had kept her above him. She saw that shield now crumble in the smiling affability of his weasel face. Desperately she searched every corner of her normally agile mind for a way to free herself from this locked corner. But her brain was as soggy as congealed oatmeal. No bright inspiration, no logical, believable reason for Coriander May, pauper and orphan, to be in possession of fifty pieces of gold presented itself.

Ezra Follett strolled back to the door, his skinny fingers plucking with seeming idleness at the pouch strings. At the door he turned to face her, the twist of a smile upon his thin lips. 'Your secret is safe with me, little Corrie. I promise you, not a soul shall learn of it from my lips. No, no, do not thank me yet.' He held up a hand to the silent, stunned girl before him. 'I am sure you will be only too eager to show your gratitude, in due course, when you have had time to reflect. Was young Sammy involved in this latest caper of yours? I always suspected him of supplying you with victuals when you led the children on that foolish and pointless hunger strike.'

'No, he was not.'

'Good, good. I am glad to hear it. I dare say he might have got away with transportation, being only an accomplice. But for yourself, now ...'

Coriander froze at the implication behind the unfinished sentence. With difficulty she forced her stiffened lips to move. 'I told you, Sammy is not involved.'

Follett bobbed his head a few times, pursing his lips in approval. Then he glanced once more at the pouch which he still cradled weightily in his fist, and the smile faded like ice on a dirty puddle. 'Is this the lot?'

'Yes.'

Eyes turned flintlike as he regarded her. 'Best come clean. If you've any more little treasures tucked away ...' He glared meaningfully at the bed where it was still pulled away from the wall.

'None,' Coriander told him, feeling a rush of blood return to her frozen cheeks.

The wintry smile flickered over the lips, but the small eyes remained hard as granite. 'Then we'll leave it there, shall we? For now.' He turned to go before a new thought struck him. 'Ah yes. I almost forgot. Present yourself to Mrs Larken in her parlour at four o'clock prompt. See that you are clean and presentable in your Sunday best. We have a visitor.' As he left the room, he drew the door closed with exaggerated care, and Coriander sank to her knees and cradled her head in her arms.

The anger which boiled in her was almost unbearable. How could she have been so foolish? If only she had not chosen that particular moment to wash her floor. If only she had not pulled out her prize one more time. If only Follett had not called just then. If only, if only. The words hammered upon her brain like pounding fists.

She sat back upon her heels, holding burning cheeks with ice-cold hands. Now she had no way of alleviating the children's hunger. No way of curing Pearl's cough. And worse, much worse, Ezra Follett had the hold over her he'd always wanted. She knew him too well to doubt he would make good use of it.

Unable to contain the irritation she felt at her own folly, she scrambled to her feet to stride back and forth, back and forth in the narrow room, beating one fist into the other small palm with despairing anguish.

If *only* she had not been so careless.

She stopped abruptly, tilting her head to one side in sudden thought. What was it he had come to tell her? 'Present yourself to Mrs Larken ... at four o'clock prompt.' And she was to wear her Sunday best. 'We have a visitor,' he'd said.

It was as if every part of her ceased to function. She stood frozen in the centre of the floor, every flicker of life deserting her as if reserving all her energy for thought. It could be none other. One stranger at the farm was rare enough, two would be too much of a coincidence. The strange, ethereal calmness helped in a way to soothe her as the dread gathered. So she was to be unmasked after all, at a time of *his* choosing. At least there would not be the agony of waiting for Ezra Follett to strike. If her first impressions of her luckless victim were correct, his retribution would be swift. And final.

With steady hands she began to pin up her hair. She intended to be the prettiest highwayman to hang this year.

Coriander stood with her hands lightly clasped behind her back, waiting for the noose to be pulled tight, or the axe to fall. Before her, in the tense calm of Mrs Larken's parlour, sat the tall stranger: dark, forbidding, impossibly good-looking and remarkably still, his eyes seeming to bore right into her.

Mrs Larken held court over the tea table, and Coriander tried not to look at the piles of cucumber sandwiches, and fluffy scones, the tiny cakes glistening with icing. It was more than she could bear even to consider such excess still existed. She could hear the wheeze of Follett's breath as he stood close behind her.

'I am correct that you do not take sugar, Mr Beringer, am I not? Would you care for lemon?'

'Pour the tea, Letitia, and have done with it.'

'Oh, yes, of course, Ezra. I do beg pardon, I'm sure.' In her haste to pour the tea, Letitia knocked over the milk jug while reaching for the strainer. 'Oh, my, now look what I've done,' she flustered.

Coriander darted forward, a rush of sympathy for Mrs Larken overcoming her own fear. She scooped up the worst of the spilled milk with a ready napkin, and poured from the depleted jug into the waiting cups, receiving a look of intense gratitude as she did so.

When the tea was finally served to everyone's satisfaction, Coriander once more adopted her stance of penitence, carefully avoiding her accuser's eyes.

He should have known, he thought, as he watched her, that Cassandra's daughter would have a stubborn, spirited streak. They would not all be in this pretty pickle if the mother had possessed a more pragmatic approach to life. But what had taken place in the distant past was not his concern today. His task must be to ensure there were no more disasters in the future. And by the look of her he was right to be concerned.

The silvery fineness of her hair, the fiercely brooding quality of those captivating eyes and the voluptuous innocence of her slender young body was enough to stir the blood of any normal male. He only wished he could claim immunity. She was quite lovely, but the most captivating part was that she seemed to be unaware of it. Her character, however, was still a puzzle to him.

'Do you think a chair might be found for Miss May? I cannot imagine why it should be, but she looks very much as if she awaits some impending doom,' said Raul Beringer drily.

Ezra Follett thrust a chair at Coriander. 'Show a little good humour to our visitor, Corrie. He will think you a sour puss indeed.'

Coriander was only too glad to take the weight from her trembling limbs. Fastening her hands firmly together upon her lap, she prayed for strength to face what was about to come. Beringer was leaning forward, elbows resting on his knees, smiling at her discomfort. How she despised him for taking such pleasure in her downfall.

'Won't you tell me a little about yourself, Coriander? In your own words.' He spoke softly and she glanced up at him in sharp surprise. Why did he not come to the point? How he loved to play upon her emotions.

'That would not take long. There is little to tell.'

'I find that hard to believe. A young girl as intelligent as yourself must have hopes, plans, dreams?'

'They have no existence, no reality, no value.'

'Do you then value only material things?' He sounded disappointed and Coriander was pleased.

'I value and trust only myself,' she told him, a wildness creeping into her eyes. 'I exist. I am a person. And one day I will mark my own path through life.'

A crease marred his smooth brow. 'I am sure none would disagree with that sentiment, but it was well spoken, Coriander. You do not mind my calling you by your first name, do you?'

'I am hardly in a position to object to anything you might choose to do,' she said smartly, and earned the pleasure of seeing his lips tighten with annoyance. She could remember those lips.

Ezra Follett took two quick steps forward and pinched Coriander's shoulder, causing her to wince with pain. Drat the girl. If she did not behave, she'd blow the whole thing. He showed all his yellow teeth in his smile. 'She is but nervous, good sir. If you could p'rhaps tell her the nature of your errand?'

Coriander marvelled at the servility in Ezra's voice. The stranger had clearly made a deep impression. Never had she known Follett sound so humble. Yet to her ears it sounded false and she waited for the reproof which would surely come. This man was not the kind to be taken in by honeyed words or an over-zealous display of courtesy. The coldness in those sea-green eyes would soon express itself more strongly in the lash of a sharp tongue. And then the noose would truly slip about her neck. But she was wrong. When he spoke his voice was mild, as if he truly cared about the effect his words had upon her.

'You are perfectly correct, Mr Follett. How very remiss of me to begin in such a way. I have no wish to frighten the child by seeming to interrogate her. And I believe you have not yet formally introduced me.' He looked expectantly at Ezra, who visibly started before clearing his throat and finding his voice.

'Of course, of course.' Removing the hand momentarily from its comforting grip upon his stomach, Ezra waved it airily in the general direction of his guest before returning it to its station. 'Coriander, this is Mr Raul Beringer, lately of the island of Madeira, come to impart some important information to you.'

For the first time Coriander regarded her adversary with open interest, and was surprised to find herself actually wanting to respond to his easy smile.

'Admirably done, Follett. Now, if you would leave us we could perhaps get this matter dealt with.'

'Leave you?' Astonishment and disappointment warred upon Ezra's face and a long icy pause followed, broken finally by Mrs Larken who bounced to her feet. With a clatter of crockery upon the tray and a spray of crumbs over the assembled company, she addressed herself daringly to Ezra.

'I do believe that would be for the best, dear Ezra. Let us leave Mr Beringer to his important and personal business.'

'I'm sure you have many pressing matters awaiting your attention,' Raul pointed out with matching courtesy, and Ezra had no option but to dip his head in acknowledgement and leave the room.

The silence which now followed was deep and all-encompassing, and, tilting her small pointed chin high, and staring with overbright eyes at some point above Raul Beringer's head, Coriander resolved that not for the world would she allow him to see her fear.

'You must have often wondered who your parents were.' His words so caught her off guard that she actually gasped.

'Would you like me to tell you about them?'

A shivering took a hold of her so that she could scarce control it. He was at her side in an instant. 'I should bite off my tongue for its lack of tact,' he said morosely, smoothing her brow with a touch that did little to cool its burning heat. 'For a man known for his long patience, I have shown little evidence of it this day. I am a clumsy oaf with words.'

She looked him full in the face, her eyes tortured. So long as he did not touch her, she could cope. 'You knew them?'

Resting back upon his heels, he returned her gaze, and in that instant an acknowledgement was made between them. Conflicting, raw, embryonic in its meaning, but none the less present.

'I knew your mother. She was very beautiful.' He held her in thrall for a moment longer before adding, 'Like you. I should have recognised you at once, but it has been many years. I was no more than a boy of ten when I last saw her, dressed much as you are now in her favourite pale blue with her hair twisted up on her head. You are she, reborn, exactly as I remember her.'

Coriander swallowed the pain in her throat, and when she spoke her voice sounded brittle, unreal, as if someone

65

mouthed the words for her. 'She is dead, then?'

Raul lifted one vulnerable hand and brushed his lips lightly upon the back of it. It was soft and warm and he enjoyed the feel of it in his own. 'I am sorry. Would that I could bring you better news.'

'Tell me.'

'I shall tell the story from the start, but I warn you it is a sad one and you may not thank me for it when it is told.'

Relinquishing her hand, he began to pace about the room, and now his tone was brisk, cool, almost matter-of-fact.

'My own mother having died when I was quite small, my father fell in love with Cassandra. She was young and beautiful with flaxen hair, and he saw her as an angel. How she saw him, a man of almost forty, with two lively sons, is hard to say, but there was certainly a wildness in her, a refusal to conform. She proved to be irresistible to him.'

'Did they marry?' For some reason hard to fathom, the prospect of being Raul Beringer's half-sister did not appeal. But he was shaking his head.

'Days before the wedding was to take place, she admitted to a passionate affair with his best friend, and the result of their union was that she carried his child.'

Coriander waited, her heart slowing to a

tremulous beat. At last she was learning of her true identity.

'The relationship for some reason had ended, and the marriage with my father seemed set to continue. Perhaps she was fond of him after all, or else she was desperate for a name for her baby. For you. But he was devastated by her frank confession and banished her from his sight. Her name even was forbidden in our home from that moment.'

'He must have loved her very much.' Coriander knew about such pain.

'No doubt. But Cassandra was not evil, only a young misguided girl who, realising her error too late, was driven mercilessly from her homeland. My father was an obstinate, proud man evidently unable to take on another man's child.'

'Perhaps she was wrong to ask him.' Coriander tossed her head. 'I would have chosen to take care of myself.'

'Than risk hurting your pride?' he taunted.

'Than risk rejection.' Violet eyes glittered through narrowed slits. 'I would beg from no man.'

'Then your mother was more trusting. She married one of her many admirers. There was no shortage of offers. He was a young merchantman and he and Cassandra set sail for England to make a fresh start.'

Raul sighed. 'I too loved Cassie in my way. Her glorious sense of fun, her impish, carefree attitude towards life. She spelled freedom and adventure to the young boy I then was, and I wept many secret tears when she left. You know the ending of their sad tale. They both perished at sea and you, a lucky survivor, were brought to Mistress Larken, a kindly widow of modest means and open heart.'

'I know Captain Benson tried, unsuccessfully, to find my family. I assumed they did not want me.'

There was a small silence as Raul looked at her with deep sadness. 'That is, unfortunately, quite correct. Cassandra's parents died within a few years, possibly from grief. My father was the only one who knew of your existence.'

'And he ignored me.'

Another pause. 'It was understandable.'

Coriander bowed her head for a moment. She did not wish him to see how his words had affected her. Then, taking a deep, steadying breath, she got to her feet. 'I thank you for coming here to tell me all this. At last I truly know who I am, or, at least, who my mother was. I can put a name and even a face to the image I carry of her. And more important I can forgive her for I see now she did not willingly relinquish me to strangers.'

'Indeed not, Coriander. She did everything in her power to build a future for you, even at great sacrifice to herself.'

'Sacrifice?'

'My father would still have accepted her, without the child.'

Coriander stared at him in bleak horror. 'Did he wish her to *kill* it? Or to give it—me—away?' Without waiting for his reply, she made for the door.

'Wait. I have not done yet.'

Of course. The gold. Slowly she turned to face him. How could she have imagined that the momentary kindness and patience he had shown to her was sincere? The line of his jaw was too tight, too obstinate for that, and the green eyes too shrewd. A tear ran from the corner of her eye down over a hot, flushed cheek. Now was the moment.

'Very well. I will confess. I stole your gold. There, it is said. I was the highwayman who robbed you.'

'I know that.'

The tears burned her throat, but she allowed no more to fall. 'Do with me what you will. I shall not beg for mercy. I have at least learned the uselessness of that from my tragic mother.'

He moved closer to her and instinctively she looked up at him, wishing instantly that she had not. The very closeness of his

69

body to hers stirred a response in her she would much rather not consider existed. Not now. Not with him. His eyes were hooded, their expression unreadable.

'Will you answer me one question?'

'If I can.' If I choose to.

'Was it for the thrill of the moment, for some jest or caper, or merely for material gain?'

She almost laughed in his face: 'You think I would risk my life purely for pleasure?' She saw a shadow cross his face, and wondered.

'Money then is important to you?'

Her temper snapped at last. The tension, the revelation about her origins. And now this patronising arrogance was all too much. 'Money is important when you do not have any, yes. So is food, and health, and medicines, and a mother, and peace of mind.' She was babbling now, and she ground her teeth into her lower lip to stop the tirade. If she did not take care she would lay her head upon his solid shoulder and sob her heart out.

'I see no shortage of any of those things here,' he said with a derisive gesture towards the two small tables still loaded with food.

'It is not always so,' protested Coriander, but knew he did not believe her.

'And where is it now?'

'Where is what?'

He sighed, shaking his head in exasperation, and she felt belittled. 'My gold. Return it to me intact and we will say no more about it. I will put it from my mind as a piece of youthful exuberance.' His tone was clipped as if he were a master reprimanding a servant. She bridled defensively, but then remembered.

'I do not have it,' she said quietly.

One scarred brow rose in caustic enquiry. 'Well, well. You must have a capacious appetite for gold if you can dispose of it so quickly.'

'I did not spend it. Why do you jump to conclusions about me?' she declared hotly. 'Ezra Follett has it. He came to my room and I—'

'Gave it to him? Is he then your accomplice?'

Coriander was horrified. Interpreting the harsh disappointment in his voice as accusation, anger flared afresh within her. 'I do not work at Ezra Follett's bidding. Do you think I toady for him?'

'Of course not,' he murmured in a falsely agreeable tone. 'I should have remembered. You say you value only yourself. However, you failed to mention that you value gold also.'

Coriander felt sick. Only the hot fury that pounded through her veins at his cruel taunts kept her from breaking down.

The door creaked open wide enough for a frizzled head to appear. 'Do excuse my interrupting, but have you concluded your business?' twittered a smiling, anxious-eyed Mrs Larken. 'Supper is served.'

When Coriander saw the supper table, her astonishment was matched only by that of the ten round-eyed children who stood behind their bench seats curbing their eagerness to fill their empty bellies with the unaccustomed riches.

A haunch of roast beef stood proudly on its platter, hemmed in by crisp jacketed potatoes. But first came soup, thick with vegetables and aromatic with thyme. And on the sideboard Coriander could see one of Mrs Larken's huge apple pies, the like of which she had not seen for many a long year. A flagon of red wine stood at Ezra's elbow, and for the children there was a jug of creamy milk.

The sight and smell of so much wholesome fare coming so swiftly upon her argument with Raul Beringer quite robbed Coriander of any appetite. Beneath his sardonic gaze she could do no more than pick at the food. She could almost see the thought print itself upon his handsome face. 'If this girl is starving she shows little evidence of it.'

Nor did the children prove her case any

better. Though they ate as well as their shrunken stomachs permitted, she noted many a slice of beef slipped up a sleeve to be enjoyed later. They well understood how easily this luxury would vanish with the stranger.

'Pray tell us about your home, Mr Beringer?' enquired Ezra, his mouth bulging with roast beef.

'I have a house in London where I am currently staying, but my main home is a small island in the Atlantic Ocean. Its name is Madeira and it is very beautiful.' The face softened with pride and love as he spoke of it, and Coriander marvelled at the difference it made to his appearance. All at once he was approachable, vulnerable. 'The sun shines all the year round and there are flowers in profusion. I am sure you would like it very much, Mrs Larken.'

Letitia blushed furiously. 'I am sure I should.'

'But what are its resources? What riches does it have?' Ezra's irritated voice jabbed in upon them, as if no time should be lost in chit-chat.

'The land is its riches.'

Ezra leaned forward excitedly. 'Does it contain gold? Diamonds? Silver?'

'No, none of those things. The soil and the mild climate are the treasures of Madeira.' Raul laughed at the look of disappointment that was laid bare upon Ezra's face. 'And the greatest treasure of all is the Madeira wine. Making that delectable drink has been my family's occupation for generations and will continue, God be willing, with my brother and myself.'

Coriander could not resist lifting her head to listen to all this, and so was in time to note the slight tightening of the wide mouth. This was not the first she had heard of a brother. But it was gossipy Letitia Larken who burst in with the questions Coriander dared not ask.

'Oh, my, so you have a brother? Do tell us about him. Is he as handsome as yourself?'

Now Raul truly laughed out loud, and even Coriander began to feel so relaxed that her lips twitched. The sound was infectious.

'Indeed, I believe he is much better looking than I. Certainly he is never short of a hand upon his arm.'

'Nor you either, I shouldn't wonder,' said Letitia daringly.

'Indeed, I wait for the right young lady to wear in such a close position.'

'No doubt there are other positions you wear them in the meantime,' muttered Ezra Follett, and received a black look from Mrs Larken as his reward.

'Really, Ezra, how coarse. And in front

of the children. Mr Beringer, you must forgive him. You were telling us about Madeira and your brother. Do you work together in the family business?'

'Since my father died we have tried to. It is not easy. My brother and I do not ...' he paused significantly '... do not see eye to eye on most matters,' he finished dully.

'How very sad for you.'

'And my father has ensured that it stays that way.' There was again the slight grinding of sharp white teeth and the ever solicitous Mrs Larken brought a swift end to the interrogation. 'Apple pie, Mr Beringer? I made it specially.'

When the last crumb of the tangy dessert had been licked clean, Ezra brought forth a bottle of brandy.

'Now, my children. You can go and play for a while,' he said expansively. 'Afterwards, you can put yourselves to bed, without Corrie's help for once. She must help me to entertain our guest, as you can see.'

In a trice the room was empty, as were the plates, the resulting silence filled only with the clink of glasses.

A rosy-cheeked Mrs Larken got un-steadily to her feet, the wine making her muzzy-headed. 'Coriander and I will withdraw and prepare tea in the parlour. Please do not hurry your brandy on our account. We shall be quite content with our own company for a while.'

The evening passed in a mockery of good manners and stilted conversation. While Letitia Larken revelled in the opportunity to display skills of etiquette learnt in a former, more affluent age, Coriander cringed beneath the probing gaze of Raul Beringer's brilliant eyes. She sensed his unease almost as sharply as her own. She guessed that he too longed for this parody of genteel society, so awkwardly enacted in a remote farmhouse for unwanted children, to end.

At the first opportunity Coriander made her excuses. 'I rise early, so I will beg your leave to retire,' she said with studied meekness.

Ezra Follett leapt to his feet to stay her with a bony hand. 'But you have not yet told us your good news, Coriander.' He beamed at her as if he were some loving uncle.

'Good news?' Her smooth brow creased with puzzlement. 'Oh, you mean the information about my parents. The news was neither good nor bad, but I am most grateful for Mr Beringer's bringing it to me. It has at least given me some peace of mind.'

'No, no, I meant—'

Raul Beringer rose from his seat.

Towering above Ezra Follett, he seemed to fill the small parlour with his presence. 'I have not yet informed Coriander of her good fortune, but I dare say it is time.'

As if to avoid the issue, he began to pace about the room. And as he fingered each of Mrs Larken's pretty ornaments, picking up each fragile piece in his large brown hand and placing it back in its spot unstudied, the expectant hush among the assembled company grew into a dark ball of suspense. 'On Madeira,' he began, 'it is often the tradition to treat all brothers equally with no preference given.'

'How very sensible,' chirruped Letitia Larken, but wished at once she had held her tongue as Raul Beringer whirled upon his heel to glower down upon her.

'I'm afraid that is not necessarily the case, madam. It can divide the land and property to breaking-point. And in our case it has been divided still further. By three.' Redirecting his fierce glare upon Coriander, he spoke in a low growl, ignoring the effect of his words upon her and upon the others present. 'It is as well you appreciate the value of gold, Miss May, for I intend to offer it to you in exchange for the land which my father bequeathed to you. Some may say he wished to make reparation, but I think it was more likely a form of twisted vengeance. He was a strange man.' The bitterness in his voice cut through her like glass.

She stared at him as if he had grown a second head. If indeed he had, she would have been less stunned. An inheritance. This was the last thing she had expected.

'It is a fine inheritance for us all,' he said caustically. 'Some of the best land on Madeira. Land which will grow grapes for the wine as well as bananas and sugar cane. But there are conditions attached. A sum of money comes with the land. But the bulk of the Beringer fortune lies in the wine company.'

'And who has inherited that?' Ezra Follett was almost panting with excitement.

'The conditions are these. Whoever makes the most profit from their inheritance in one year from the date of the bequest will gain complete control over the wine company and the Beringer fortune. I regret to say there is a long-standing power struggle between Maynard, my brother, and myself. Not uncommon, I dare say, but no less unpleasant for that.' The wide lips lifted into a sneer. 'My brother makes up his own rules by which the game is played.'

Coriander was appalled. He was fortunate enough to have a brother, a family of his own, and he spoke of it with open contempt. What kind of man was this who did not realise his own good fortune? 'You think of it as a game to disagree with your own brother?'

He looked at her for a long moment before answering. 'Indeed it is. A game of life and death. One my brother intends to win. And so do I.'

In the small, startled silence that followed Ezra Follett cleared his throat. 'You spoke of gold for Coriander. What exactly did you mean by that?'

A glint almost of amusement was back in the eyes, softening their bleakness. 'I know well how she appreciates its pretty colour.' He gave again the light laugh, but this time there was little mirth in it and Coriander was chilled. 'She has no part in our feud, in our battle for power. Running a wine company is not a job for a woman and it has been in my family for generations. We did not know of Coriander's existence until the reading of the will, but we wish to be fair to her. Upon this point my brother and I are in agreement.'

'I am glad to hear it,' said Coriander with uncharacteristic sarcasm.

'We will offer you a fair price for your bequest. Sufficient to set you up in comfort here in England. We can promise you a modest income for life in the form of shares in the company. You will never need to worry again.'

It was a generous offer and Coriander recognised it as such. But then she thought of the land, and freedom. She thought of her mother banished from her home, and of the man responsible who had made a will in this peculiar way. What kind of a man had he been? And from whom did he seek vengeance and why? Surely not upon herself who had never known him?

She looked at Ezra Follett and saw the lascivious greed upon his face. He would never let her be free. She knew that now.

And what kind of a man was Raul Beringer? This dark, brooding stranger. She could trust no one. She had been hurt and rejected enough for one lifetime. Even Mrs Larken had failed her in the end. But there was something intriguing about him. What was it? She gazed up into the clear green of his eyes and knew her answer. On no account must she allow him to come too close.

'I must beg leave to decline your kind offer,' she said. 'My share, great or small, is not for sale. I shall return to Madeira with you and carry out your father's wishes, to the full.'

CHAPTER FOUR

The china figurine fell to the ground and splintered into tiny fragments, the sound seeming to echo for long seconds afterwards into the shocked silence of the room. Ezra Follett leapt forward into the void.

'Take no notice of her. She must have lost her head. What you thinking of, girl, refusing such a generous offer? The likes o' you aren't made for gallivanting overseas.' His small eyes flashed warning messages at her. 'Thank the good gentleman and then be off to your bed.'

Raul Beringer was staring at the dismembered china figure scattered about his booted feet. Coriander wished he would speak, or at least look up so that she could see the expression upon his face. But when he did at last raise his head, the features were held in a frozen calm and quite unreadable. Completely ignoring Coriander, he whirled upon his heel to offer a small bow to Mrs Larken.

'I crave your pardon, madam, for my carelessness. I will, of course, pay for its replacement.'

Letitia Larken, flustered and blushing with confusion, emphatically refused his offer, saying the figurine was of no consequence and she had always disliked it.

Coriander quietly drew breath into her lungs. She must not let him see how his outward calm unnerved her. Beneath the bland words of courtesy beat an altogether different message. He was furious. She felt every wave of suppressed anger that vibrated from him. But she must not let it touch her.

'I assume that there is no compulsion for me to sell?'

'None.' The word was bitten off as if his tongue were a traitor to form the word.

'Then I see no reason why I should,' she continued reasonably. 'As I have no family ties, this inheritance surely gives me the right to choose for myself. I cannot stay in the orphanage for much longer. It is well past time for making my own way in the world.'

'You would be well advised to accept my offer, none the less, and make your way, as you put it, on English soil. It would certainly be far safer.'

'Safer?' she challenged. 'For whom? For you perhaps.'

'It was your safety which was on my mind. Events are moving fast in Europe.

Perhaps you are not aware of it, way out in the country here, but Napoleon has escaped from Elba and is even now mobilising new forces. He has been seen in Lyons declaring his intention to save the French from degradation. We have not seen the end of the little Corsican yet.'

'Oh, Coriander, then you must stay here where you will be safe,' cried Mrs Larken anxiously.

One single glance at Ezra Follett's smirking grin made Coriander stiffen her resolve. It was very much in Follett's interest for her to take the payment offered. It would go nicely with the money he had already accumulated, and the gold he had stolen from her. And if that were not enough, she hated to be told what she could or could not do, particularly by a man as patronising and domineering as Raul Beringer appeared to be. Besides, the idea of seeing new places was exhilarating.

'You, apparently, are not so ill informed of Napoleon's actions.'

'You would be much better to stay in London,' he repeated stonily. 'Besides Napoleon, there are ... other dangers you could face.'

A giggle erupted irreverently from Coriander's throat. 'There is no need for you to take your role of guardian quite so

83

seriously. I am perfectly capable of taking care of myself.' She smiled impishly at him, and for a moment he saw only her natural enthusiasm and not the problems her decision would create. 'It is far more exciting to travel to a faraway island and see my inheritance for myself than to stay safely at home.'

'It is quite impossible for you to accompany me without a chaperon and I see no way round that one, since you have neither family nor friends to support you.'

For one startled moment, Coriander floundered. The proprieties of the situation had never entered her head, but she could understand how it would look for her to travel alone with an attractive man, even one some years older than herself. Raul Beringer clearly did not relish the prospect. Perhaps it offended his sensibilities, his being a gentleman of standing. Apart from which, it would perhaps be wiser for her own sake, for she was ashamed to admit that she found him strangely compelling. What could she do? When the answer came to her she almost laughed out loud with delight.

'You could not be more wrong,' she said and, stepping quickly forward, knelt before Letitia Larken where she sat on her pretty fireside chair. 'You were once a good friend to me, Letty, through all my troubles and your own. I know I have not been an easy burden, but I beg you, most humbly, to come with me now for the sake of that friendship we once enjoyed.' Before Ezra Follett spoiled it, she might have added, but chose not to cause her friend greater distress. 'We will begin a new life, together. What do you say?'

Astonishment and delight set fire to Letitia's plump cheeks. 'Oh my! Can you mean it?' A hand flew to her cheek in consternation. 'But how would we manage, two women, alone in a strange land?'

'We will manage very well, as we always have when allowed to, you and I.' Coriander flicked a challenging glance across at Raul Beringer. 'And we will not be quite alone. I am sure Mr Beringer's brother will have some say in the manner with which we are treated.' She saw by the change in his expression that her barb had thrust home.

'But the children?'

'They can be found good homes, or employment. Some of the boys are old enough to be apprenticed with a kind farmer. Even the younger ones are good workers and can do much to earn their own keep.' A better one than they get here these days, she thought. 'They deserve a chance at happiness,' she finished more earnestly.

Letitia cast an anxious glance in Ezra's direction. 'And what of you, dear Ezra? Would you mind if I went with Coriander? Or perhaps you would prefer to come, too, else how would you manage without us?'

Coriander got slowly to her feet and, turning to face her enemy, smiled fully into his face. 'Mr Follett is, I am sure, well able to take care of himself.' Deliberately presenting her back to him before he had time to frame any words on his mobile, spluttering lips, she stepped up to Raul to direct her teasing words with relish.

'Letty will be my chaperon, since you require your honour to be protected. I also wish for Pearl to accompany us. She is but ten years old and is like a sister to me. She will be no trouble. So you see, I am not quite so alone as you might think. Your little problem is solved.'

The twisted brows drew together in a dark look. 'It would seem so.'

'As far as is practicable, we would wish to retain some degree of independence as we travel. I think the least we have to do with each other, the better, don't you?'

'I doubt old Boney himself would not do all in his considerable power to avoid tangling with you.'

Coriander's eyes positively twinkled with

triumph. 'Then it is agreed?'

A long expulsion of breath and then in a low voice, scarcely above a whisper, 'It is agreed.'

In less time than Coriander could have believed possible, they were on their way. It had proved surprisingly easy to place the children, either because an extra pair of hands was always welcome with country chores, or else the way had been eased by a more tangible form. Where the children's happiness was concerned, Coriander chose not to investigate too closely. Pride was an expensive luxury she could ill afford in this instance.

Much attention had been given to the spreading of dust sheets in the now empty farmhouse, and issuing instructions to the loyal Molly and her husband who were to take care of everything during their mistress's absence. Sammy, Molly's son, was ordered to sell the two horses and this, for Coriander, had brought more tears to the ones she'd already shed in parting from the children.

Pye, her old comrade of many secret outings to procure food for the children, regarded her with a knowing eye as she buffed his coat down one last time.

But there was little time to waste on sentiment. Raul Beringer was not a man to tolerate delay. A chaise was hired for herself, Letitia and little Pearl, and their small amount of luggage. Raul intended to lead the way in his own newly repaired curricle and was evidently anxious to depart.

And so here they were, settling back comfortably upon the leather seats, well wrapped in warm cloaks with their feet on hot bricks against the coolness of the green spring day.

'What I do not understand,' began Letitia, almost as soon as they had set off, 'is what can have happened to dear Ezra. One moment he was there and the next gone. I really do think he could have bade us goodbye.'

'I dare say he had his reasons,' said Coriander. Such as not wishing his secret, and no doubt substantial, hoard of gold too closely investigated. He had been gone for some days. Poor Mrs Larken. It was evident to Coriander that she had no inkling of the extent to which her small fortune had slipped into Ezra Follett's cunning hands. The land had been the first to go. Then one by one Letitia's treasured pictures and ornaments had been sold off, and each time the children would be indulged by Letitia and food would be plentiful again. But all too soon the surprisingly meagre sums realised from the sale of these heirlooms was exhausted and once more she struggled to make ends meet, turning again and again to 'dear Ezra' for help in managing her affairs. It had seemed to Coriander that when all items of value had been sold, it was then that Ezra Follett had moved into the farmhouse as if preparing the way for his final take-over. Compelled at last to reveal her suspicions, Coriander had found she was too late, for Ezra's hold upon Letitia was by that time unbreakable. Her blunt words had succeeded only in fracturing their long friendship and Coriander could do nothing but watch helplessly as the farmhouse continued to be stripped of its assets.

Letitia now dabbed a lavender-scented handkerchief to her nose. 'Friends can be so unreliable.'

'Not Corrie,' put in Pearl's soft voice. 'You can trust in Corrie. And me. I shall never leave you, Aunt Letty, without first saying a most proper goodbye.'

This caused them all great amusement, and Coriander squeezed both their hands together with her own in a sudden excess of emotion. 'We shall at least be together. Almost a family. Good riddance to Ezra Follett, I say, and good luck to us all in our new life.'

'What do you think the island will be

like, Corrie?' asked Pearl, eyes shining with curiosity and excitement.

'I think it will be very beautiful and we shall have to work very hard.'

'Why? Do you want to win the prize that the old man promised?'

Coriander laughed. 'Not at all. What should I do with a wine company? No, indeed. All I want is for us to be secure. If by our own efforts we can build an agreeable life for ourselves, what more could anyone ask?'

'But I know nothing of growing grapes or sugar cane,' declared Letitia. 'Indeed, once my poor dear late husband passed on, such land as we did have was a great worry to me.'

'I am certain we will find people who can show us what to do.' This last point had caused Coriander a few sleepless hours, but she had no intention of letting that be known.

'Could we have a garden, do you think?' enquired Pearl tentatively. 'One like Lady Mildred has up at the manor.'

Coriander hugged her close. 'Why not? A garden of our very own to walk in would be delightful.'

It was not a comfortable ride, as the hired vehicle lurched and bumped over the rutted roads in its attempt to keep pace with the flying curricle in front.

Sometimes they were forced to hang on tight to the straps in fear of certain death. When surmounting a particularly large rut or taking a corner too fast, it seemed as if the entire vehicle was hurled into the air before crashing down again, tossing its occupants about like dice in a gaming cup. In no time at all Pearl was complaining of a queasy tummy, Letitia was quite green and Coriander herself could not lay claim to any better state of health. It was with profound relief that the ladies climbed down the folding steps on to solid earth the first night, eager to refresh themselves and rest in a wayside inn.

The landlord's good lady herself led them to the pair of rooms they were to share, an ample four-poster in each, with a small truckle-bed for Pearl. Chairs, washstands and a table laid with guinea fowl and apple dumpling before a blazing log fire completed the picture. Though it gladdened her heart to look upon the appetising scene, Coriander could not help but wonder where Raul was choosing to take his own repast, for he had taken her at her word when she had made her plea for independence. They were to dine alone.

She watched with deep pleasure as Pearl finished every morsel. Already, new plump flesh pushed out the shrunken cheeks. Letitia, also watching the eager concentration the young child applied to her food, gave a low shuddering groan.

'I should have known they were hungry. I should have seen.' Blue eyes were bright with tears and the fat cheeks wobbled dangerously close to loss of control.

'Put it from your mind, Letty. He had mesmerised you in some way. We shall never speak his name, nor see him ever again. The children are happily tended to and we are free of him. I can only hope our new companion is more of a gentleman.'

'Oh, but he is. I am sure of it,' Letitia avowed. 'And so dashing. Only see how he looks at you.'

Coriander's heart lurched in an extraordinary manner. 'Looks at me? What are you saying? How does he look at me?'

'As if he cannot tear his eyes from you,' said Pearl with a gleeful giggle. 'I believe he is falling in love with you, Corrie.'

'What nonsense.' She leapt to her feet at once. 'And it is past time you were in bed, young lady. Your eyes are so big with need of sleep I can see my own image in them.' An image that disconcerted her by its nervy reaction to the child's playful teasing.

'I think we shall all be the better for a good night's rest,' agreed Letitia with a stifled yawn. And to Coriander's great relief the prickly subject of Raul Beringer was dropped.

But if they'd imagined that the gentleman in question would allow them much time for resting, they were soon disenchanted. Before even the cockerel had sensed dawn, Raul had them packed back into the chaise and they were bowling bumpily along once more with the promise of a stop later to break their fast.

They could scarcely see each other in the chaise as black night still held back the day, and were soon lulled back to sleep by the jingling of the harness and the rhythm of the horse's hoofs on the hard-packed earth of the road. The golden haze of the coach's lamps brought to Coriander's mind a picture of glittering coins, falling, falling. But soon, even dreams melted away with heads nodding upon each other's shoulders and Pearl wedged warmly between them like a softly curled dormouse.

Nevertheless, the end of the journey was greeted with a sigh of thankfulness as they climbed down from the chaise on wobbly legs, dress, hair and general demeanour having lost all pretensions of order.

Coriander followed Raul up the five steps of his tall town house, whereupon a pair of doors, bristling with polished brass, were swung wide to reveal a hall of impressive proportions. Even more overwhelming, certainly to Coriander, was the stately figure who performed this simple task. Clad in green and gold livery, the man was the very epitome of London graciousness. She found it hard to credit that he was no more than a servant, so grand was his dress, so condescending his manner as he threw her the merest glance before welcoming his master home.

Raul strode briskly into the hall, flinging off greatcoat and gloves with relief as he did so. All too keenly aware of her own dishevelled, rumpled appearance, Coriander held her cloak firmly in place as she pattered after him.

'Burton, will you find Mrs Tavannagh and ask her to prepare rooms for our guests?'

'And where shall she put them?' asked Burton, looking down his nose as if they were tadpoles requiring a pond, thought Coriander with irritation.

Raul looked thoughtful. 'The pink suite, possibly.'

'My lord?'

'Yes, hmm. Why not? The pink suite it shall be.'

Seemingly satisfied that all was in hand, Raul strode to the wide staircase. For a moment Coriander watched him go, almost mesmerised by the swing of powerful shoulders beneath the fine grey cloth of his coat. Coming to herself, she stepped quickly forward to address him from the foot of the stairs.

'If you prefer it, Mr Beringer, we would be perfectly happy in the servants' quarters.'

The click of boot upon marble stair halted abruptly and the silence which followed was appalling. Raul stood stock-still in mid-stride before slowly pivoting round to regard her with a long-suffering patience. 'Must you always attempt to countermand every decision I make?' he enquired, the perfect teeth snapping together with icy contempt. 'You may look like a laundry maid, but there is no necessity to behave like one. We have ample accommodation available here at Funchal Place, and always treat our guests with respect.'

She did not miss the insinuation that her reception of him at Larken Farm had been anything but welcoming. With difficulty she held her tongue as he continued up the stairs. But then he stopped again as a thought occurred to him.

'Burton. See that the silver is locked away, will you?' The triumphant glimmer in the cool green eyes mocked her mercilessly before he offered a sweeping bow and, departing rapidly up the stairs, left Coriander afire with fresh fury.

She was given ample opportunity to

cool down, however, as they were left waiting for some considerable time while a servant was found to show them to their quarters.

Coriander could not help looking about her with interest. The black and white marble hall with its Corinthian pillars and marble busts in niches was, she judged, typical of a London town house meant exclusively for a man of affairs. Yet it was cold and comfortless, lacking any welcoming ambience in its classical lines. She felt belittled by its size and had a sudden urge to turn and run back to Larken Farm and its shabby familiarity.

Following a diminutive maidservant up the black marble staircase, Coriander noticed that there were no ancestral portraits adorning the bare walls, surely unusual for a man of Beringer's status. The severity of the décor was relieved only by sparkling patches of colour from a domed window set high in the ceiling. It was as if he wished to emphasise his lack of interest in his family, and she shivered. A man of pristine taste but no humanity.

The girl gave a cheeky grin. 'Like a palace, eh? But a bit too dark for my liking. And quiet. As the grave sometimes. Me, I like a bit more life going on.' Coriander could well believe it. Dressed in a lilac dress that fell in

96

straight lines from her pert bosom where a neckerchief was pinned cornerwise about her, to her slippered, black stockinged feet tripping lightly upon each step, the little maid positively bounced with life. Even the regulation cap was set at a jaunty angle, showing off the chestnut curls to perfection.

She opened a door on to a spacious salon. The golden afternoon sun shafting through the tall sash windows gilded the gracious beauty of the pink and white room. Its sumptuousness was breathtaking and did little to restore Coriander's diminishing confidence.

'Shall I unpack, miss? The bedrooms are through there.'

Thinking of the poor contents of the bags, Coriander quickly declined.

'Well, should you require anything, just call for Alice. That's me.' Again the smile, this time accompanied by a cocky wink.

'Thank you, but we shall manage very well, I am sure.'

The perceptive, inquisitive Alice had missed nothing of the faded, outmoded, too-short gown, for all it was hidden beneath a classic red wool cloak which had itself seen better days. But Alice knew that country folk often wore the same clothes year in, year out. Hadn't her old aunty worn just such a cloak and she was the third in her family to wear it? Alice preferred something a bit more stylish herself. Still, it wasn't for her to judge. The young woman spoke well enough, for all she looked like a beggar-woman. But how Mr Raul would take to her looking like this was another matter entirely.

'Begging your pardon, ma'am, but will you be changing for dinner? I could see that your gown was aired and pressed.'

It was difficult to know how to answer this one, since nothing Coriander possessed could come anywhere near fit to wear in these fine apartments. She dared not consider what the grandeur of the lower floors would reveal, and she certainly did not feel up to coping with the problem now. 'Perhaps we could take a light meal up here this evening. It has been a most tiring journey.' Without causing any offence to the young girl, who was well-meaning enough, Coriander managed to dismiss her, and watched the door close with a thankful sigh.

Letitia and Pearl, however, elected to forgo a meal.

'I vow I shall sleep for a sennight, and I doubt my old bones will ever find their proper place again,' groaned Letitia feelingly.

Coriander laughed. 'Pearl is asleep on her feet, I fancy.'

'There are pink angels, Corrie. Can you see them high on the ceiling?'

Coriander looked up to where the child pointed. 'Cherubs, darling. They are playing their trumpets in heaven.' An incongruous touch for a house which seemed to have been planned in funereal tones.

Alice returned with warmed towels to help Coriander take full benefit from the jugs of hot water and wooden tub left ready by one of the unseen army of servants. After satisfying herself that her fellow servants had seen Pearl and Letitia into their warmed beds, Alice set about combing through the silvered web of Coriander's hair, remarking upon its prettiness.

'Mr Raul wishes you to take your evening meal in the blue salon, with him,' Alice informed her. There was a shade of anxiety in the maid's tone and Coriander surmised that Mr Raul was accustomed to having his wishes obeyed. For a second she was almost tempted to accept. A civilised meal with an attractive man would be a rare treat. But then she remembered his mocking disregard for her comfort, and the state of her one good dress. Her appetite instantly deserted her.

'I'm afraid that on this occasion Mr Raul

must be disappointed,' she said firmly. 'I want only my bed.'

'Begging your pardon, ma'am, but if it's the dress ...' For a moment both girls, close in age, regarded each other with a guarded caution. Then Alice seemed to take courage from what she saw and continued more forcibly. 'Seeing as how you're a bit travel-stained and unprepared, as you might say, I could look out one of Miss Isabella's dresses. She's about your size.'

'Miss Isabella?'

'The Viscount's intended.' Alice giggled. 'Mistress, more like. They do say as how she was Mr Raul's mistress once upon a time, and may still be for all we know. She was going to marry him, but then he was disinherited for a while and she changed her allegiance.'

'I see.' Coriander was beginning to see a good deal. 'When you speak of the Viscount, you mean Raul's brother, Maynard?'

Alice nodded vigorously as she busily combed the tendrils of hair into curls over her fingers. 'Reckon Miss Isabella's waiting to see which way the cat jumps.'

'The cat?'

'The inheritance. Not much point in marrying a Viscount if the younger brother gets all the money, eh?'

'I-I suppose not.' So they fought over women as well as property? Coriander felt sickened by this further evidence of his ruthlessness. Were she fortunate enough to have a brother of her own, she would not spend her time quarrelling with him.

Alice, having concluded her task, finally left Coriander to the privacy of her thoughts. As time passed she grew almost languid sitting dozing by the warmth of the fire. The thoughtful maid had brought her a Chinese silk robe, and, tempted by its soft mauves and pinks, Coriander had slipped it on over her homespun nightdress. Rubbing her cheek against its cool softness, she felt as if she were in some kind of beautiful dream. One from which she had no wish to wake. Even the glowering disapproval of her new guardian could not curb the nut of excitement that glowed in her heart. Perhaps even he would soften towards her in time. She would make an effort to be agreeable, try to explain the difficulties she had had to cope with. Would he understand her fear of Ezra Follett and her concern for the children? Could she prove her innocence? Somehow his good opinion of her was important.

'But soon I may wake and find myself back in my narrow hard bed, with Ezra Follett knocking on the door,' she murmured sleepily to herself. A prospect which hardly bore thinking about.

As if in embodiment of these thoughts there came indeed a light tap upon her door and the handle rattled, sending Coriander leaping to her feet in startled confusion, heart pounding wildly in her breast.

Who could it be at this hour? Cold reality froze the very blood in her veins. She might have led a sheltered life, but Coriander was no fool. She knew instantly who it was. No, this was no dream, but a return of the old nightmare. She might have managed to hold out against Ezra Follett, but this man was not so stupid and would not be so easily diverted from his purpose. Her requests had been agreed to; she had been placed in a home of enviable luxury and promised a fortune. But there was always a price to pay. Raul Beringer had come to collect his dues.

The knock came again. A single, imperious rap. Coriander would have liked to ignore it, to climb between the enticingly warm covers and pretend to be asleep. Drawing the silk wrap close about her, she went to open the door.

The sight of Raul Beringer leaning against the door-jamb made her catch her breath. He had changed and looked fresh and handsome in a dark green silk jacket over the whitest of silk shirts and slim, close-fitting trousers in night-black.

She felt suddenly gauche, and shy as a new arrival at Mrs Larken's orphanage.

'So it is not that you are overtired from the journey that you choose to ignore my invitation?' The tone was mild but condemning, robbing her of any defence and leaving her momentarily speechless.

'Nor, unless those flushed cheeks indicate the onset of a fever, do you look sick.' Pushing himself off the door-pillar, he strode past her into the room.

'How dare you march into my chamber without permission? Is this the normal behaviour of a city gentleman?'

He looked mildly askance at her. 'This is not your bedchamber. It is a small sitting-room and perfectly respectable for you to receive visitors here. Do you imagine that I mean to ravage you?'

She balled her hands into small fists at her sides. Her palms were sweaty but she was ready to protect herself. To her great consternation he burst out laughing. 'You did think so. Foolish child.'

'I am not a child.' She felt belittled by his attitude. Did he mean to use such a condescending tone?

The smile slid from his face and he looked almost contrite. 'Quite true, Coriander. You are not. You are, in fact, quite a lovely young woman and I can understand your alarm. Forgive me my thoughtlessness. I shall leave at once.'

His sudden consideration nonplussed her. How could she trust a man who swung so wildly from one emotion to another?

'I believe my privacy should be respected,' she said quietly, moving to the door in readiness to open it for him.

'And what of my hospitality? Do I deserve no recompense for that?' he quietly asked, and saw again the shuttered look come down upon her face. She was the most vexingly difficult person to get to know. He determined to try again. 'Could you not at least have dined with me and put an end to this petty squabbling? We could try to be friends, if only to make the journey more tolerable. It was not very sociable to not even reply to my perfectly reasonable invitation, was it?'

She began to squirm inwardly with shame. 'It was perhaps ill-mannered of me. I apologise.'

His face visibly brightened and he took a small step towards her, almost as if he couldn't help himself. 'Then perhaps tomorrow evening?'

She hesitated, unable to say no outright, for he suddenly looked so boyishly eager and she felt again that warm compulsion to please him. Yet, when she considered what his underlying motives might be, panic washed over her in hot, undulating waves. Ezra Follett had been courteous once, and she had trusted him before his friendship had become overly intrusive. And on one occasion he had almost ...

Raul's brows drew together in a puzzled frown. 'You are shaking, Coriander? What is it? Why are you afraid of me?'

'I am not,' she replied, with an effort at conviction.

'Then what the deuce? Ah ...' The brow cleared and, before she had time to realise what he was about, he whirled upon his heel and in a few quick strides entered the inner sanctum of her bedchamber.

CHAPTER FIVE

Coriander was after Raul in a moment. 'Where are you going? What do you ...?' But she was too slow to reach him as he flung wide the closet door to reveal her three shabby dresses hanging limply within.

'As I thought.' Gathering the gowns from their hooks, he tossed them on to the bed in a crumpled tangle. 'This situation must be rectified at once. Why did you not remind me of the paucity of your wardrobe?'

She felt herself colouring to the roots of her hair. 'It was none of your concern,' she said proudly. 'I could have dealt with it myself, in time.'

'It is very much my concern. Do you imagine I would expect you to go about town proclaiming yourself for a waif?'

'But that is what I am.'

'Not any longer. Nor have I any desire to be seen with a dowd.'

Coriander hesitated. She could see the sense in this observation. Nor, in truth, had she any wish to appear as such. Should she ask about access to her small inheritance? Even as she considered the best way to approach the subject and still retain some dignity, Raul Beringer was calmly settling the matter.

'I shall speak with Mrs Tavannagh in the morning. She is certain to know of a suitable gownmaker who shall be asked to call forthwith and furnish you with more suitable attire.'

'Oh, but I could not possibly accept.'

'Whyever not?' His voice was disbelieving.

'Only if the charge were to be made against my inheritance.' She could feel the pulse beat in her head and a small ache start. She was far too tired for this bartering of words.

'Your independence does you credit, yet

it is flawed.' She thought she saw the shadow of a smile at the corners of his lips and it grated upon her frayed nerves.

'What is so amusing? If there is to be some form of income, however small, may I not be told of it so that I can budget sensibly for our needs?'

'I doubt it will cover the cost,' he said, with some amusement. 'For a woman of your tastes.' Taking her firmly by the shoulders, he turned her about, examining her with his piercing gaze as if she were a piece of merchandise. Once she was facing him again, he said, 'Such a delightful figure deserves only the best, do you not think?' His hands slid over her shoulders and down the silky flowing sleeves that covered her arms. 'I have already learned that you are a woman who appreciates beauty, and quality. The pink in that gown suits you very well, my clever Corrie.'

Her cheeks flamed as if to match it, as she caught the significance of his words. He was speaking as if she were some common woman who could be enticed and bought with gold coin, fine clothes and soft words. In her mind she wrenched herself free from his grasp. In reality it took a moment or two longer before she rid herself of his closeness. A sigh, almost of regret, escaped her lips as she drew away from him.

'I will not be treated in such a way,' she roundly scolded him. 'If I may be allowed to speak with your late father's lawyer or man of affairs, the matter of an income could be dealt with more agreeably.'

'Indeed, an excellent idea,' he surprised her by acquiescing without argument, but then continued, 'however, the immediate problem of your wardrobe will be solved by me. Tomorrow. One which is more befitting to your changed circumstance.' He regarded her mutinous expression with apparent interest. 'There is no necessity for you to fall upon my neck with gratitude.'

'I am glad to hear it.'

'Nor do I expect obdurate disobedience which shows complete lack of common sense. On Friday, for instance, we are to dine with Lord Wilchester. Several Members of Parliament will be present, together with many notable and titled personages. Which of your many gowns would you select for such an occasion?'

All colour drained from her face. He had driven his point home so piercingly that she stumbled over her next words. 'I-I could trim my Sunday blue with new ribbon.'

'And most ridiculous it would look, too.' Picking up the offending garment, he grasped it firmly in hands which could easily span the waist of its owner and just as easily separated the bodice from the skirt and split the latter quite in two. The sound of worn cloth being ripped to destruction made Coriander gasp, but it moved him not a jot.

'Now we will have done with foolish pride and this over-fertile imagination of yours which fancies that all men are out to rob you of your virtue, and concentrate instead upon more sensible, mundane matters such as how you are to be presented into society.'

Cold fury was simmering within her. 'You rob me of my pride as if it were of no account and mock me with your game of Lord Bountiful. But what is it you expect in return? There is always a price to pay.'

Raul fixed her with his probing gaze. 'I dare say you are accustomed to making payments of a certain nature, my little highwayman. Did not those clandestine visits of Ezra Follett to your private bedchamber at Larken Farm betoken some agreeable arrangement twixt the two of you.'

'Never.' She almost choked upon the word, but could see at once that he did not believe her. 'That was not of my choosing.'

'So you say. But I have only your word for that.' He laughed, and the harsh sound of it pressed upon her ears. 'Do not play the sweet innocent with me. Any woman who can carry out an armed robbery with such professional skill, and bargain so artfully for her share of an unexpected inheritance, can have few moral scruples. Did you plan it, or your protector?'

'Ezra Follett was not my protector.' Emotion tightened like an iron band around her heart, its one saving grace being that it squeezed out all possibility of tears.

His fingers reached out to stroke the fine skin of her jaw and curl themselves silkily about her throat. The effect upon her was stunning, the sensation of his touch vibrating through her like a playful breeze in corn. He would never believe her motives for the hold-up to be just. She knew that now with a dreadful, awesome certainty.

Feeling her quiver, he abruptly released her as if she contaminated him, and, lifting his hands in mock surrender, he curled his lips with sarcasm. 'I forgot. You do not like to be touched. Presumably you prefer your lovemaking to be spiced with the element of danger. Is that why my patient courtesy irritates?'

Before she had chance to respond, one hand grasped a bunch of her wayward curls and he pulled her face to his. As she opened her lips to protest, his mouth closed upon hers in an all-consuming kiss. There was no gentleness in it, no consideration, not a morsel of humanity. Coriander did not protest, nor attempt to escape from his hold which crushed her body intimately close to the steely hardness of his own. Like a rabbit caught in a snare she submitted, while holding herself rigidly ready for flight the instant it became possible. There was no sign now of the patient courtesy, only a searing passion which demanded to be sated in the only natural way. Here, at last, was proof of the ruthlessness she'd suspected lay beneath the veneer of charm. This was her nightmare taken physical form. Lips devouring hers, moving with relentless urgency, hands exploring each intimate curve. She knew what came next. Hadn't she dreamt it a thousand times? But the sensation in the pit of her stomach was not that of fear. It was recognisable to her as being akin to that she had experienced in the velvet mask, only more probing, more demanding and infinitely more urgent.

Excitement mounted in her, astonishing her by its intensity. The rapid pulse that beat in the hollow of her throat cried out for its share of caresses and, as her body softened in pliant surrender, she knew her hands for traitors as she felt the shine of silk between the clinging fingers. A whirl of emotion spiralled through her, and as the kiss deepened she knew she was behaving like a wanton, proving his accusations to be true, yet she could do nothing to braid her desire.

When he finally put her from him, they stood in silence, not touching, not looking at each other. The need to return behind the safety of her closely guarded shell was strong as Coriander kept her eyes downcast and concentrated on regaining control of her breathing.

And Raul was fighting his own inner conflict. He had meant the kiss as an insult, to hurt and to wound her, but he had been unprepared for his own reaction. A strange humility, almost an overwhelming protective tenderness for her, enveloped him. He had wanted to hate her, to lash her with his tongue and physical lust as a revenge against the destruction of his carefully laid plans, because her very existence had rekindled the hatred between Maynard and himself, and because she was not Isabella. Instead, he found himself suffering the agony of shame for his harsh treatment of her. He saw how her lips, rosy from his kisses, trembled. He noted the swathe of dark lashes, striking in one so fair, beaded with unshed tears where they fanned the curve of flushed cheeks. With a gentle finger he wiped the pearl of a tear from her cheek.

'Did I hurt you?'

Raising her brimming eyes to his, she gazed at him without speaking. After a long moment, he turned upon his heel and left.

True to his word, a seamstress followed swiftly upon the clearing of the breakfast dishes. A busy little body and as thin as the measure which hung about her neck, she whisked it about Coriander with a practised skill, making small tutting noises in her throat.

'Impossible,' she kept muttering. 'Quite impossible. I might have one gown done by Friday, but a half-dozen? Tut, tut.'

'What Mr Beringer wants, Mr Beringer usually gets,' said Mrs Tavannagh with crisp finality.

Wisely Coriander held her peace while swatches of fabric were held up to her cheek, laces and trimmings selected or rejected in a positive fever of activity. She guessed, accurately enough, that in distant rooms somewhere in the city a veritable army of young girls would soon be stitching their fingers raw for her.

Over the following few days this procedure was to be oft repeated as fabrics of every hue, coats, hats and pelisses were pinned and unpinned upon her, borne away to be stitched, and returned for the whole performance to start again. Any temptation to call a halt to all the fuss was stifled by the sight of little Pearl being likewise petted and preened. The effort she exercised to hold herself so unnaturally still was such a delight to watch that Coriander could do little but laugh.

For herself there was a lavender organza with rows of wide ribbon trim of a deeper tone about the ankle-length hemline. A deep turn-down collar finishing at the high waist was likewise decorated. The sleeves were short and puffed, with a long slim undersleeve which frilled at the wrist. Then there was a deep cobalt-blue walking dress with a stiffened skirt rich with embroidery. It had a neat, buttoned bolero, again with the same style sleeves and a neck frill. To match was a feathered bonnet which Coriander found quite dashing. There were parasols and white stockings, gloves, boots and silk pumps, several muslin day dresses and many more bonnets. She felt quite dazed by such excess, and, despite herself, thoroughly entranced with the whole thing.

But her favourite gown by far was an oyster silk satin which slipped softly about her slender figure, its hemline weighted with ruching. The arms were left bare beneath the full short sleeves, and the neckline was so daringly low it made Coriander blush just to think of it. This was the dress chosen for her first outing into society.

Her hair was dressed for the occasion by Alice with particular care, the bulk of her curls being gathered into a top knot and interwoven with narrow blue ribbon. She wore white stockings decorated daringly with clocks at the ankles, and silk pumps. A hooded cloak of midnight-blue velvet completed the ensemble.

As she crossed the black and white hall, she did not dare raise her eyes until she stood demurely before Raul, and only then because of the long silence which threatened to quite unsettle her confidence. Looking up at last, she could see at once that her efforts had been worthwhile. Raul's smile of greeting warmed her heart.

'Where is the waif now?' he teased. 'She has been replaced by a princess.'

She met his sparkling gaze with a shy smile, attacked with a sudden burst of nervousness, for he looked even more handsome in his black and white evening attire. 'I only hope I can live up to your expectations and not disgrace you. You must tell me how to behave. I have never attended anything grand in my life before.'

'Then you must trust to your notable

instincts for survival.'

She glanced up at him sharply. Was he reopening combat? But the smile upon his face looked sincere and something very like admiration. He was offering up his arm and, after the very smallest hesitation, she placed her gloved hand upon it to be led to the waiting coach.

If she had expected grandeur she was not disappointed. The invited company assembled in the green drawing-room of Lord and Lady Wilchester's town house in Curzon Street. One glance at her surroundings and fellow guests was sufficient to confirm Coriander's worst fears. No matter how beautiful the gown, how artfully coiffured her hair, she felt as out of place as a lily in a hothouse of roses. The gorgeous attire of the ladies, fiercely rivalled by their escorts, was outshone only by the sheer opulence of the room. Each apple-green damask-covered wall was hung with gilded mirrors all along its length from one huge marble fireplace to its fellow some thirty or more feet facing. These reflected the kaleidoscope of colours of the ladies' dresses, illuminated by the brilliance of the two immense chandeliers which hung from the Italian painted ceiling. Embellishments flourished on every pillar and cornice with hearts, crowns, carved roses and lattice-work of intricate detail gilded in gold leaf. And, though no one showed the least inclination to break from their social chit-chat to make use of them, richly ornamental gilt chairs, upholstered in palest rose, were strategically placed about the room.

Had it not been for the firm pressure of Raul's hand upon her elbow, steering her through the noisy crowd, Coriander guessed she would have turned and fled.

Footmen in crimson and gold livery carried trays of sparkling champagne, but Coriander blushingly declined.

'Come, you must try it,' Raul insisted, reaching her a glass.

'Oh, but I have never—'

Nuzzling his mouth close against her ear, he whispered, 'Never be afraid of new experiences. And it will at least keep your fidgety fingers occupied.'

She stilled them at once, but accepted the long-stemmed glass. Since he was so clearly watching her with ill-feigned amusement she was forced to try a sip. It was deliciously cold and slid over her tongue as easily as if she'd been born to it. She met his smile with delight upon her own face as she handed him back the empty glass.

'It's lovely. May I have another?'

'No, you may not if you drink with such abandon,' he laughed. 'A lady should sip her drink, and only nibble at her food. She must never be seen to actually enjoy either.'

Her eyes grew round with disbelief. 'I think you are teasing me.'

'I swear I am not.'

'Then I shall be the exception, for I intend to enjoy every morsel.' This made him laugh all the more so that she joined in, relaxed and mellowed by the champagne and by the warmth of his good nature.

'Do tell us what is so amusing. And why should you keep this charming young lady all to yourself, Beringer, you young rogue?'

Coriander, turning to learn the owner of this merry voice, was enchanted to meet a smiling face of girlish delicacy. Fair-skinned and dark-haired, Lady Wilchester looked considerably younger than her shapely full figure suggested. She wore a dress of palest pink satin crossed at the rounded bosom and revealing a fine sweep of shoulder as white as any Dresden shepherdess.

'So this is your little protégée? Why did you not tell us she was so lovely?' Lady Wilchester took hold of Coriander's two hands and held them out while she examined her. 'Would that I had had such a daughter instead of grumpy, difficult sons,' she complained with a chuckle, but

Coriander sensed the sons were not in such great disfavour as might be suspected, for pride shone in the lady's eyes.

'Christina, you rascal. Let me kiss you before everyone else does. I swear you grow more beautiful every day.'

'Pretty talk will catch fair lady.' A finger bobbed playfully upon Raul's nose and he laughed with delight, planting a firm kiss upon each round, rouged cheek.

'Allow me to introduce Coriander. She is learning her way about in the world, but with surprising speed.'

Once again, Coriander experienced conflicting emotions. Was there a barb to his teasing wit or was she being unduly sensitive? Good manners demanded she let it pass.

'And where have you been hiding yourself, Raul, all these months? I thought our wonderful army had concluded its task and you were free at last?'

'Not quite.' Raul looked grim. 'Fighting could break out again at any time. Once more Louis has been deserted by his troops, including Marshal Ney, and has been forced to flee for his life, taking his family to Belgium. Bonaparte has retaken Paris and is gathering his forces either for a repeat of last year's battles or some new offensive of which we are still ignorant.'

'And are we ready to meet him?'

' Raul's lips tightened momentarily. 'England and Prussia have agreed to put up a force of a hundred and fifty thousand men. Austria and Russia will almost double that number by the summer, but by then it could be too late.'

'But you will not fight?' she demanded.

'No, I will not fight.' Coriander glanced sharply up at him. There was almost raw satisfaction in his voice, as if he were proud of taking no part. Surely he did not revel in cowardice?

'Would you not do your duty, sir?' she bravely challenged, and brought both pairs of eyes upon her.

'And what is that, pray?'

'To your country? I know you live in Madeira at the moment, but I understood you to be English.' Coriander was hurt and astonished that he could boast so openly of refusing to take arms against the enemy of his country.

'You understood correctly.'

'Then why will you not fight?' she persisted smartly. 'Do you wish Napoleon to succeed?'

Lady Wilchester cleared her throat. 'I see you quite have your hands full with this young lady. I shall leave you to it, my dear boy, and see to my less illustrious guests. We must talk some more later, my dear, so we can become better acquainted.'

Lady Wilchester, scooping up her train and drifting away from them with a smile, was already directing her charms to another of her many admirers. 'My darling Mr Mackay, you shall take me in to supper. Now put down that vase, you naughty boy, before you break it. I vow I cannot leave you alone for a second, you are such a fidget.'

As Raul led her into supper, Coriander supposed she should feel honoured to have been included in Lady Wilchester's invitation. Yet somehow the disagreement with Raul, coming so soon upon their amicable truce, had left a bitter taste in her mouth.

She cast a sideways glance in his direction as he led her down the length of the dining-room to their places at table. Why did he refuse to fight for his country? What kind of man could speak so firmly in favour of a dictator and tyrant? Certainly not one she could trust.

'You use the fish knife and fork first.' Raul indicated the implements in a low whisper as Coriander stared in wonder at the bewildering array of cutlery, plates, glasses and finger bowls set before her. What to use, how and when, was a terrifying puzzle to her. Dish upon dish was presented to her from soup, turbot and lobster sauce, through cutlets, various roast meats, game and vegetables, to raspberry tart, orange ramekins and roughed jelly. She did not need any reminders of etiquette. She was far too overawed by the occasion and her heart too raw with disappointment to do more than nibble at any of them.

But the beauty of the table alone with its glistening silver set upon a stark white cloth made her catch her breath. The placement of every spoon and crystal goblet was a work of art, culminating in a grand centre-piece of golden flowers and green and gilded leaves arranged around a small fountain, as if it were a fairy garden.

Yet more brilliant still was the company seated around it. Coriander was to learn that the so called 'less illustrious guests' included Lord John Russell, Baron von Humboldt, the naturalist and traveller, Lord Lansdowne, Sydney Smith, whose intellect and witty conversation left her mind in a whirl, and Lord Byron, the much revered poet who enchanted them all by reading an extract from one of his latest romantic poems. There was also a number of politicians, artists, authors, and eminent figures from such notable journals as *The Gentleman's Magazine*. She rightly guessed that an invitation from Lady Wilchester was greatly sought after.

This was evidently the place to meet anyone of note, while basking in the warm favour of Lady Wilchester's captivating bossiness, which nobody seemed to mind in the slightest.

Raul seemed to be acquainted with most people present and showed a new side to his character by the skill and wit of his conversation. His smiles and charm were unsurpassed and Coriander watched with covert interest. He was undoubtedly a man of many facets, or one capable of assuming any role to suit the occasion. But, too, a man of duplicity and counterfeit manners, she decided. For beneath the veneer of seeming good humour and sweet patience she knew a different Raul Beringer: one riddled with bitterness; one ruthless in his passions, whether of lust for her or hatred for his brother and greed for his inheritance. More than anything, Coriander loathed and mistrusted anyone who had such little regard for family.

After dinner as they played a rubber of whist the conversation once more drifted back to the coming confrontation of French and English armies. Coriander heard how the commanders had fled home from Vienna to muster a national force in order to block Napoleon's determined bid to add England to his dream of a single united Europe under his own control.

'Do you not despise Napoleon for his greed for power?' Coriander persisted.

He paused before answering. 'Bonaparte is a man with a dream. Over-ambitious perhaps, but one who will go down in history as one of the great commanders and tacticians of all time.'

Coriander stared at him in shocked surprise. 'But he has caused untold misery and hundreds of innocent people have been killed. Surely you cannot forgive such an outrage?'

'It is not for me to forgive, but I can observe. He has dominated Europe for almost twenty years and changed the face of warfare into a strategic art never before contemplated.'

'I see little laudable in such a claim,' said Coriander heatedly. 'He is a tyrant and a bully.'

'Possibly. But to be fair to the man, he has brought order out of the chaos that was Europe. Say what you will, he has a brilliant mind, can grasp the central significant point of any argument in an instant, has many interests, including law and education, and is a talented mathematician.'

'Is it true that he even dictates to his secretaries while bathing in a white marble bath?' queried Lady Wilchester, raising her fan slightly to disguise her chuckles.

Raul smiled. 'So it is said. He is certainly reputed to work long hours and is totally single-minded.'

'Like you?' said Lady Wilchester with a provoking smile.

Coriander, appalled by his light-minded attitude, clenched her fists fiercely into the skirt of her gown. 'For the rest, he has brought nought but trouble upon us all.'

'Indeed no. His influence has not been all bad,' Raul assured her. 'Were it not for Bonaparte there would be no fine display of art and sculpture in the Palace of the Louvre, readily available for all to enjoy. Is that not a good thing?'

'I think you defend him too vehemently!' Coriander cried.

Raul smiled benignly upon her. 'I believe it is you who are expressing vehemence. And quite ruining that satin gown in the process. For my part I will only say that Bonaparte is a great man, albeit a man of obsessions, and he certainly possesses charisma.'

'Charisma,' Coriander scoffed, none the less lowering her voice and smoothing out the crumpled fabric. 'What does that signify in comparison with an issue as huge as Europe?'

His equanimity was infuriating and there

was a positive glint of mischief in his eyes as he said, 'Now, Corrie, do remain calm and recognise that there are always two sides to any argument.'

Acutely aware of the close proximity of her hostess, Coriander tried not to be too forceful in her opinions. 'I will accept that Napoleon has showed great taste in the Arts, but only consider how he acquired those treasures.'

'And how did he acquire them?'

'By theft, of course, as you well know. He took them from their rightful owners.'

'In the interests of the nation.'

'It was none the less stealing.'

'And stealing is wrong?'

'Most certainly.'

In the small silence which followed, again he only smiled at her, eyebrows slightly quirked in humorous enquiry while Coriander felt the colour flood upwards from the low-cut neck of her gown to the roots of her silver-blonde hair, so artlessly curled and braided.

Lady Wilchester tapped her fan upon the card table. 'Children, children, enough. You have done nothing but squabble over politics all evening. I am sure I would be the first to welcome a young lady with opinions, my dear, but if anyone knows about Napoleon, it is Raul. So let that be an end of the matter and let us speak of more homely topics.'

'I do beg your pardon, Lady Wilchester,' murmured Coriander, instantly contrite, and for the next several minutes devoted her attention to the game. But in her head there remained the echo of Lady Wilchester's words. If anyone knows about Napoleon, it is Raul. How could that be unless he were personally acquainted with the man?

'Coriander has decided to return with me to Madeira,' said Raul, in a voice carefully devoid of expression.

'Indeed?' Was there a new respect in the lady's tone, or something else? Surprise? Disapproval? Concern? Coriander could not decide, so felt bound to dismiss it as mere fancy on her part. 'And when do you leave?'

'Not yet. I have important matters to attend to first.'

'Of course. I do worry about you, my dear boy.'

'Then you should not. I am well able to take care of myself, sweet Christina. I shall always return, if only for your most delightful suppers.' He bent over her hand to kiss it and the expression in her eyes was soft, almost adoring for an instant before being superseded by the charm of the skilled hostess once again.

Coriander looked on with curiosity and interest, and something more. Jealousy? Why should she care if Raul Beringer directed his smiles at others and not at her?

Yet as the evening progressed it grew impossible to maintain an air of disapproval. Raul was all she could have hoped from an escort on her first outing into society.

'I'm afraid I do not follow the fashion for dancing,' he said, when the card game was concluded with Lady Wilchester and her partner the much satisfied winners. 'Would you be bored if we sat in the music-room and listened to Christina's Italian singer?'

'Not at all.' Coriander had never heard an Italian singer, but was soon entranced by the beauty and resonance of her voice and quite forgot her disappointment at not dancing.

She found it pleasant sitting next to Raul, for occasionally he would lean closer to ask if she was enjoying the music or to whisper snippets of information about the piece into her ear—a small courtesy which she appreciated. When a short interval for refreshment was called he led her out into the garden for a breath of fresh air, and, looking up at the winking stars, she was reminded of the night they had first met.

Turning to him, about to risk a tease upon the subject, she found him gazing down upon her with such a thoughtful expression upon his face that for no reason at all she flushed.

'You were one of the loveliest women in the room, Coriander,' he said quietly. 'Almost beautiful.'

'It is merely the starlight,' she whispered.

He shook his head. 'There was no starlight in the music-room.' He drew in a deep breath then said. 'Coriander, I wish to apologise.'

She was surprised. 'For what?'

There was no smile upon his face as he steadily regarded her. 'A gentleman, if he is worthy of that name, does not take advantage of a young girl in his care. It was unforgivable. I cannot imagine what came over me, yet I crave your forgiveness. It will not happen again, I do assure you.' Lifting her hand he touched the palm with soft lips, before tucking it into the crook of his elbow. A deliciously warm feeling flooded through her. Nothing she had ever experienced before had prepared her for the sheer pleasure of this simple action. 'Perhaps I will take you in to dance after all,' he said. 'Such beauty should be displayed to full advantage. And we did take considerable trouble over the dress, did we not?'

She looked into his eyes and a great gurgle of laughter rose in her throat as she agreed that indeed, yes, they had taken considerable trouble over the dress.

The rest of the evening passed in a whirl of colour and music and laughter and new emotions. His eyes scarcely seemed to leave her face and she found herself equally enthralled, smiling up at him through dance after dance.

'Are you tired?' he asked her once after a particularly lively galliard. But she shook her head fervently.

'Not at all. I could dance till dawn.' She laughed up at him, eyes sparkling with delight, and he found himself responding to her good humour, which was quite genuinely infectious. He was beginning to see a different side to Miss Coriander May, thief of the road and grasper of fortunes. She held common-sense views upon politics and had a quite delicious sense of humour. He couldn't remember ever having enjoyed himself quite so much.

Catching her slender figure close, he pressed his cheek to hers for one daring, breathless moment. 'You are very nearly irresistible, Miss Coriander May, do you know that?'

And so was he, she thought, a tremor stroking the warm glow in her heart. That was the trouble.

CHAPTER SIX

In the days which followed, the magic of that night was to fade while the mistrust grew and festered, for Lady Wilchester had intimated that Raul knew Napoleon well. No matter how hard Coriander tried to deny it, this worrying information kept returning to trouble her. As if to emphasise her growing suspicions, not a day passed in which Raul was not visited by a stream of gentlemen callers. None of these was introduced to Coriander, who was left to amuse herself in the pink salon as best she might. On the days when the house did not echo with the ring of strange footsteps, or the confused tones of hushed voices, Raul was absent, and these absences lasted long into the night.

'Are we to spend our entire time incarcerated in our apartments like nursery children?' Coriander finally burst out to him on one of the rare occasions Raul chose to take dinner at home. It had been a merry enough meal, at which they had all enjoyed a particularly fine piece of sole in a mushroom sauce, followed by a large custard tart of which Pearl had eaten far more than was good for her. But they were only too glad to have his company, for it had been a particularly dull afternoon, too damp for the three ladies to enjoy their usual stroll in the park, accompanied by Alice and a footman, of course; and time was hanging heavy on all of .hem. But the moment that Letty had taken Pearl upstairs to her bed the question had popped out unbidden as Coriander and Raul enjoyed an after-dinner coffee in supposed harmony.

He glanced enquiringly at her. 'Growing weary of the London scene so soon?'

'I did not request to be part of the London scene,' she pointed out, trying to keep a hold on her temper. 'It was my understanding that we were to be leaving shortly for Madeira. Why can we not do so? I really think this is no life for a child.'

His brows drew together in a troubled frown. 'We cannot travel yet with matters in Europe so unsettled. And it was your idea to bring little Pearl, remember, not mine, therefore she is your responsibility.'

The truth of this forced Coriander to bite down hard upon her rebellious tongue before it ran away with her. Though she could not resist adding, 'But nothing has been settled. I have no independence, no income by which to take care of her. I am still totally dependent upon you.'

'Income? Is that all you think of?' He looked at her, almost sadly. 'At least this way I have some control over what you do and where you go. You want for nothing. Do you not have gowns enough?'

'It is not gowns I speak of.'

'Then what can you possibly require that is not already amply provided here in Funchal Place, a fine house, ably run by a multitude of expensive servants?' He held out his hands to encompass the splendours of the library, richly lined with books and furnished with exquisite taste in gold and green, and Coriander felt a prickle of shame.

She had known real need, and the life she was now living should inspire in her nothing but gratitude. Yet she felt the lack of something so strongly that she was growing more and more unhappy. Had it all stemmed from the magic of that one night, or had it begun long before, on another evening of mystic beauty when the April mists had hung low over the land? There was little sign of that magic now. She had the grace, however, to show no mortification in her expression as, sighing, she walked over to the window, away from the shrewdness of his gaze. 'You must forgive my seeming ingratitude. I simply grow restless. No doubt it is the inclement weather.'

'I can see that for someone used to a life of crime and adventure, being confined to drawing-room pursuits must prove restricting,' he said crisply, and she whirled upon her heel to face him.

'Why must you always think the worst of me?'

He regarded her with lazy insolence for a moment. 'Did I then dream that you stole fifty gold pieces from me? And have still to return them, for all your cry of poverty?'

'I do not have them.'

'Should I be blamed if your accomplice did not give you a fair cut of the loot?'

She knew with a heavy sinking of her heart that there was enough of the truth in his accusation for her to be unable to offer any real defence. Abandoning all argument, she withdrew to her room without another word and went early to bed, nursing her hurt in secret as if it were a bruise that must not be seen. She lay tightly curled in the darkness, far from sleep. What had she done? Because of her own impulsiveness, Letitia had left her home, Pearl had lost her friends who were living goodness knew where, and she had failed them. How naïve of her to believe in a promised land, one which it was doubtful she would ever see, if it existed at all. And for what purpose? To find a family who did not even want her.

Though weariness lay heavily upon her lids, she slept fitfully that night and woke uncharacteristically depressed, gripped by remorseless guilt and crippling self-pity. Raul's night had been little better, for as soon as she left he rang for the brandy bottle and embarked upon an equally uncharacteristic and prolonged bout of heavy drinking.

But as the weeks passed and she saw less and less of Raul, frustration gave way to anger. She became convinced that he was avoiding her, that he had no intention of taking her to Madeira because he did not wish her to share in his inheritance. Her welfare was of no importance to him.

One evening Coriander, Letty and Pearl were attempting to form a cosy group, sewing quietly before the screened marble fireplace in the pink salon, believing that if their fingers were fully employed their minds would be likewise. But the fallacy of this was proved when Pearl, finally overcome with boredom, threw down her sampler upon the floor and folded her arms in protest.

'I'm doing no more of it, Corrie. I don't care what you say. I don't believe we shall ever have a pretty garden. I don't believe we shall ever do anything, ever again.'

Coriander gazed at her in dismay. Pearl was expressing what they all felt. They needed security, a purpose in life, not idle diversions. Jumping to her feet, she tossed aside her own embroidery. 'We shall have no more gloom. These matters will be settled forthwith, this very night.'

Pearl's eyes lit up. 'How? What are you going to do? Do you have one of your schemes brewing, Corrie? Oh, do tell us, do.'

'Oh, my.' Letitia's hand flew to her mouth in distress. 'Now, Coriander, think before you act. Do not, I pray you, be over-hasty. Pearl is simply in a pet which is most unbecoming.'

'I am not in a pet.'

'I'm sure you do not mean to be, my lamb, but you are causing Coriander unnecessary concern. We are perfectly well placed here. I'm sure for my part I do not mind in the least having no one to talk with, so long as we are so warm and comfortable.'

'But it is so dull, Letty. What can you do, Corrie?' Pearl persisted, clinging to Coriander's hand. 'Please, please, do something. You are so good at making things happen.'

'Yes, indeed, sometimes more than she bargains for,' said Letitia drily.

Coriander stroked the child's hair. 'If I

could, I would, you know that.' She looked across the child's head to Letty, who smiled reassuringly, dimpling the plump cheeks with characteristic good humour, though to Coriander the forget-me-not eyes looked unusually bleak.

'Do not fret about me. I am content enough. I shall ask Mrs Tavannagh if there is not some task I can do for her.'

Letty's brave words did not fool Coriander. The older woman was lonely, despite all her efforts to the contrary, and was experiencing a creeping feeling of uselessness in this unusually inactive life.

The only answer was to find Raul and settle the matter once and for all. No longer would she allow him to ignore their presence so callously.

Even as she ran down the stairs she saw him stride out through the front door. Though she crossed the wide hall as quickly as she could, her pumps slipping, and sliding on the marble floor, there was not a sign of him in the street by the time she reached it.

In desperation she rang the bell for Burton. Facing the autocratic manservant, she nourished the small amount of courage in her breast, hoping it would grow.

'Would you kindly tell me where Mr Beringer has gone?'

Burton's eyebrows shot up with the

shock of her temerity. 'Mr Raul does not find the necessity to explain all his movements to me.' He meant to her, of course. Coriander had not the smallest doubt that he knew Raul's movements, almost to the hour.

'Then can you at least tell me when you expect him home?'

Again, if it were possible, the brows climbed higher so that the forehead above became lined with deep furrows of displeasure. 'I could not say, miss.'

Coriander abandoned her fruitless inquisition and dismissed him. Or rather, she would have done so, had he not already departed in high dudgeon. Burton let it be clearly understood by the stiffness of his back what his opinion was of inquisitive females prying their noses into his master's affairs.

But if he had been more closely acquainted with the so-called softer sex, he would have known better than to expect this particular female to concede defeat so easily. Without pausing for thought, Coriander flew to her room, gathered up her cloak and purse, and, waking John, the coachman, from his station, ushered him from the house before he had time to recover his wits.

'Did you drive Mr Beringer out this evening?'

'No, ma'am. He did drive himself, as he often do these days.'

'Do you know in which direction he has gone?' When she saw how he hesitated, she guessed that he knew well enough, but that he dared not tell. Gossip could lose him his job. Coriander thought quickly. She would follow and discover what he did do so late at night and settle this other problem at the same time. 'It is imperative that I find Mr Beringer.' She put her hand softly upon John's arm and looked at him with beseeching violet eyes. Even before she pressed home her suit he was lost. 'No blame will attach to you simply by conveying me. You may depend upon me to see to that.'

He drove her in a small closed carriage along darkened streets empty of everyone save late carousers and those about night business which was best not investigated. She did not ask where he took her nor make any comment when he drew the vehicle down a small sideroad and brought it to a halt, save to ask if this was the place.

'It's where he often is at this hour. You had best wait within, miss, while I find him. T'wouldn't be safe for you to be abroad at this time of night.'

He disappeared through a door, leaving Coriander alone in the dim closeness of the carriage. John had drawn the curtains against any prying eyes, but a flicker of nervousness still, sparked into life and a steady pulse began to beat low in her stomach. What would she say to him? What had possessed her to act so rashly? It was Raul Beringer's fault for using her so ill. Waiting had always galled her, and here, alone in the dark, it was none too pleasant. She needed action to hold the fears back. Turning the handle with soft care, she opened the door and stepped down from the carriage.

She found herself standing in a dark street with not a single light showing at any windows, if indeed there were any. Four steps rose before her and she climbed them hastily, hating the unidentifiable rustlings scraping the darkness behind her. The door was unlatched and she felt safer once she was on the other side of it. Whose house this was she did not know, but apparently she was entering by a side-door. No doubt John's attempt at discretion. Which must mean that the house belonged to a gentleman. But who? Was he one of the men who visited Raul at Funchal Place so frequently? And what was Raul doing here? Could such a meeting, held so late at night, be entirely innocent? Did this gentleman, whoever he was, also share an acquaintance with Napoleon Bonaparte?

With her own fear beating against her eardrums, she crept down the short lobby on the silent toes of slippered feet. A further flight of stairs led up into the house and somewhere above she could hear the low murmur of voices. She climbed them quickly and found herself pressing an ear against a panelled door, trying to hear the voices within. Unfortunately, because of the thickness of the panel, it was impossible to distinguish individual voices, let alone words. She could not even be certain if Raul was present. She leaned closer and suddenly the door seemed to give way beneath her pressure. At precisely that moment it had been thrown open from within, and, unable to hold her balance, Coriander pitched forward on to a rug to gaze in stupefied horror at a pair of all too familiar black boots.

The silence in the room was appalling. When she finally plucked up the courage to lift her head, she saw herself the focus of several pairs of eyes, belonging to a group of gentlemen seated around a large oval table. She did not need to inspect the amusement highly evident among them to know how completely foolish she looked. She waited for fury to fall upon her in the shape of Raul Beringer's hand.

His calm voice rang out across the room.

'Allow me to introduce to you my ward, or partner, or what-you-will, Miss Coriander May. She is new to society but, as you can see, does not allow that to be a barrier to her adventurous spirit.'

Whatever she had been expecting, it had certainly not been cool indifference. It somehow left her rather deflated.

'Miss May?' A hand was extended to her and she was being helped to her feet by a kindly looking gentleman with white whiskers. 'Are you hurt? Dear me, we must have that door seen to. Come and seat yourself and gather your breath.'

He led her to a chair where Coriander kept her eyes cast firmly downwards. But she was not allowed to retreat for long as she heard Raul curtly dismiss the coachman, promising to speak with him later.

'Oh, do not blame John. It was all my doing. I made him bring me. And he knew I would have found some other conveyance to take me around all the London Clubs of which you might be a member, if he had not.'

She became acutely aware of the astonishment in the three other gentlemen's eyes at her words. They must think her quite demented to venture half across London at this hour, alone but for a coachman. It required very little imagination to realise she had caused Raul acute embarrassment.

'Is my house on fire?' The icy stillness in his voice warned her of a coming storm. She could only pray it did not break before this avidly curious audience.

'N-no,' she admitted.

'Have Pearl, or Letty, or anyone at Funchal Place been struck down with some terrible accident or incurable disease?' Raul felt his only hope was to let her appear as a foolish besotted girl or else his well-meaning friends would start asking questions he felt ill-equipped to answer. Therefore she must temporarily be made to suffer considerable embarrassment for this undoubted breach of etiquette. Which was a pity in a way, but with luck his friends would be merely amused. Twin spots of heightened colour were warming her cheeks and he could not deny she was holding the attention of the assembled company quite easily.

'I doubt you would care if they had, since you are never there.'

She surprised him by her spirited reply. 'And as you are not my wife, nor my keeper, is it any concern of yours how I spend my time?' he pointed out with some justice.

'Dash it, Beringer, but the girl has spirit. Pray take care not to scold her too severely.'

Coriander bestowed her sweet smile upon the bewhiskered gentleman who so gallantly defended her, but Raul was not so easily mollified.

'Perhaps you thought to partly take on a wife's duties and surprise me with my mistress?'

Coriander actually gasped out loud at this. 'I would not presume to ...' she began, but stumbled to a halt, for indeed the thought had crossed her mind, and she turned her eyes from his face in case he should read her thoughts.

'Seeing his mistress here, eh? I reckon Christina has more sense than to tangle with this young puppy.'

Guffaws of laughter greeted this remark and suddenly Coriander began to relax. The gentlemen were enjoying the joke, but not simply at her expense. Perhaps she could turn the situation to her advantage after all, for she now had a good idea where she was. She certainly had nothing to lose, she thought, flashing an impish glance in Raul's direction and noting with satisfaction a sudden wariness enter his eyes. She raised dark lashes in a knowingly provocative fashion to smile shyly with sweetly curved pink lips and sparkling violet eyes upon the assembled company.

'I am so sorry to have disturbed you gentlemen.' Growing bolder, she swiftly took in the details of her surroundings, the small panelled room, evidently a gentleman's retreat, and the forgotten cards upon the leather-topped table. 'To interrupt your game was unforgivable. I swear I would not have done so had I not imagined myself abandoned.' She gazed up at them from glistening eyes and the three gentlemen moved perceptibly closer.

'Abandoned?'

Accepting the kind offer of a handkerchief, she turned her face into it for a moment as if controlling her emotions, before continuing.

'I dare say Raul has told you that I was an orphan when he found me in a remote farmstead, and of my inclusion in his father's will?'

Faint surprise and glances of enquiry in Raul's direction greeted this intriguing information.

'Yet he refuses to take me to his home in Madeira so that I can begin my new life. Where else can I go? I have no one in the whole world, no home of my own except that provided by Raul, and I so long to have one. So when I could not find him, for some reason I became convinced that he had left without me.' There was enough of the truth in her plea to make genuine tears spill from the brimming eyes, but Raul's growl of disgust caused her sudden concern. Could she have gone too far, overplayed her hand? She looked up at him and now, at last, she was afraid.

He clapped his hands slowly together as if in applause. 'A good performance, Coriander May. Why do you not finish the act and tell the whole sorry tale? Her talent for disguise is renowned, my Lord. Perhaps that is where her future lies. Upon the stage.'

'That was an unnecessarily cutting remark, Beringer.' The white-whiskered gentleman rose to face him. 'Can't ye see the poor gel's upset? And if you've neglected her as much as I suspect, I'm not at all surprised.'

Matters were not going according to plan. It should be Coriander who was suffering embarrassment and yet it was he who was being placed in a compromising situation, finding himself cast in the role of villain, as if he meant to harm her. How could he explain that the very opposite was the case? She sat before him, so determined, so independent, so touchingly beautiful, and the desire to scold her melted away from him, overwhelmed by another more urgent desire and in a form which astounded him. In all the years he had spent with Isabella he had never experienced this humbling need for a woman's approbation. What could possibly have come over him?

Coriander was being helped to her feet by her gallant saviour. 'You'll not know me. I am Lord Wilchester, m'dear,' the bewhiskered gentleman informed her, though she had already guessed. 'We'll see what Christina has to say about all this.' Casting a severely disapproving glance back at Raul, he conducted Coriander from the study to his wife's private sitting-room, where she was enjoying a small nightcap of spiced wine. A cup was drawn for Coriander and soon that good lady took it upon herself to gently coach Coriander in the proprieties of being 'an untroublesome dependant.' A prospect which filled Coriander with no comfort whatsoever, though she took care not to let these feelings be known.

Lady Wilchester shrewdly summed up the situation and immediately declared that Coriander must stay on for a few days. John was duly dispatched to return before noon the next day with Pearl and Letty, and a small but essential wardrobe for their stay.

'Seems to me the matter needs steering by a firm hand,' said that good lady decisively.

Lady Wilchester's two lively boys, little older than Pearl herself, fell in love with their new playmate at once and instantly whisked her away to share the delights of the nursery wing. Within days, Letitia and Lady Wilchester were calling each other by their first names and declaring themselves to be fast friends. Since Christina had recently lost her companion, Letty was only too pleased to fill the gap.

'Now what shall we do to entertain you, Coriander?' asked Lady Wilchester as soon as these domestic matters had been settled to everyone's convenience.

'You must not trouble yourself on my account,' Coriander hastened to assure her. 'Soon we will be leaving for Madeira, I know it.'

'Hmm,' was all Christina felt bound to say upon that little matter, and Coriander hurried to her room and her embroidery, feeling even more of an imposition here in Curzon Street than she had at Funchal Place. And with even less opportunity of seeing Raul. Matters, as far as she was concerned, had taken a turn for the worse.

But if Christina chose to say little to Coriander, she did not feel the necessity to curb her tongue with the girl's guardian.

'I declare, Raul, you grow more obstinate with each visit home.'

'Madeira is my home.'

'Don't be provoking, you know well

enough what I mean. You have had that poor child staying with you a good five weeks, or is it six? And have you attempted to please her, show her the sights, visit the gardens, introduce her to some other young people? Not a bit of it.'

'I hardly feel it is my place,' said Raul, the coldness of his tone softened slightly by his affection for his old friend.

'Not your place? What utter nonsense. The child is lonely. You told me not to call as she was not ready to receive visitors. And like a fool I believed you. This cannot go on. You have brought her to London, therefore you must make it your responsibility to do all of those things.'

'All?' Raul raised a questioning brow.

'All.'

'Christina, I know you possess a soft heart, but I do have other matters which demand my time.'

The pretty, girlish face tightened with displeasure, the small lips firmly pursed, the blue eyes narrowed as she frowned at him. Then, just as he began to shift in his seat with discomfort rather like a naughty schoolboy, she bestowed upon him a smile so beauteous, and at the same time so wickedly provoking that he almost, but not quite, laughed out loud.

'Have you noticed how lovely she is?'

'I am not blind.'

She clicked her tongue with impatience. 'For how long are you going to allow this vendetta to eat into your heart? Is it not time that you put it behind you and looked to the future?'

'What future do I have?'

'Do not think I have not noticed the number of times you have found the need to call during these last few days while she has been here, nor how your eyes follow her about the room.'

'You speak as if I were some young boy in his first flush.'

'Perhaps she makes you feel that way.' Christina smiled at him so enticingly he found himself responding with a smile of his own.

'Perhaps she does. But you are well aware that I can find no place in my life at present for complications.'

'Is that what she is?'

'It's what she could be, if I do not take care.' Raul got to his feet to stride about the room in obvious agitation. 'Dammit, Christina, I do understand how the girl feels. None better. She doesn't trust me. She doesn't trust anyone. Abandoned as a baby, denied by those in a position to help her. Didn't my father deny me almost as completely, for years?'

'You made your peace with the old

150

man before he died, and he with you. Be thankful for that. As for Maynard, if what you say about him is true, then you must not give in. It is your duty to the memory of your father, however hard he was upon you in your early years, to ensure the safe future of the company he built.'

'I never forgave Father for allowing Cassandra to go away. I think that was what originally alienated him from me,' said Raul, sadly.

'But now you have found her daughter.'

Raul grew thoughtful. 'Yes. Now I have found her daughter. The question now is, do I have the will to take on another battle? Sometimes I grow weary of fighting. Does it really matter who owns the company, so long as it continues to thrive?'

Lady Wilchester snapped closed her fan with exasperation. 'Do not play the coward with me, Raul Beringer, I know you better than that. Of course it matters, for if it continues in Maynard's hands you have said yourself that it will not thrive. This is one battle you can and must win, I am sure of it. But is there any reason why you must do it alone?'

Raul stood before her, his green eyes bleak as frosted glass. 'Many, many reasons, dear Christina.'

'Hmm.' She walked past him to the door, then, turning back, she gently tapped his arm with the folded fan, 'Before you leave, give this child some pleasure. Do it for me, if you refuse to consider your own happiness.'

She sailed from the room, leaving him to his guilt, and to the reawakening of that obstinate need. He would like to do something for her. Perhaps he did owe Coriander that much. And it would not be unpleasant to try to improve her image of him. Odd how they were growing to like each other, yet each was unwilling to offer complete trust.

The next morning Raul surprised Coriander at breakfast, offering to show her the sights. She clapped her hands with pleasure.

'Oh, that would be lovely. Give me one moment to fetch my cloak.'

Raul felt strangely touched by the genuine delight she showed. Surely such simple sincerity could not be a disguise for a more grasping, greedy nature? How could this delightful, fun-loving girl be a hard-hearted, calculating thief?

He took her for a sail up the river. He showed her Hampton Court, the Tower, and Carlton House where the Prince Regent lived. And though he tried to remain aloof, as if he were doing no more than performing a duty, little by little he found himself warming to her charm and fun-loving nature. She was enchanted by everything he showed her, asking endless questions, smiling and laughing with him as easily as if they had known each other for a lifetime. The awkwardness in his manner faded and the relationship which had flowered on that first evening at Lady Wilchester's began once more to flourish between them.

As the summer progressed, he found himself devising new treats, simply to watch the excitement and joy flit across her face. He took her to see a balloon dispatched high into the sky, and when it almost crashed into a tree, seeming as if it would ditch its daring occupant, she clung to him in fear, and hugged him with relief when the moment of crisis was over.

Not one to follow fashions, he none the less would have needed to be blind not to notice the care she took to look pretty in the rainbow of muslin dresses he had ordered for her. On numerous occasions she looked so delicious he had difficulty restraining his natural urge to take advantage of her charms. Yet always he held back. He could see her trust in him growing and had no wish to spoil it.

As for Coriander, her heart was so full she felt she could not bear any more joy. No longer did she avoid his touch, rather she unconsciously sought every opportunity for the fleeting brush of fingertips, like a caress against her velvet skin, for the pressure of his powerful shoulders next to hers in the carriage, for the warm whisper of his breath across her cheek.

'Perhaps I should spirit you away soon to my magic island, where we can hold hands and sit in the sun all day,' he murmured softly one evening as they strolled in the Vauxhall Gardens.

Blushing furiously, Coriander resisted the urge to slip her hand into his at once, not least because Letty and Pearl were chaperoning close behind.

She smiled up at him, unaware of the adoration shining forth from her satin-soft eyes. 'One day you shall take me around the world.'

'Is that what you want?'

She nodded fervently. 'Yes. I would love to travel, but I want only to go with you.'

His eyes held hers for a long, long time before he answered. 'I think that that is what I want too, Coriander.'

And on the day the news burst that Wellington had defeated Napoleon at Waterloo it seemed that the whole world rejoiced. Fireworks blazed and exploded over the parks, people feasted and danced, and toasted each other in wine, champagne or ale, whatever they could afford.

To Coriander the celebrations seemed to go on for weeks. This was the climax of her happiness, for what was there now to prevent their travelling abroad? The world had changed and nothing would ever be the same again. Unfortunately this was also true for Coriander, though she was as yet blissfully unaware of the fact.

Until one morning in late July when she awoke to find another day filled with sunshine but empty of Raul. He had left for Madeira without her.

CHAPTER SEVEN

Maynard Beringer stretched his muscled body beneath the silken sheets and rolled over on to his back to gaze lingeringly at the voluptuous curves of his mistress's body as she slept peacefully beside him. Isabella was almost beautiful in repose, with the dark waves of her hair fanned out across the pillow and sleep softening the hard lines of her full scarlet mouth, silencing its pithy taunts. He could understand any man wanting her, even his goody-goody brother. Maynard allowed himself a lazy smile. Perhaps that was why he had wanted her for himself—because she had belonged to

Raul. Hadn't it always been so throughout their boyhood together? But he had not been disappointed. Isabella had proved to be a willing, if unpredictable mate, with a healthy appetite for sporting between the sheets.

But she was growing lazy and less inclined to please him these days. He nudged her ankle with his foot. How much sleep did a woman need? Perhaps when Raul returned the spark of competition which always excited her would rekindle her interest in him. She enjoyed the piquant sensation of being wanted by both brothers. Maynard ground his teeth together. He could not rid it from his mind that she was servicing Raul's appetites as well as his own. Sensual as a cat, she was completely without scruples. He nudged her again, more forcibly, and she groaned, a deep, rumbling purr of contentment that stirred the dark corners of his mind.

Sliding her arms from beneath the sheets, she curled them about his neck. 'Is it morning already?'

'Morning? It's past noon. I should have been slaving away long since instead of dallying here, with you.' He stroked the curve of her shoulder, pulling the sheet away so that he could feast his eyes upon her. 'I wonder why I am not?'

She chuckled, a deeply rich tone as

she smiled up at him, eyelids hiding the triumph in her dark eyes. 'I wonder,' she purred, pulling him unresisting towards her.

Later, with his appetite once more pleasantly sated, Maynard lay with his hands behind his head, contemplating the ceiling. The sweet scent of bougainvillaea drifted in through the open window. Birds sang in the sun, and time, as far as he was concerned, stood still.

'Raul must return soon,' he said irritably. 'He has never stayed away so long before.'

'Perhaps it is the pretty English miss reluctant to leave her schoolroom.'

Maynard's eyes narrowed. 'She would not refuse to come. She must not.'

'Raul might refuse to bring her. You cannot control him. He is his own man.'

Maynard's hand shot out to grasp her about her slender neck and she let out a tiny squeal of fright. 'You are wrong. I can control anyone I choose, including you, my little snake. Raul will bring her because he must. I demanded it.'

'You are hurting. Let go of me.' She sighed with relief when he took his hand away, but curled herself provocatively around his body in case he should forget she was present. She was ever afraid he might grow tired of her. Strangely, he always wanted her more when Raul was there, as if he needed to constantly prove to his brother of the pleasures he was missing. Perhaps he could see that Raul still excited her.

'I wonder what she is like, this by-blow of Cassandra's?' he mused.

'I thought the mother had married?'

'What of it? She did not marry the father. And, more to the point, she did not marry my father. The child has no real claim to either our land or our fortune.'

'Then why do you wish for this woman to come to Madeira?' Isabella asked, peeved at the interest he was showing in her.

Maynard smiled a mirthless smile that chilled even the insensitive Isabella. 'Because I intend to make it my business to see she does not have either for very long.'

Coriander knelt, ashen-faced, at Lady Wilchester's feet. 'What am I to do? How could he do this to me, just when I was starting to trust him?'

'I vow this is most unlike Raul. It is not normally in his nature to be so heartless, and he has grown fond of you, child.' Christina looked with genuine sympathy upon the girl before her and remembered the pain of first love. Curses on all men, she thought, for their callousness. And

158

she had believed Raul Beringer to be different.

'Grown fond?' Coriander's eyes were big and wide, dark with misery. 'How could he have grown fond when he can leave without a care? Not a word of goodbye, no apology, no acknowledgement of our friendship. Nothing.'

Christina cleared her throat. The situation was most delicate and she must tread softly. 'Did he by any chance, my dear, make any provision for you?' She hated to speak of money, indeed she rarely thought of the subject, nor carried any upon her person. But for this child, matters were entirely different.

Coriander could only shake her head.

'But what of this inheritance of which you spoke?'

'No mention has been made of the sum of money involved, nor have I received any. I believe there is some land.'

'And may you sell this land? Could that sum be used to invest in some kind of annuity for your future?'

Coriander had no wish to own to Lady Wilchester that such an offer had already been made, and she had refused it. There must be some other way out of her dilemma, a way which would not embarrass her patient hostess. A thought struck her, and filled her with such hope that she grasped hold of Lady Wilchester's hands in relief.

'Perhaps John is wrong. Raul could be visiting the company's shipping offices before he prepares to leave. He did say that he had some business to attend to.'

Lady Wilchester looked doubtful and more than a little sad. It grieved her to disenchant the child and wipe the look of hope from her lovely face. 'That is not how I understood it, but there, you might well be right.'

Coriander was not entirely convinced by her own theory either, but they had grown so close this summer. There must be some rational explanation. The alternative, that he had deliberately abandoned her so as not to share the inheritance with her, nagged at the back of her mind, but she would never know the truth of it unless she could follow him.

'Tell me, child, do you love Raul very much?'

The abruptness of the question knocked the breath from Coriander's body. She had never said so, not in words, nor in thought, even to herself. But what did that signify? Did she love him? The answer burst from her subconscious, whirling to the forefront of her mind like the glorious colours of a Catherine wheel. But she dared not confide the intensity of her emotion to

160

Lady Wilchester. She hid her blushes in a shy smile. 'I dare say I too have grown fond,' was all she said.

Christina shook her neat head in disbelief. 'I know what I know. Listen to me, child, there is something you must understand about Raul. His father was a hard man, with little patience for sentiment.'

'So I believe,' replied Coriander drily.

'None the less Raul worshipped him. He built a fine wine company in Madeira, exiling himself from the rest of his family in order to do so. It was not easy. The British were not so loved at that time as he might have wished. He had to win the respect of the local people, which he did. But, perhaps because he worked so hard, or because of family problems, or simply because of a flaw in his character, he was unable to show Raul how much he cared for him. He was not, you see, a demonstrative man.'

'Why are you telling me all this?' Coriander asked, intrigued.

'Because I suspect there is a touch of the old man in Raul, no matter how he might deny it. He too finds it difficult to demonstrate his affections, and his family life has made him even more introspective. Oh, I know he has had his adventures, and bears the scars to prove it. What young man has not sown a few wild oats in his time? But he is in truth a sweet, quiet, caring gentleman, for all he has a stubborn streak, who has been a dear and loyal friend to me for many years. Even when, for reasons we will not go into now, society as a whole spurned me, he ignored all gossip and remained steadfast. Raul may well be in need of love, my dear, but he is unaccustomed to its face.'

There were tears blurring Coriander's vision, and burning her throat. Despite all her efforts, she dreaded they would fall. 'What must I do?'

Christina pushed away a tendril of fine hair from a damp cheek. 'I think you know that already.'

After a small silence Coriander said, 'I must speak with Pearl and Letty before I leave. I promised to take them with me.'

'You must indeed ask them, but I think you might find them content to stay here, with us. And I declare I would love to have them. Letty is a dear companion, and as for Pearl, well, the boys would be heartbroken if she left. Make no mistake, my dear, that you will have your hands full enough.' The blue eyes sparked. 'But I doubt you are the kind of girl to take flight easily.'

Coriander hugged her new friend close for a moment. 'Whatever would I have done without you?'

There was no time to be lost. If Raul intended to leave on the next tide she must pack at once. He had said he wanted to sail around the world with her. He had held her hand, and kissed her cheek. He had told her how lovely she was and how much he enjoyed being with her. So why should he wish to go to Madeira without her? She would surprise him by meeting him on board ship when his business at the shipping office was done, and save him the trouble of returning to fetch her.

'We are grateful for your coming so swiftly to our call, Beringer. You were our first thought when we received this news.'

'It is an honour. I am always at Your Highness's disposal.' Raul bowed deeply before the Prince Regent, marvelling how the ample girth seemed to have considerably increased in circumference since his last visit to Carlton House a few months previous. It was not politic, however, to mention the fact, for the Regent preened himself upon flattery. 'May I say, sir, how very well you are looking?'

His Royal Highness handed over a letter, by way of his aide, for Raul's perusal.

'Upon my soul, Beringer, it is a very proper letter. We said as much when we received it. More than we've ever received from Louis.'

Raul quickly scanned the single sheet he had been given. As he'd suspected, it was from Bonaparte, begging asylum in Britain. 'I put myself under the protection of its laws,' the letter stated, 'which I claim from Your Royal Highness as the strongest, most consistent and most generous of my foes.' No wonder the Prince Regent was impressed by it, the flattery was blatant. Raul handed back the letter, consideringly.

'May I ask if any plans to deal with Bonaparte have yet been finalised, sir?'

The Prince seated himself comfortably in a yellow striped brocade chair, worry scoring deep lines upon his florid face. While Raul was sensible of the honour of being received in the Chinese drawing-room, he could not help but contemplate the vast sums of money spent upon it. Over six thousand pounds upon silk alone, so he had heard. And this at a time when the Corn Laws were causing near starvation in many parts of the land. As for Prinny himself, the signs of indulgence grew daily more apparent. Raul put a hasty end to his idle speculations, for the Prince was about to speak and it would never do to appear inattentive.

'My brother, the Duke of Sussex, influenced no doubt by Castlereagh, is suggesting Bonaparte should be allowed dignified restraint in Scotland.'

'And what does Your Highness, and, of course, Your Highness's prime minister, think, sir?' Raul chose his words with care. It would never do to imply the Regent had no mind of his own.

'We would feel happier if the tyrant were in distant exile. Lord Liverpool for one is not prepared to risk a revolution on our own shores by harbouring the rascal.'

'A wise consideration.'

'Indeed, indeed. We cannot have him take us for a fool.' The Regent rested his foot upon a brocade stool. It had been aching a good deal lately, caused undoubtedly by the dampness in the air and all the recent problems from Europe. The sooner this matter was settled, the better, then he could put his mind to persuading his daughter, Charlotte, to a suitable match. The girl was almost as obstinate as her mother, thankfully now far from this land. Best thing too, to judge from the tales which reached him from the continent. But this self-styled emperor must be dealt with first. A threat to all Europe while he lived. Since there was little hope of hastening his end, better to put him as far from the central buzz as possible.

'The fellow has a vexing way of recruiting

his would-be gaolers. He has escaped once before, therefore we do not feel in a position to be at all generous. St Helena has been marked out as a likely place. You know of it?'

'I have heard tell it is a rocky, lonely spot, given to mists and a damp climate.'

Let the Emperor suffer rheumatic pains as princes do and see how he liked it, thought the Regent with not a trace of sympathy. 'Ideal,' he said aloud.

'It would serve Your Highness's purpose well, I should think,' said Beringer agreeably.

The Prince leaned forward suddenly, as far as his bulk would permit. 'But it won't stop the plotting, eh?'

'I doubt it. There'll be plenty pleased to see Boney free.'

'That's why we thought of you. Keep an eye on the fellow for me, will you? When you return to that island of yours.' The Regent leaned back in his chair with a satisfied sigh, and Raul accurately judged the interview was drawing to a close.

'From Madeira?' he ventured.

'Is that what it's called? Charming, charming. See he reaches this cold, damp spot, will you, Beringer. And stays there. Keep your ear cocked, eh?'

'Indeed I will, Your Highness.' Again the deep bow before Raul withdrew from the Royal presence. Once outside, he carefully viewed this turn of events with an experienced inner eye. The summons had not surprised him, nor the request, but the timing of it could not have been worse. How was he to reconcile it with his other commitments? And how would it affect his developing and fragile relationship with Coriander? This was not going to be an easy assignment by any means.

Lady Wilchester had been right. Letty opted to remain with 'dear Christina,' readily owning to a fear of the 'dread unknown'. Since Coriander must venture out into the world alone, Letty was at pains to offer a small homily on the good of patience to the soul.

'It would not do, Coriander, for you to proceed in your usual daredevil way.'

Coriander conceded the value of this advice and promised to be more circumspect in her behaviour.

As for Pearl—she was fervent that Tom and Edward could not, at present, do without her, and so the matter was settled.

'My first plan will be to secure our inheritance—I think of it as ours. The Beringer family owes Cassandra that much at least. Then I shall find us a house and start upon that garden.'

'Will the house be big enough for Tom

and Edward to come and stay?'

'We'll make sure it is,' Coriander assured Pearl, smiling serenely, while wondering why her vision of her little friend had become suddenly clouded.

Later, safely hidden in a corner of the chaise, Coriander let the soft tears fall at last. With every passing mile she was severing her connections with everything and everyone she knew. And before her was an uncertain welcome, a possibly dangerous sea crossing and who knew what kind of future at the end of it?

How she would cope if Raul did not want her after all, she dared not think. How could she cope without him for the rest of her life? Drying her tears, she determined to think positively. It was not in her nature to be a defeatist. In the short time she had known Raul Beringer he had changed her life. Whatever those changes brought, she would face it.

'This is the place, miss.' John handed her down from the chaise and began to unload her boxes. Arrangements were soon made to row her out to the *Bella Regia*, Raul's schooner, which stood at anchor in the river.

The boatman was not a little curious to be conveying a pretty English miss late on this summer afternoon when he knew the ship was about to sail. It was none of his business, he supposed. Still, it wouldn't do no hurt to test out the waters, as it were.

'Is the master expecting you, miss?'

'I mean to surprise him,' Coriander told the man, then added hastily, 'But I'm certain he will be pleased. We are great friends.' She wondered fleetingly if that was perhaps stretching the truth a little, but she let it pass.

The boatman nodded. 'That's all right, then. Only Mr Raul, he don't much care for his plans to be changed without his say so.'

A small silence followed this depressing titbit in which the dip and splash of the oars seemed to echo in her head. She rather thought she would remember that sound for a lifetime. Then the boatman spoke again.

'I'm Ned, if it please you, miss.'

'I am enchanted to make your acquaintance, Ned.'

He grinned. 'You do know there b'aint much comfort aboard? Most of her space is taken up with cargo. The wine have been unloaded and sold a'course, but the hold is now filled with bolts of cloth, ironmongery and other products we'm be needing. I hope's you won't be mindin' that, miss?'

'Not at all. I shall enjoy it. You just find me a job to do, then I can be useful.'

The old sailor cast a sidelong glance of

surprise in her direction. Not the usual sort of girl the master bothered with, this one. Had a mind of her own, that was for sure. But he couldn't hardly imagine her working in the hold, for all her brave words. Too pretty for such hard labour.

'Have you worked for Raul long?' Coriander enquired.

'For as long as I can remember I've worked for the Beringers. Most of his sailors are Madeirans or Portuguese, but I came over with his father many years ago and stayed. I only come back to England with the ships occasionally. The wine run was my special province in my younger days, see. The *vinho da roda* was always the very best wine.'

'*Vinho da roda?* What is that? You mean exporting the wine from Madeira for sale?'

'*Vinho da roda* are wines of the round trip.' Ned dipped the oars with a strong, patient rhythm. 'Nearly there now, miss. See, the Madeira wine has a special flavour, which you'll soon discover for yourself. It all started long ago when a shipment of fortified wine was returned from the East Indies because of non-payment; it was discovered that the journey had improved the flavour and the aroma of the wine. It was said that something magical had happened during its long months at sea, so ever after that every shipment of Madeira wine was sent off for a few months' tour of the tropics. Some still like to do it that way, but we know now it is the heat and the shaking and not magic which improves the quality of the wine, so steps are taken to do that at home and save the expense of the crossing.'

'How fascinating.' Coriander was so enthralled, she was almost sorry when the boat bumped up against the side of the *Bella Regia*. 'Thank you Ned, for bringing me safely, and for this new knowledge. I shall remember it.'

If she had realised how prophetic were these simple words, Coriander might have had second thoughts at boarding the Madeira-bound vessel so eagerly, and without permission. As it was, on being told that Raul was absent, she asked for and was granted a suitable cabin, and tried to ignore the expressions of doubt in the faces of the crew at having a woman aboard.

Wasting no time, she began at once to unpack such of her belongings as she would need for the journey, and stow them neatly away in the cunningly devised mahogany drawers and lockers specially built for the purpose. For all Ned's warning, the cabin seemed luxuriously appointed, if of rather cramped proportions. But she did not mind that. She was not accustomed to spacious apartments, in any case, and she was sure she would be a good sailor. When her task was complete and a cabin boy had come to remove her empty boxes, she sat upon her bunk and wondered what she should do next. How best could she fill the time before Raul returned? Surely he would be pleased to see her? But as time passed confidence began to fade.

How should she receive him? With humility? No, she had every right to be here. And had done with begging long ago. He had promised to take her to his island, so here she was.

It all very much depended upon what Raul's reaction was to her sudden presence aboard his ship. Would he be angry, or philosophical? Would he welcome her with an understanding, if not a loving smile? And how best should she respond to him? With joy? Should she stop trying to hide her growing love for him and let it shine forth? Surely he would not let that foolish hold-up sour all hope of a future together? He could not be unaware of the feelings which had been growing between them all summer. Would he then take her in his arms and kiss her as she longed to be kissed, with tenderness and deep emotion? Would he tell her how glad he was she had taken this initiative upon herself? She

172

frowned. Perhaps he would not say quite that. For didn't he like to plan things in his own way? No, she must keep her distance yet, and her dignity. It would never do for him to think her forward and quite without moral standards.

Finally exhausted from the emotions of the day and tired of struggling to find an answer to her problems, she curled herself upon the bunk and slept. Lulled by the slap and fall of tide, she was unaware of the bustling activity upon deck. She slept on as the tall ship was piloted out through the channel. And as darkness deepened, so did her sleep. She did not even hear the cabin door open. Nor was she aware of a figure standing by her bed for several long moments before quietly leaving her undisturbed.

When Coriander woke and stretched her cramped limbs, the sun was pouring through the tiny cabin window and she was furious with herself for having slept at all. Hearing the creak of old timber and the stamp of feet upon a wooden deck, realisation came that the ship had left her berth and was under way. And with it came intense disappointment. Where was Raul? Why had he not come to her?

A sick feeling crept into her stomach as for a moment she wondered if she'd mistakenly boarded the wrong ship. But then she remembered Ned and his tale of the wine run. No, this must be the *Bella Regia*. Perhaps Raul had been too fully occupied sailing the ship to come to her yet, or perhaps no one had told him she was here. In that case she still held the element of surprise. She could not wait to see his face.

Swinging herself out of the narrow bunk, she was out of the door and running along a narrow passage, climbing the rungs of a wooden ladder, gasping as a salt breeze caught at her lungs. She saw Raul before he became aware of her presence, and she checked her dash to sink into the shadows behind the bulkhead where she could watch him, unobserved.

Stripped of his jacket, the fine linen shirt clinging to the powerful muscles of his broad shoulders, he was working alongside his men. She could not deny that he was a fine figure of a man, and her heart turned over at the sight of him. The men were chanting a song as they hauled up ropes into massive coils, and Raul was singing with them, laughing good-naturedly at their dubious musical skills.

But as Coriander stepped smiling from the shadows, the harmonious notes dried in the air and the scene before her eyes ceased its fluid movement and froze into a tableau as if painted on canvas. Hiding her sudden attack of nerves with a determinedly bright smile, she walked briskly up to them.

'Can I help? This looks fun.'

It was the wrong thing to say. In the stunned silence which followed, she saw the look of hostility in the men's eyes as they stared at this slip of a girl in the lavender muslin dress who stood so perkily before them. Raul kept his head down, as if he gave all concentration to the task in hand, and, though she longed to see his expression, she could not. But she was all too painfully aware that he had offered no welcome. Once again, it seemed, she had breached etiquette and embarrassed him before others.

But it was a bull of a man behind him who addressed her. 'Fun? Do thees woman think we play games, hey? She should stick to her laundry and bilhardam. That is what women good for.'

Raul tilted his head and regarded her with a laconic smile. 'He means gossip, Coriander, so you can remove the self-righteous shock from your face.'

'Oh. Well, I do not approve of gossip.' She felt the heat rise up her neck, for she had indeed thought the sailor had meant something else.

All the men laughed, as if she had made a joke, and Raul was joining in. More words, which she did not understand, were exchanged between them and the men laughed again.

'He thinks that cannot be so. Gossiping and washing are women's pleasures. This is men's.'

Coriander drew herself up with pride. 'I beg your pardon if I have interrupted you. I meant only to—to—'

'What did you mean to do? To surprise me? I heard of your surprise from Ned. Pity you didn't make mention earlier of your intention to board my ship.'

'A pity you did not trouble to tell me you were leaving,' she answered swiftly, the pain in her breast so intense she could scarce find her breath.

'I could have saved you the trouble of following me, had I known,' he continued, as if she had not spoken. 'For you cannot sail with us.'

CHAPTER EIGHT

Coriander was astounded. 'Not sail with you? Why ever not? You promised me. In any case I am here now, and we are already at sea.'

'Ees bad luck,' said the huge sailor, gesticulating a brown hand at Coriander's.

'I beg your pardon?'

'Ees bad luck to have woman aboard. We take you back ashore at once.'

Coriander glanced at Raul, expecting him to deny this. His green eyes were as translucent as the sea, and as cold. Following the direction of his gaze, she looked out over the water. Letting out a small gasp, she ran to the side. They were heading into land even as they spoke. Before them lay a bustling harbour, packed with ships of every size and description from tall, masted schooners to tiny fishing-boats weaving in between them like buzzing flies on a pond.

'Where are we? Surely this cannot be ...?'

'Madeira? Hardly. Not even the *Bella Regia,* sleek as she is, can circumnavigate the seas so quickly. No, this is Torbay.' He came to stand beside her, cool, impassive. 'I have to put in here to attend to some business. I shall make arrangements for you to travel by mail coach back to London.'

She whirled to face him. 'Mail coach? But, Raul, why?'

He answered her with a smile that at best could be described as vague. 'Not as comfortable as a private chaise, admittedly, but it will serve in the circumstances.'

Embarrassingly aware of the intense

177

interest of the listening crew behind them, she slipped her hand upon Raul's arm, giving it a gentle tug, forcing him to look down and meet her gaze. Staring back up into those green eyes, she sensed his withdrawal, as if he went through the motions of looking at her but refused to see her. It was the last thing she had expected. She could have better coped with his anger than this apparent indifference.

'May we speak somewhere in private?' He did not answer her. She took her only thread of hope from the fact that he did not break away, but she felt an increase of tension in the muscles of his arm. 'Please, Raul?' She put all her heart and soul into that plea and prayed silently for a response.

'I will come to your cabin later,' he said, and for a second her heart leapt, but then he added more casually, 'When I can find a moment to spare. Now go below. There is much for us to do and it is dangerous for you to walk upon these slippy decks. Besides, it upsets the men.'

In a daze she turned from him, the curious stares of the onlookers burning into her back. Her planned surprise had turned sour, for Raul had rejected her. He sounded uncaring, coolly indifferent to whether she was beside him or miles away still in London. She withdrew her hand from his arm and her fingers shook so much she was forced to clasp them together for control.

'I shall wait for you below,' she said, not looking at him. As she walked away, she wondered if his eyes followed her.

They did not. Raul at once returned to his men, but as he worked the image of her beautiful, sad face thrust itself into his mind. He had deliberately spurned her, crushed their budding friendship with the chill of a callous glance. Yet what else could he have done? This was no place for a dispute and she would never have agreed to leave the ship peaceably. How many times he had tried to talk her out of coming, and yet she persisted. If he had learned anything about Coriander these past weeks it was that she kept stubbornly to her own chosen course. A rope slipped from his hand, upsetting his balance so that he almost fell in the path of an iron hook being swung into position.

'Watch your head there!' came the cry, and Raul ducked instinctively, not a moment too soon.

Idle thoughts were dangerous. He must concentrate on what he was doing. Later, he would speak with Coriander in her cabin and soothe her ruffled feathers. He and Maynard had battles enough to fight; she would be nothing but an encumbrance.

He must think of some tale to convince her.

But when the ship was safely at anchor and Ned had brought her to his cabin as requested, he saw at once the uselessness of his attitude. He would have to be honest with her. One glance at her mutinous hurt expression convinced him of the impossibility of lying. He allowed himself a small, wry smile. Of all the women who had readily clung to the glib excuses he had made when he'd grown tired of their shallow charms, it had to be this one who resisted. Why was she so different?

'Would you take a glass of Madeira with me?'

Coriander shook her head. Ignoring her, Raul poured a glass for each of them, handing her the rich amber liquid shot with shards of fire. 'Try a sip. It will make you feel better.'

Without a word Coriander obediently sipped, and as the warmth of the liquor ran through her there came in its wake a new strength and she was able to look up at him and return his smile.

'I'm sorry,' she said. 'I do seem set on embarrassing you, don't I?'

'I'll forgive you this one more time.' His eyes seemed smoky in the dim light of the cabin, hazy with some inner emotion she could not read. She sipped again, a mellowness pervading her limbs.

He had no wish to hurt her. He had seen the shuttered look come down over her face when he had broken the news to her that she could not come with him after all. Drat Christina and her romantic notions. This was the very thing he had dreaded, for he knew well the pain of rejection. Raul was crouching down before her, taking the glass from her trembling fingers and setting it upon the central desk. He held her gaze with his own for a long moment till almost of their own volition her lips parted, expectant for his kiss.

'Coriander.' His voice, husky with desire, stirred the flames of her own as his arms came about her, cradling her gently, his lips seeking hers as if that was the only place they belonged.

In that kiss she told him of her love, and believed she recognised his for her. With a soaring joy they gave one to the other, certain that nothing else could matter but the revelation of this moment. And in that moment, like all new lovers before them, they believed they could conquer the world. It was a wild, heady power that for as long as it lasted blotted out all other considerations.

When they drew apart, this time there was no shyness, no guilt, no reluctance to meet the other's gaze. The opposite was, in fact, the case. Each pair of eyes moved over the other's face as if every beloved feature must be memorised now, for all time. Raul captured her cheek with his hand and she leaned into it, revelling in the possessive comfort it offered.

'Coriander,' he murmured again, his lips unable to resist tracing a trail of kisses over her soft cheek and down the line of her throat to her breast where she arched her body readily towards him. He knew she was but a pulse-beat from surrender. Every natural instinct cried out to take her, yet he resisted. The feelings developing within him for this young orphan girl with the stubborn will were such that demanded far more than a mere hasty coupling. He sensed that to take her now would bruise her beyond redemption, like a crushed rose petal. He could not do it. Besides which, wanting her was only a part of his problem. 'I cannot take you with me,' he said.

She pushed him from her with shocked hands, clammy with sudden fear, shaking her head in a stunned, bemused fashion. 'I-I don't understand. What are you saying? What is it you are trying to tell me, Raul? That you do not care for me? That your lips lie?'

'No, Corrie. That is not what I am telling you. But, while I cannot deny what exists between us, I can and must deny it room for growth.'

'Why?' It was a cry from the heart, and in it was all her need of him, all the loneliness she had ever experienced.

He gathered her floundering hands between his own, holding them tight and safe with his warmth. 'Listen to me, Coriander. I will try to explain. The reason I cannot take you with me has nothing to do with the way I feel.' He paused a moment, a thoughtful expression crinkling his brow. 'And yet, in a way, I suppose it has everything to do with it.'

'You speak in riddles. Are you deliberately trying to confuse me?'

The desperation in her voice cut him on the raw and he gave her hands a reassuring squeeze. 'The problem lies with my brother.'

'Your brother?'

Relinquishing his hold upon her, he began to pace about the room, his boots sounding hollow on the wooden-planked floor. 'I have no wish to bore you with old tales of my childhood, but if I fill in a little of the background you might better understand.'

Coriander ran to him to impulsively fling her arms about his neck. 'Nothing you could ever say or do would bore me,' she said. But smiling quietly at her, he removed her arms from his neck and bade her sit quietly in the armchair.

'When we were boys together, Maynard was jealous of everything I did, everything I owned. He was jealous if our father singled me out for any special favour by offering some treat or word of encouragement for excelling in archery or the wrestling we both loved. Whatever I had, Maynard made it his business to steal it from me, if he could not acquire a better one of his own by some means or other. Whether it was my favourite bow or my father's love.'

'But that is dreadful.' Horrified by what he was telling her, Coriander could not help but speak out, yet Raul seemed unaware of it, his mind turning back the years with a pain that was evident in the planes of his handsome face.

'As the years passed and we grew older, he did not change his attitude, only his methods grew more unscrupulous, even devious at times, so that I was often blamed for his misdemeanours and my fractured relationship with my father grew ever worse.'

'Why did you not explain the truth?'

Raul gave a helpless shrug. 'That is easily said, but not so easily carried out. How does one go about telling malicious tales about one's own brother, however true they may be?'

Coriander was silent. She could well understand the hurt he must have suffered as a young boy eager for his father's approbation and perplexed by the cruelties of a jealous sibling. 'What of your brother's attitude now that your father is dead? Has it changed?'

Raul was so long in answering, she almost thought he had forgotten the question. 'Now he is even more ruthless, and I dread to think what he might do to gain what he thinks is rightly his.'

He knelt before her again, placing his arms protectively around her waist. 'Do you not see, my love, that if I take you with me Maynard cannot be blind to the affection and understanding developing between us and will do all in his power to spoil it?'

Reaching up a hand, she stroked his cheek, smooth and scented of the salt and sea. 'He could never do that,' she murmured.

'You do not know him. He can do anything he sets his mind to.' Raul's brows drew together, the scarred one crookedly ominous, hardening the face which a moment ago had been soft with love. 'First he will steal you from me, then he will poison your mind against me. All that concerns him is power and money. He will be utterly ruthless in robbing us

185

both of our heritage.'

'I think you underestimate me,' she said quietly against his ear.

'No, Coriander.' His hands were gripping hers so tightly now, they hurt, but she did not cry out. 'You must not come. Madeira is too dangerous a place for you while I have this score to settle. One day, if all goes well, it will be different and then I will send for you. In the meantime, go back to little Pearl and dear, old-fashioned Letty where I know you are safe. When all this is settled, I will return for you.'

She wanted to believe in him. If the problems with his brother were indeed genuine, perhaps there was some sense in her staying in England. But how could she be sure that he would return for her? Promises were not always kept. Hadn't she long ago discovered that? Coriander was smiling and shaking her head, the wayward curls slipping down her neck as she fervently refused to be browbeaten by his dire words of warning. 'My place from now on is by your side, Raul, and nothing and no one can change that fact. Even if your brother is all you say, and I cannot believe that he is, there are two of us against one of him. He cannot beat us both; our strength together is invincible.'

Her eyes were wide and warm with her love. She looked, he thought, as if he had already made love to her instead of merely wanting to. Tantalising kisses were brushing his brow, his eyes, his cheek. God, how he wanted her. He knew it was madness, but he could sense his resistance sliding from his control. 'How could I bear it,' she murmured, 'if I could not see you each and every day?' Her soft, slender body was pressing ever closer against his.

He made one last valiant effort to regain some calm logic. 'No, Coriander. I beg you, stay here where you are safe. I will deal with your share of the inheritance for you, and with Maynard. Only then will it be possible for us to be together. Do you not see?'

She put her mouth tenderly against his, and at the touch of her soft lips he was lost. Feeling as he did, what could he do but kiss her and agree to anything she said?

'It looks better on you than on that rapscallion of a cabin boy, miss,' chortled Ned.

Coriander had sensibly changed her lavender muslin for more practical attire, not dissimilar to that she had once borrowed from Sammy. Could it only have been four short months ago when she and Raul had fortuitously met on that lonely road? At least he had stopped accusing her of less altruistic motives for that night.

Leaning over the rail of his ship, she watched with pride as he was rowed off in the clinker-built tender. She had not asked what business brought him to Torbay, but she hoped it would not take long. Apart from the fact that this area brought Ezra Follett once more to mind, an aspect of her life she preferred to forget, having set out on this journey, she was now all eagerness to reach her destination and begin her new life with Raul.

Cupping a hand to shield her eyes from the sun, she watched the small boat approach another, much grander ship, standing at anchor. The boat seemed to be drawing alongside it and, as she watched, she saw a rope-ladder uncoil over the side and Raul begin to climb.

'Does he not make for land?' she queried of Ned, who still stood watching beside her.

'Nay, miss. His business do take him aboard that vessel.'

Coriander, squinting in the bright sunlight, was unable to identify it. 'Which ship is she?'

'The *Northumberland*,' Ned informed her. 'Bound for the South Atlantic.'

'Is she a cargo ship, like the *Bella Regia?*'

Ned gave a low chuckle. 'Aye, you might call her a cargo ship, but hers is of a special kind.'

Coriander glanced at his face, eyes sharp as a terrier's after a rat. She was intrigued.

'What kind of cargo?'

'She carries the bogeyman himself to what will hopefully be his last resting place.'

As Ned ambled off, she turned this information over in her mind. Bogeyman? Who ...? Of course, that was the name given to Napoleon Bonaparte, used to frighten children into good behaviour. But if Bonaparte was on that ship, Raul must be going to visit him.

Her heart gave a low thump of disappointment. Whenever she started to trust him, something happened to sow a further seed of doubt. What possible reason could Raul Beringer, wine merchantman, have to pay a call upon a one-time dictator? She could think of none.

Coriander kept her position at the rail until half an hour later, when she saw Raul climb back down the rope-ladder and swing into the bow of the small rowing-boat. He smiled and waved as he approached the *Bella Regia,* and as she ran to meet him Coriander put the problem from her mind. She would not ask him. This was the man she loved,

189

and however difficult it might be for her, unskilled in the art as she was, she must learn to trust him.

She was filled with excitement at the prospect of a long voyage ahead with she and Raul together each and every day. She would allow nothing to spoil it. The sun shone, the sea was calm and in no time at all she felt as if she belonged to the *Bella Regia*.

During the day, Raul was kept fully occupied with the duties of sailing the ship, but in the evening he always managed to find the time to dine with Coriander in the privacy of his cabin, when they would chat and joke together as they had come to do in England.

'What would Letty think if she were to see me here alone with you in your cabin?' teased Coriander. 'I doubt she would approve.'

Raul smiled, then added crisply, 'I assure you, you are perfectly safe. I shall not lay a wicked finger upon you.' His eyes told her that this was much against his natural inclination, but she responded in equally light vein.

'How very unflattering.'

'I dare not,' he growled teasingly, 'for I doubt my powers of control if I did.'

'Then we will talk of more prosaic matters,' she said demurely. 'You have still told me very little about Madeira, or about your wine company.'

Raul laughed. 'An omission I should perhaps rectify, since you insist on taking up this cursed inheritance.'

'Cursed? Why do you say it is cursed?'

'Is it not a curse to be forced to share anything with someone you do not trust, nor even like?'

Coriander saw the muscles of his jaw clench and she wondered, with a skip of her heartbeat, if he could possibly be referring to herself, but then remembered his ruthless attitude to his brother. Calming the slight tremor in her voice, she continued, seemingly unperturbed. 'I know that I look forward to being a part of a real family,' she said with simple honesty. 'I shall be forever grateful to your late father for at last making that possible.'

Raul looked steadily at her. 'Do not expect too much, Coriander. You may find that things are not what they seem. My late father may not so much have granted you a favour as taken a final act of revenge.'

'How can you speak so about him?'

Raul gave a wry smile. 'Because that is the kind of man he was.' He looked pensive for a moment before quietly adding, 'And Maynard is very like him.'

Coriander remembered how Lady Wilchester had declared Raul to be very like his father in some respects, but she made no mention of that now. She hated to see the shadows fall across his face, and anxiously wished she could lighten whatever burden he carried. 'You were about to tell me of Madeira,' she prompted, hoping to draw his mind away from worrying family matters.

Raul seemed to shake himself mentally, and, leaning back in his chair, took a long sip of his wine as if forcing himself to be at ease.

'Madeira is a pleasant, rocky island with an equable climate set in the Atlantic Ocean. Its people are hard-working, cheery and generous, and I'm sure you will get along famously with everyone.' He smiled at her and she gave a little sigh of relief, glad to see him more relaxed.

'I'm sure I shall.'

'It was discovered in the fifteenth century by a Portuguese called Zarco. He was one of Prince Henry the Navigator's explorers and took shelter on the island during a storm. He found it to be uninhabited, rich with fruit and flowers, gushing with fresh mountain streams and thick with forest. He named it Ilha de Madeira, island of wood.'

'How delightful. Did Zarco stay?'

'He was governor of Madeira for forty years. That was his reward for proving

Henry the Navigator's theories to be scientifically correct. Until that time, few sailors ventured far from the sight of land, without at least following the prevailing winds. Prince Henry proved a ship can be navigated regardless of such considerations. He set the pace for all the famous navigators and explorers who followed, including Christopher Columbus, who lived for a while on Porto Santo, Madeira's sister island. I shall take you to see his house, if you like,' Raul offered, and only too gladly did Coriander accept.

'Where, on Madeira, do you and your family live?' she asked, enthralled by this historic tale.

'We live in Funchal, named after the Portuguese *funcho* for fennel, which grows wild all around that area. It is a fast-developing town, with a busy, easily navigable harbour. Many ships call for fresh water and supplies on their journey south through the Atlantic to Africa or India, or north to Europe. It is often called "the meeting place of the Atlantic". And, of course, our own ships loaded with wine, fruit or sugar embark from there.'

'I hope to learn much more about your wine industry,' she told him, and he glanced sharply at her. When he spoke, though the words were lightly spoken, a certain wariness came into his eyes.

'Why? Do you then intend to compete for the prize of the company?'

'No, no, of course not,' Coriander hastily assured him, feeling again that swift withdrawal of his confidence. 'But surely it is only right for me to take an interest, since I now own a portion of it.'

There was a small uncomfortable silence, during which Coriander had time to reflect upon the sensitivity the whole subject of the inheritance and the company engendered. The thought crossed her mind that perhaps old Mr Beringer had hoped to use her as a catalyst, a means by which his warring sons could be brought to work together, in peace. Coriander's soft heart soared at the prospect. What an achievement that would be, to restore harmony to the Beringer household. For the moment though it was perhaps a subject best avoided.

There was one other topic which met with similar resistance, and that was the frequent sighting of a second vessel, which, although always at a distance, seemed to be keeping pace with the *Bella Regia*.

When she ventured a question about it, Raul told her briskly it was the *Northumberland*, and walked away, as if he wanted no further probing. Wisely, Coriander never mentioned the ship again, though its presence on the horizon continued to concern her from time to time whenever she caught sight of it.

In the main, however, their relationship grew ever stronger with each passing day. Though Raul seemed to take a particular care never to touch her, as if he did not quite trust himself, their eyes would often meet, and linger, silently speaking what their lips dared not. And if sometimes she caught a more wary expression in them, she chose not to give it credence. The sea-faring life evidently suited both of them, for they were soon glowing with good health, sunshine and happiness. Even the crew came to accept the sight of a small figure working strenuously beside them, though they proved to be every bit as protective as Raul. Even if she carried a bucket of water to share in the general swilling and scrubbing of the decks, he was there beside her.

'Put that down. It is too heavy for you.'

'I have carried pails before today,' she told him firmly. 'Do you not recall?'

'Not on the heaving deck of a ship you haven't,' he replied tersely, taking the object from her, much to her annoyance. She wanted to be a part of this vessel, a part of his life. Sitting in a cabin and pleating her fingers all day until he had a spare moment to talk with her was not the life for Coriander May.

Raul, however, thought differently. He found that if he did not watch her at every moment, she was liable to do herself a great mischief by trying to tackle something beyond her capacity. She obstinately refused any advice he offered to fill her time, saying she much preferred to be out in the fresh air and he must simply treat her as one of the men. As if he ever could!

Then one day he discovered her scrambling up the rigging with the other men. In seconds he strode across the deck.

'Get down from there at once.' His voice bellowed up over the sound of wave and wind, so frightened was he to see her swinging so perilously high above decks. Why must she always stretch his equable temper beyond endurance?

Coriander waved to him, acknowledging his presence, but calmly finished her task of unknotting a sail before climbing carefully down to be met by a ball of fury which almost swept her from her feet.

'Don't you ever do that again,' he snarled.

'Why ever not? It was fun. And I was perfectly safe. Christoph was with me.' She indicated a grinning sailor who stepped on to the deck behind her.

'I'll deal with you later,' Raul informed

the suddenly anxious man, then, turning back to Coriander, 'Get below.'

'But—'

'*At once!*'

Even she was not equal to combating such fury, deciding it was more politic to obey without argument in this instance. Down in his cabin it was another story. Resolutely she turned to face him.

'I understand your fears,' she said calmly. 'But I assure you I am quite used to taking care of myself, am very nimble upon my feet and felt perfectly secure up there.'

'Christoph was mad to take you.'

'You must not blame him.'

Raul snorted with fury. 'I do not. What is it you do to men that robs them of all common sense? Christoph is not dear reliable John, and this is not London. This is a ship on the high seas and you could have fallen to your death.'

'I very much doubt it—I was fastened to the rigging with a leather strap.'

His face did not soften a fraction at this reassuring news. 'You will oblige me by keeping your nimble feet firmly on deck.'

'And if I refuse?' She tilted her chin in impish defiance.

'Then, dammit, I shall lock you in your cabin,' he said harshly. 'Do not doubt that.'

She let out a small gasp. 'You would not.'

'Try me.' The warning sounded ominously genuine, but Coriander's talent for recklessness pushed her to challenge him further. Stubbornly tossing her head, the silken curls at least safely confined beneath a woollen hat, she met his fierceness with a glowering rage of her own.

'You do not own me, Raul Beringer, and have no right to tell me what I can or cannot do.' Still not content to leave it, as she saw his lips tighten, she went further. 'If you are permitted to freely fraternise with the enemy, then I'm sure I am entitled to equal freedom on board a British ship. Who are you to deny me?'

The wide lips were tinged white with the coldness of his fury. 'This is not a British ship, and *I* am her master.'

'But you are not *my* master,' she retorted, springing closer to him to better impart her sting.

Catching hold of her wrist, he pulled her into his arms. 'By God, but I will be, Coriander May. I'll make you mine.'

A soft cry came from her as she leaned against him, all the anger draining from her, flooded out by the rising tide of her desire. She put her arms up around his neck and he at once bent his head to kiss her, the battle over, with no winner declared. But this kiss was as unlike the first as it could ever be. This kiss was a shared experience which gently explored the new boundaries of caring as well as longing. Their need for each other was so strong, their bodies clung as if one could become a part of the other by sheer will-power. Even the dispute was a result of that need. Raul expressed as much a moment later, as he abruptly put her from him, dropping his hands to his sides in seeming despair.

'This cannot go on, Corrie,' he said. 'You know that as well as I do. It was wrong for you to come. I only have to look at you and ...' He turned from her and she smiled inwardly at the proof of his agitation as he took his usual refuge of pacing the cabin floor. Surely this concern must prove his love for her?

'You would make me your mistress?' Coriander softly enquired, but he whirled upon his heel to scowl at her.

'No.'

As the word sank into her consciousness she knew sudden and deep regret. She would gladly have accepted such a role, and given freely of her love. It did not occur to her to expect anything more. She did not ask other than that he love her, and his blunt refusal indicated to her that he did not.

'I would make you my wife.'

If his earlier anger had astonished her, this quietly spoken statement riveted her to the spot. Time, the motion of the ship, even the beat of her heart seemed to pause as his words slowly seeped into her soul.

As for Raul, he too heard the words as if they'd been uttered by other lips than his, words he'd never intended to speak to any woman. He had complications enough in his life without the added one of a wife. For that reason he had confined his interest to women who were generous of heart and willing to suit his needs without commitment, though many had learned to regret such a policy as they'd come to know him. Now he faced an altogether different woman. One who had such an extraordinary effect upon him that he could not merely kiss her goodbye and move on to the next. But, delightful and amusing as Miss Coriander May was, could this bout of over-protectiveness he felt for her be called love? Even as his wife she might not be safe from Maynard, and he would have sacrificed his freedom for nothing.

Then she was in his arms, whispering words of endearment and acceptance against his ear, the warmth of her small body entwined with his own. And even as he kissed her again he was thinking, dear

God, what have I done? Marriage would bring nothing but misery and anguish. What had possessed him to do such a thing?

CHAPTER NINE

Coriander watched the approach of land through starry eyes. Never had she seen such an up-and-down, tumbling-over-the-edge sort of place. High mountains poked their craggy peaks up into misty cloud, while a crazy patchwork of green terraces and red-roofed houses clung around its skirts, dangling dizzily over knife-cut cliff edges as if at any moment Lady mountain would rise and shake the lot into the sea. It was the magic island of her dreams. She knew at once that this was a place to which she could belong, the place where she would become part of a real family. And, though she flushed warmly even to think of it at this stage, perhaps the place where she and Raul would start a family of their own.

But as the ship drew closer to land, she cast anxious glances in Raul's direction. He had been strangely quiet of late. A small worry niggled at the back of her mind that perhaps he was beginning to regret his offer of the other evening. 'Which of those pretty roofed houses is yours?' she asked, swallowing the small constriction that threatened to block her throat.

He kept his attention firmly upon the wheel lightly held in his strong brown hands as he replied, 'This is Funchal. The wine company is here, but our home, called a *quinta*, is situated high above the town in the country.'

'Then I can enjoy some walking and start my garden?' She could not prevent the small bubble of happiness revealing itself in her tone, and he turned his head a fraction to look at her and with relief she saw his expression thaw. Reaching out an arm, he pulled her into its shelter. 'Is that what you want, my dear love, to start a garden?'

'You know it is.' He had called her his dear love. 'I promised Pearl that I would make her one.'

'And promises must be kept.' There was almost a bitter note in his voice which Coriander felt she could no longer ignore. She had almost devised a way to broach her fears when he spoke again. 'Until we marry, and the sooner that is done with, the better, it would be wise if you defer to me in all things, and stay close to the house.'

It was the most unromantic statement she had ever heard and all her natural love of freedom rebelled against it. 'Close to the house? But I wish to explore the countryside, meet the people and feel free to pursue my own life.'

The wheel jerked in his hands and he cursed mildly beneath his breath as the call went up to drop anchor. 'This is no time for rebellion, Coriander. The interior of Madeira is rocky and equally precipitous as the cliffs, with many crevasses and thick forests. It is unsafe for you to wander alone in such terrain. I should never have a moment's peace.'

Reaching up, she popped a kiss lightly upon his cheek. 'You fret too much about me. If I am never allowed out, how could I tend my land?' she persisted.

'Arrangements will be made for that. It need not be done by you. As you can see the terraces are steep, which makes working the land an extremely hard and dangerous task.' He saw the start of tears forming in her eyes and was instantly saddened that he should be forced to place these restrictions upon her, but how could he tell her the truth? How could he explain the extent to which his own brother might go simply to get his greedy hands on her fortune? With her idealised view of family life she would never believe it. 'I warned you not to expect too much. You must learn to do as I say,' he told her crisply, striding away.

Only the beauty of the island soothed her sore heart as her land-hungry eyes devoured the red and purple clusters of bougainvillaea, the giant orchids, the roses, geraniums, lilies, carnations and masses of exotic flowers of every hue, many quite unknown to her, which brightened the hillside.

'But I shall make it my business to learn them,' she told Raul as they rowed to shore in the small boat. And as the other men in the boat seemed not to be taking any notice of them, she dared at last to speak her worries, albeit in a whisper. 'If you are entertaining second thoughts about marrying me, I shall understand and not hold you to your promise. You may feel quite free to retract the offer.'

There was the smallest, infinitesimal pause before he squeezed her hand in his own and planted a small kiss upon it. 'No. I shall feel better once it is done.'

It was not a particularly reassuring reply, but a swift glance at his face told her it was the most she could hope for.

As they stepped ashore she set her fears aside in a determined effort to find joy in the experience of this new land, remarking with delight upon the flower sellers in their crimson skirts, prettily embroidered bodices over soft white blouses, and dashing red capes. Fish sellers cried their exotic wares in a strange tongue, young boys vied to help unload and earn themselves a coin or two, old women with round brown faces offered scraps of embroidery, and everywhere great wicker baskets lined with cabbage leaves overflowed with sweet-smelling fruits. The warmth, the sudden noise and fervour was almost overwhelming after the quiet days at sea and Coriander stood irresolute; a pale, almost forlorn figure in a blue coat dress neatly trimmed and buttoned, oddly out of place among the more colourful figures that bustled about the quayside.

'It will be some time before I am done here,' Raul told her. 'You will have to wait. Ned will stay with you.' The two men exchanged a long speaking glance. Ned had his instructions to keep close by and nothing short of an act of God would keep him from that duty.

Coriander, however, anxious about the fragile state of her relationship with Raul, tried to be co-operative and rushed in over-eagerly with an offer to find her own way to the Beringer *quinta*. 'I am sure one of these young boys would take me, so that you would not then be deprived of Ned's assistance.'

Raul drew a patient sigh and said in his

satin-soft voice, 'Do as I ask, Coriander. If you will. Gird your impetuosity for half an hour or so and I shall return to conduct you home myself.'

She watched with fast-beating heart as he strode away, bleakly aware of a sense of failure and a seepage from the sensitive cup of her happiness. Unable to pinpoint its precise cause, she put it to one side, resolutely conjured up her more equable good nature and benefited Ned with a dazzling smile. 'A stroll would be pleasant.'

Ned grinned. 'Aye, to find your land legs again, eh?'

They walked along wide avenues lined with blue jacaranda trees, past the sixteenth-century fort, Fortaleza de São Lourenço with its huge gates and high, white walls dotted with tiny green shuttered windows. From here they made their way along the Avenida Zarco and came at length to an open plaza paved with black and white mosaic where there were more flower sellers with baskets glowing with blooms of every colour and description.

'What are those little black skull caps with the long tail on top which the flower sellers wear?' asked Coriander, intrigued.

'It is the traditional head gear, called a *carapuça*, and is believed to have been brought over as a form of turban by

Moorish workers many years ago. It has been adopted by both men and women, though very often you will see the men wearing a woollen hat with warm ear flaps, very useful when going up into the mountains where it is much colder than here.'

Seating herself upon a low wall, Coriander stopped to catch her breath. She gave a soft gurgle of laughter. 'I speak of climbing the mountains and here I am out of breath from one short hill.'

Ned fixed her with an anxious stare. 'You mustn't wander on your own, little miss. You stick by Ned and you'll be safe.'

Coriander gazed all about her at the colourful scene and gave a small happy sigh. 'How could I be anything but safe and content in this beautiful place?' Then getting to her feet she turned to shade her eyes as she looked out over the sea. 'Do you think we should be getting back now? Surely Raul will have finished his business by this time.'

'I reckon we could,' Ned agreed, and turned to lead the way back to the waterfront. 'T'aint a pleasant place along some parts o' this quay, miss. Tis a bit boisterous for the likes of yourself,' he told her gravely, much to Coriander's amusement.

'Indeed I should not dream of venturing there,' she assured him, with equal gravity.

'Pirates once frequented this bay, coming to plunder and pillage,' Ned added in awesome tones as they walked amicably along together. 'One such was a French pirate named Bertrand de Montluc who stayed for sixteen days carrying out his torments. Quite a character he was. And on Porto Santo 'tis said there are many sunken ships with holds full of silver ingots, gold, and fabulous treasures, that have been overcome by storm and sunk beyond trace. One is said to contain gold and silver stolen from the South Americas by the notorious Capt'n Kidd himself.' He gazed at her wide-eyed and Coriander listened with all evidence of believing his fanciful yarns, seeing nothing more sinister in them at all.

'There's many would like to get their hands on that, I can tell you, the Beringers included.'

Coriander laughed. 'I doubt even Raul knows how to pull up a sunken ship.'

'T'wasn't Master Raul I was thinking of,' mumbled Ned. 'Now you mark what I say.'

'I promise you, Ned, that I shall stick close by you, despite the apparent tranquillity of this beautiful island.' She smiled reassuringly at him and he grinned

208

back, seemingly content.

Back on the quayside she looked about her for Raul but could see no sign of him. 'Where do you think he can be?' she asked her stalwart guide.

Ned, squinting his eyes against the sun, looked out over the water then thrust forward a blunt finger. 'There he be, just returning by boat with the British Consul.'

'The British Consul?'

'Aye. Henry Veitch. He'll have gone to see if there be anything our special guest would be requiring while in port.' Ned pursed his lips tightly as he nodded. 'Reckon this'll be his last chance.'

Coriander was at first bemused, but a closer inspection of the ship told her all. 'Ned, she is the *Northumberland?*'

'She is that.'

'And the special guest. Would that be Napoleon Bonaparte?'

Ned gave a brisk nod before turning to lead a reluctant Coriander away, back to where the baggage had been stacked. 'Put aboard the *Northumberland* in Torbay from the *Bellerophon,* now he's almost at his final destination. Boney will not find St Helena so comfortable as you'll find Madeira, little miss. Nor will we be content till this business be safely wrapped up and concluded to our satisfaction.'

Coriander dared ask no further questions, though her mind teemed with them. What kind of business? The last chance for what? Exactly what would bring satisfaction? And why was it that every time Napoleon Bonaparte was mentioned or his ship glimpsed, Raul was somehow involved?

Her boxes were soon located and Coriander perched upon one, composing herself to wait. Raul's baggage, however, seemed more elusive, much to Ned's consternation. He didn't like to speculate what his master's reaction would be if his personal belongings and private papers disappeared. A patient man he might be, that was for sure, but he had his limits. On learning of his anxiety Coriander was at once full of concern.

'You must go and look for them. I shall be perfectly comfortable here.' Her merry eyes shone. 'I promise not to wander off with any pirates.'

With duty so evidently in conflict Ned hesitated, but at last demurred. 'You stay right there, then, little miss. I'll not be above a minute. If Capt'n thinks I've let you down he'll use me for cannon fodder.'

Coriander chuckled. 'You are much too plump, Ned, to fit down a cannon. Besides, Raul would never risk losing you. Now hurry, else he will be back before you.'

Warmed and reassured by her words, Ned slipped away into the crowd, constantly looking over his shoulder to check Coriander was staying put. He knew just where Mr Beringer's baggage was stowed. Somebody, probably that fool of a cabin boy, had forgotten to fetch them off, and there they'd stay till they collected green mould if it weren't for him. It wouldn't take more than a minute to fetch them out himself, then he'd make that young rapscallion's ear burn.

Smiling to herself, Coriander watched his stocky body thrust its way through the crowd. Already, in the short time she had known him, he had come to be a dear friend. Raul was lucky to receive such loyalty, or a special kind of person himself to be able to promote it. The smile deepened as she thought how special Raul was to her, only to be marred by the thin lines of a frown as she struggled to solve the conundrum of his feelings towards her. However much she tried to bear in mind Lady Wilchester's words about his being undemonstrative, she could not help but secretly long for a more positive display of his emotions.

She had to admit too that his proposal of marriage had been done in a most unconvincing manner. And, ever since, he had shown all the signs of a man who had spoken in haste and now repented at leisure. Her upbringing might have been unusual, but not so sheltered that she was unaware of the difference in the needs of men and women. With a heavy sinking of her heart she faced the unpalatable fact that, even when she'd been in that delectable moment of near surrender in his arms, Raul had never said that he loved her.

'A frown must not be allowed to mar such pretty features.' A soft voice spoke in her ear and Coriander started, turning eagerly to its familiar cadence, but experiencing a pang of disappointment as she saw that it was not Raul who stood beside her.

This man was as fair as Raul was dark, with golden hair that curled unfashionably long upon his neck. The lean lines of the cheekbone and the straightness of the nose were very like, but there the similarity ended. Where Raul's unmatched brows were a dark crag over pools of green, these were narrow and pale as if drawn by nature's finest brush. The mouth did not have Raul's wide generous sweep, but was smaller and neater with only the fuller upper lip, showing signs of sensuality, to give it any degree of character. The slightly receding chin gave an indication of weakness, though this was not apparent in the eyes which were of the palest grey-blue and filled now with a quizzical, admiring interest which was not unpleasing. Coriander was in no doubt as to his identity and, jumping lightly to her feet, offered a bob of a curtsy and a merry smile which would have melted the hardest of hearts.

'Cousin Maynard, I presume. Do you mind my addressing you thus?'

'I'd much rather you refrained from dubbing me by any title but that of friend. Maynard alone will do.' He smiled at her and, taking her hand in his, bade her be seated once more upon her perch. 'I see that you have been abandoned already by my thoughtless, selfish brother.'

'Oh, no, not at all.' Coriander was anxious to disprove any such lack of attention on Raul's part. 'Ned was with me, but he had need to make a hasty visit to the ship. He will not be above a minute. I am so glad we have met at last,' she continued. 'I have heard so much about you.'

Maynard smiled. 'And not at all good, I warrant. My brother and I are not bosom pals. Never have been.'

'Then I sincerely hope that situation will change. I shall certainly do all on my part not to worsen your relationship.'

' Maynard studied her with serious attention. Could she be as well-meaning and naïve as she sounded? 'That would not be possible,' he informed her sadly. 'You may as well accustom yourself to the fact that nothing I do will ever please Raul's perfectionist standards. I have tried to please him, but he must do all himself or, in his eyes, it is useless.'

'He says that you envy him,' Coriander gently pointed out.

'We have ever been competitive, it is true,' Maynard conceded with a wry smile. 'But when Raul is away, which he has often been these last years, he expects me to run the company exactly as if he were still here issuing his orders. How am I supposed to know what he would wish? And if I guess wrong and do something which displeases, there's no end of a rumpus when he returns. You would never guess that I am the elder by a full twelve months, he makes me feel so ineffectual.' Maynard put his hand to his eyes for a second, as if wishing to hide his emotion. 'But there, I must not burden you with our family problems. I live in hope that one day they will be resolved.'

Coriander listened wide-eyed, heartened by this unexpected and touching confession. It would seem that she had been right to suspect there would be another side

214

to this breach between the two brothers. 'I have noticed that Raul can sometimes come down hard upon one, as patient as he claims to be,' she admitted. 'I was certain all along that the trouble between you two was probably no more than the result of simple boyhood rivalry. We must do all we can to help you both overcome the memory of those times and to become better friends. For your own good as well as the company.'

Maynard adopted a suitably contrite expression. He couldn't believe his luck; this was going to be easier than he had anticipated. She was quite charming, and delightfully anxious to be friendly with not a sign of the alienation he had expected after weeks spent in Raul's company. 'I can see you have a soft heart,' he told her, and, as she half turned from him to welcome a huffing Ned on his return, took the opportunity to run an experienced eye over the rest of her person. She was pretty too, if not as voluptuous as he liked. But the duty his father's will now required of him would not prove unpleasant.

'I couldn't find the Capt'n's baggage anywheres,' said a distraught Ned, red in the face from his exertions.

'Ah, is that all you seek?' put in Maynard pleasantly. 'I saw it all stacked. here and had it carted home. Had I realised, Miss

May, that this was your own baggage I would have dispatched that too, but there, we can soon remedy the matter.' Turning about, he called two rough-looking fellows and, after a swift and softly spoken discussion, the several boxes were collected and borne away on wide shoulders without any more ado. Coriander thanked him for his kindness since Ned seemed disinclined to do so, probably through lack of breath after his run. 'Where is my elusive brother, by the way?'

'About his business,' said Ned, succinctly.

'I'm sure he won't be long.' Coriander was suddenly smitten with uncertainty, and a reticence to equal Ned's, not to divulge Raul's actual whereabouts. The growing suspicion that Raul could be involved in nefarious transactions concerning a certain prisoner of note, and the security of her country, was beginning to cause her considerable worry. She had no wish to lay him open to further critical comment from his own brother when relations were already delicate between them. 'And do please call me Coriander, or Corrie, if you wish.'

Maynard lifted her hand and placed his lips lightly upon it in a gentle salutation. 'As pretty a name as its owner. I think we shall soon be fast friends, Corrie,' he told her, much to her blushing confusion. 'But now, I do not see why you should kick your heels upon this quayside any longer waiting for that neglectful scoundrel when you could be settling into your new home.'

'Mr Raul expressly bade her wait for him here,' Ned butted in with righteous firmness.

'I am sure he did, but he could not know that I was here and able to conduct Corrie safely. Even Raul could have no objections on that score, particularly if it saves Corrie a long, tiresome wait.'

'Then we shall both come with you,' said Ned, anxious not to lose his charge.

'You will stay here, my man, and inform Raul of our whereabouts, or how else will he know?' Maynard fixed Ned with a firm and unremitting smile, so that Ned subsided into disgruntled silence, and was left to anxiously worry over how he would explain all this to his master as he watched the two of them walk away, Coriander's hand upon her escort's arm and her pretty face smiling up at him in a way which would not please the Capt'n one bit, were he to see it.

At precisely that moment, Raul was in fact doing his utmost to extricate himself from the excessive hospitality of the British Consul. Ensconced in the Consul's comfortable office, he was already on his second glass of Madeira with not a sign of being able to escape without a third.

'We shall send Bonaparte a cask of our very best vintage. That should see him through,' Henry Veitch was saying with unsentimental lack of tact. 'The seventeen ninety-two, I think. An excellent year. Can't complain about that, can he?'

'Indeed, no,' Raul hastened to agree. His mind was showing an alarming tendency to wander. He found himself thinking of Coriander, worrying over her waiting for him. 'Not forgetting the fruit and the books he requested,' Raul reminded Veitch.

'Naturally, naturally. We mustn't give the impression of shoddy treatment.' Veitch poured himself a third glass and replenished Raul's despite his protests. 'Wouldn't do, in the circumstances, would it?' He beamed, and, sighing softly, Raul was forced to agree. 'He seems in good spirits, anyway, spending much of his time at chess and vingt-et-un.'

'At least he leaves his winnings on the table for the servants, or so I'm told,' put in Raul drily.

'Not much to spend it on now, eh?' Veitch looked thoughtful. 'Sir George

Cockburn is entirely loyal. It will take nothing less than a tornado to prevent his seeing Boney safely to his final resting place.'

'I agree.' Raul wondered how soon he could make his excuses.

'I hear you brought a passenger with you on this occasion,' the Consul probed. 'A pretty waif, eh?'

Raul felt himself bridling at hearing Coriander described thus. 'Not any longer. She has been amply provided for by my late father's will.'

'Of course, of course. I never meant to imply otherwise. Do you think she is likely to pose problems for your family, eh? Or restrict your movements in other directions?' There was a shrewdness in the gaze which unsettled Raul, making him relinquish his glass scarcely touched and get briskly to his feet.

'I shouldn't imagine she could create any more problems in my family than already exist,' he said with careful blandness. 'As for that other matter, you can be assured that I will do all that is required, as soon as opportunity permits. The Prince Regent has prior call upon my duty, but after that ...' Raul paused for a moment before continuing more firmly, 'After that, as I said, I will do what is necessary.'

Their glances locked in a shared agreement. 'Good man. We cannot risk upsetting the Portuguese. It has taken too many years to achieve this degree of friendship between us.'

'I am aware of that, sir. You can rely upon me, as always,' Raul assured him and, with the usual salutations, left as hurriedly as he was able without causing offence, to make his way at once to where he had left Coriander. Even before he reached the spot, he could see that Ned was alone, uncomfortably shuffling from one foot to the other in obvious anxiety, and alarm rattled through him like clanging bells.

'Where is she?' Raul demanded with peremptory bluntness, and Ned hastened to reassure his master as best he could that the little miss had not been stolen by anyone other than his own brother. Though he was well aware that that would prove little comfort, their always being at loggerheads one with the other.

'She'm quite safe and there by now, I shouldn't wonder,' he said, risking a smile.

'Damn you, Ned. I told you to keep her here. Why does she never listen to a word I say?' He was inwardly astonished at the way his heart thudded so alarmingly.

'There wasn't nothing I could do, though

I tried,' mourned Ned with deep shame at having failed his beloved Captain. Recognising this, Raul slapped him with a rough kindness upon the back.

'No accounting for women, Ned. They will always please themselves.'

Ned grinned with relief. 'That's true, sir, indeed 'tis. Shall we be on our way ourselves, then? Mr Maynard have already dealt with the baggage.'

'He seems to have dealt with matters with exceptional efficiency,' said Raul quietly. 'For once.'

'That he does, Capt'n.'

'Most unusual, wouldn't you say, Ned?'

Ned frowned. 'Jest what I thought myself. Reckon we'd best be keeping our eyes open a bit wider in the future.'

Raul fixed his long-serving comrade with a piercing gaze. 'We have seen some hard times together, Ned, in the long war. But what is to come could tax us to our limits. We are well equipped to cope, I know that, but Coriander may not be so well prepared. She is dazzled by the prospect of family life, of having a fortune of her own to spend, and has already shown a somewhat light-minded attitude towards money. Nevertheless, I would be obliged if you would make it your business to keep an eye on her, particularly if I am engaged on other, shall we say, more pressing business? Do this for me, Ned, without regard to my brother's wishes on the matter.'

'I understand, Capt'n,' said Ned, solemnly drinking in every word and nuance of his master's instructions. 'You can be sure that I'll not fail you next time.'

'It is Coriander you must not fail, Ned. Neither of us must. I think it could be very important that we do not.'

CHAPTER TEN

Coriander was to be transported to the *quinta*, or country estate of the Beringers, by the most extraordinary means imaginable.

'I could not possibly ride in a hammock,' she stated bluntly when first presented with it.

'It is known as a palanquin or serpentine,' Maynard told her, 'and quite the best way to travel in Madeira. Our *quinta* is a good five kilometres from here in Monte, all uphill. You could not possibly walk so far, particularly in those shoes.'

Coriander, glancing ruefully down at her embroidered blue slippers, could not deny his argument seemed valid. Already she felt hot and sticky, despite the lateness of the August afternoon and the light offshore breeze, but she hated the prospect of being a burden to anyone and going anywhere except upon her own two feet.

'My men are very strong and can easily carry you.' Maynard indicated for her to climb aboard, which she judged would be none too easy an exercise. 'Allow me to arrange the cushions for you.' He shook up the print cushions which lay upon the prettily flowered fabric that comprised the hammock, shaded from the sun by a fringed canopy. Coriander's lips twitched upwards into a smile.

'I dare say it will be an experience,' she conceded, and wished suddenly that Raul were here to help her decide.

It was the cheerful amiableness of the bearers which in the end persuaded her. Dressed freshly in white, their breeches stopping just below the knee, strong leather boots upon their feet and the now familiar black tailed hat which they courteously doffed to her, nodding and smiling all the while, '*Obrigado*,' they said.

She glanced at Maynard for enlightenment.

'They thank you.'

'What for?'

'The honour of carrying you. They would be heartily offended if you declined to travel with them.' There was nothing for it now but to gracefully accept, so, sitting tentatively upon the lip of the hammock which swung from the two poles carried by the bearers, she tried to ease herself gently into it. The palanquin wobbled crazily for a moment and she clasped the edge in fright, giving a little squeal of laughter.

'They won't drop me, will they?' she ventured, a tremor of laughter still in her voice and, as she watched, Maynard swung himself expertly into his own.

'They have never lost an English lady yet,' he replied by way of consolation and, as the men set off at a surprising rate up the steep, cobbled streets, Coriander clung tightly to the thick fabric, not sure whether to be delighted or terror-struck by the experience.

But as they climbed away from the town, the sweet scents of the jacaranda drifted to her, and despite herself she began to enjoy the gently swinging motion. Her view was restricted as yet, but occasionally she caught breathtaking glimpses of the mist-blue mountains ahead, and excitement was born in her. A new future lay before her, a new beginning. How could she doubt but that it would be a good one? Why could she not trust that Raul had meant it when he had asked her to be his wife, and be happy about it? Of course he loved her.

What other reason could he possibly have for wishing to marry her?

'We'll take a short detour,' Maynard called to her as they came out upon the small square before the church at Monte, and he ordered the bearers to strike out along a track which led off into thick woodland.

Coriander's immediate reaction was to resist and to long once again for the comforting, familiar presence of Raul. She was beginning to wish that she had stayed on the quay and waited for him as he had asked. Her head was starting to ache, for the voyage had been long and tiring, though pleasant enough. Despite the entertaining novelty of this present mode of transport, she felt more than ready to stop moving for a while. She was in no position, however, to argue and so resigned herself to bear with the detour as best she may.

The bearers walked along a rough track for some distance before Maynard called a halt and came to help her out of the palanquin. Drawing her to a low wall which bordered the edge of the track, he flung out a hand to encompass the panoramic view below them.

'I will show you Beringer land,' he said, excitement ripe in his voice. 'You see where this river cuts down from the mountains into the ravine?'

Coriander nodded, instinctively stepping back a pace when she saw how sheer was the drop below.

He laughed. 'Do heights trouble you?'

'I must be more tired than I thought,' she acknowledged. 'But you may continue, I am perfectly all right.' Resting one hand on the stone wall before her, she used that as a support, avoiding leaning too far over.

'The land on this side of the ravine is ours. In addition, we own several of the terraced fields above us, and many more beside the house which I will show you another time. Fields in Madeira are always small because of the steepness of the terrain.'

'How can you tell which is yours and which is Raul's?' she tentatively asked in a soft, enquiring voice, impressed by the extent of the estate.

'Or which belongs to Miss Coriander May?' Maynard added quietly, quirking one fine brow in amusement and looking disconcertingly like Raul as he did so. 'We know,' he told her, 'because my beloved father decreed it all in that wondrous document, his will.'

'I see.' Coriander subsided into silence. Something about Maynard's attitude disturbed her, but she could not pin-point exactly what it was, and put it down to her own tiredness and the sheer dizzying fall of the land below them which sloped away in tilting terraces down into the ravine where the ribbon of a river gushed madly onward to the sea. Squares of fertile land were laid out all around, like neat green handkerchiefs left to dry in the sun.

'How he arrived at his momentous decisions we cannot tell,' Maynard was saying. 'He knew how fiercely Raul and I would contest every hectare, and so he left detailed maps and plans to avoid that.'

She turned to look at him more fully, genuine interest and concern prompting her to probe more deeply. 'Why do you compete so fiercely? Is there not enough for all? Could you not share the company?'

Maynard laughed and the sound echoed hollowly across the hillside. 'You might as well ask the espada fish to fly in the air,' he mocked. 'Once, long ago when we first came to manhood, father gave us a parcel of land to do with as we wished so long as we were both in agreement. I wished to build a small summer pavilion set in a beautiful garden.' His eyes lit at the recollection. 'There would have been nothing like it on all Madeira, a gem of classical architecture set high above a sapphire sea. I intended to sit in it, enjoy the landscape and find a respite there from the hurly-burly. Somewhere tranquil

I could go to write my poetry. And for all time the name of Beringer would have been remembered.'

It was easy to imagine this golden-haired young man sitting in a beautiful white pavilion, writing poetry with his fine-boned hands, yet the picture was somehow cold and unfeeling and Coriander wondered why. Watching him closely, she prompted, 'And did you build it?'

The lower lip jutted almost to a pout as he answered. 'Raul would have none of it. Waste of money and good land, he said. Insisted we plant vines, as if the island doesn't have enough of them already.'

'Were you very disappointed?' Coriander was thoughtful, unable to decide which brother had been right.

'We came to blows over it.' Maynard threw back his head and gave a shout of laughter. 'I won that battle at least, for he carries the scar to this day.'

Coriander was shocked. 'Do you mean the mark on his brow?'

'Most certainly.' Maynard looked almost gleeful in his recollection of the event. 'Quite a spat, that was.'

'With fists?' she wanted to know, trying to place herself in their position. The one a poet and artist, the other practical and single-minded, his one consideration the good of the family business.

'Indeed not. I called him out with swords in the time-honoured tradition.'

Violet eyes shot wide open as she took his meaning. 'You fought a duel with your own brother?' she gasped, and saw at once how she had annoyed him by her question. 'I-I did not realise that was what you meant.'

'Of course it was what I meant,' he snapped. 'We were not children, to play at fisticuffs. I was twenty-one, a man, and should have had my way as the elder. Raul is too selfish, too obstinate. He refused at first, declaring he could always beat me easily so why run the risk of injury?' Maynard chortled with laughter. 'But I showed him. Lucky I didn't slice his nose off.'

Coriander felt suddenly and awfully sick with a longing to be gone from this place which held such bitter memories. Glancing back, she saw how the bearers were some distance away along the track, resting and smoking their pipes. She returned her gaze to Maynard and saw him quiver like some child caught out in a misdemeanour.

'No need to look so accusing,' he burst out. 'I was injured too. And he swore that he would kill me for it.' Wrenching up his sleeve, he revealed a long white scar that ran from the bony wrist halfway up the forearm, its edges blue and puckered like a badly sewn seam. Coriander closed her eyes tightly as her head swam. She could see Raul's angry face, the shining sword slicing through the air, boyhood rivalry erupting into cruel violence. Had she been right all along? Was Raul's patience no more than a surface gloss covering the ruthless core of him? Determined not to show her weakness, she opened them again almost instantly.

'I should like to rest now. I am very tired,' she said, and calmly returned to the palanquin, noting with thankfulness that Maynard repaired to his own without question.

The *quinta*, when they reached it, was a low, white handsome building set squarely upon a plateau. A series of red-tiled roofs perched like the *carapuça* hats upon the separate sections of the buildings, while small windows had their black-painted shutters thrown open to enjoy the pleasing vista of distant seascape. Below the house was a series of terraced gardens, intersected with gravelled walkways and stone palisades. Its beauty served to blot out the dreadful pictures Maynard had presented to her. And then she saw that they were not alone.

A woman sat curled upon the white steps before the house. Dressed in the traditional scarlet costume, her long black hair tumbling in deep waves down her back and over her slender shoulders, she was the most strikingly beautiful woman Coriander had ever seen. Black eyes darted in their direction, expectant, watching the little procession approach, glinting in her oval olive-skinned face. A face which held a wistful quality in its voluptuous beauty that was oddly moving. As the woman scanned the extent of the hammocks, disappointment registered in the quick swoop of shielding lashes and in the droop of her scarlet mouth. Getting to her feet with a sinuous grace, she slid away as silently as a cat, not looking back even as Maynard called out to her to wait.

'Was that Isabella?' Coriander asked, and when Maynard replied in the affirmative she was thankful the girl had not waited. She really did not feel up to facing Raul's one-time mistress while still suffering the debilitating effects of the long journey. Tomorrow would be soon enough, in particular to break the news of their impending marriage. Eager to feel solid ground below her feet, she began to struggle free of the hammock's restraints as she complimented Maynard upon the magnificence of his garden, noting how he preened himself with pride at her words.

'There are many fine statues and

fountains in my garden here, which I have had specially built,' Maynard said, coming towards her. 'I do like things to be orderly, and have provided secret arbours where you can sit in peace and enjoy it. When you are rested you must view it properly,' he said and, reaching her just in time, caught her in his arms as the hammock swung wildly, threatening to up-end her as recklessly she tried to jump from it without assistance.

Clinging tightly to him, she gurgled with merry laughter. 'I almost went at once, did I not? My head is still swirling dizzily from all the bobbing and swaying it has endured,' she said, and they both laughed at her undignified and hasty exit from the hammock. She tried to extricate herself, but much to her chagrin the giddiness turned into an odd light-headedness and she crumpled into his arms, faintness sweeping over her.

'Corrie, are you all right? You have gone deadly pale.' He could smell the sweet scent of jasmine upon her hair and his arms tightened possessively as he held her. There was an air of fragility about her which reminded him of a rare butterfly. He had used to trap them as a boy, and pin them out upon a board where he could admire their pristine beauty.

'It is nothing,' she declared with an

232

attempt at firmness, steadying herself by grasping his shoulders. 'I have been travelling too long, that is all.' She gave a giddy little laugh. 'And everything has been so exciting.'

'And more than anything you do love excitement, do you not, Coriander?' Whirling from the confinement of Maynard's arms, she ran to Raul, not at first noting anything amiss in his expression, but the crispness of his next words froze the laughter upon her lips. 'I can see now why you chose not to wait, so eager were you to meet with my elder brother.'

Seeing her there, so comfortable in his brother's arms, eyes overbright with excitement, he had experienced an intense longing to pull her into his own arms and forbid her ever to see or speak with Maynard again. An impossible hope. A pointless exercise. Blinded by her apparent vulnerability and his own foolish weakness for a while, he had forgotten what an opportunist she was. A weighty purse, a small inheritance were easy to snatch, so why not a Viscount? And, since she did not yet know which brother would win the golden prize of the wine company, what better than to make herself indispensable to both? He loathed himself for having these doubts, but was helpless to banish them. Jealousy raged through him like the forest fires that had consumed this island once in its infancy.

'You must take care not to be taken in by her, Maynard. She possesses consummate skill as an actress.' While to Coriander he said only, 'How soon your patience grows thin.'

Coriander's natural independence and penchant for rebellion broke through her anxiety not to cause any ripples of disquiet between the brothers and, rallying herself valiantly, she tilted her chin in obstinate defiance at him. 'Since you chose to neglect me, as is your wont, why should I refuse Maynard's kind offer of transport?'

'I have been showing her the land,' Maynard agreed, and Raul was smitten with a keen sense of disappointment. He had not realised how much he had looked forward to performing that function himself.

'You have always to interfere.' Raul fixed his brother with an unnerving stare. 'I think it would be better if it were made plain from the outset that Coriander and I have come to an agreement.'

'What kind of agreement?' Maynard's eyes narrowed with suspicion. He should have realised that Raul would have gained some advantage from having Coriander to himself these last weeks.

Watching the way the two brothers'

hackles rose as they faced each other, like two dogs who waited only for the word to tear each other apart, Coriander felt a chill frame her heart as all hope of reconciling them died stillborn within her. More than anything she hated the quiet smile on Raul's face, which, if it was meant to be conciliatory, failed miserably, for the keen glass-green of his eyes flashed a different story.

'I have asked Coriander to be my wife and she has accepted.' He spoke with a cold precision, making even his proposal of marriage sound like a business transaction.

'The devil you did,' said Maynard softly through gritted teeth, and, turning to Coriander, 'What did he use to bribe you? The promise of a fortune, of owning a wine company?'

Coriander was appalled at this interpretation of their love. 'No,' she gasped. 'Not at all. That never entered my head.'

'I'm sure it did not, for you are a sweet innocent in the ways of men. But my brother is another matter. Did it not occur to you that by marrying you he immediately disposes of half his opposition?'

'Wh-what do you mean?' She asked the question but guessed the answer, and fervently wished that she did not. There was a strange singing in her head, like the sound sirens might have made long ago in ancient mythology when they lured unsuspecting travellers on to the rocks. Had she been so lured by Raul?

'With control of your share as well as his own, he is in a strong position to develop those two portions into a sizeable fortune by the end of the prescribed period of one year. How could I, one man alone, compete with such a dual attack?' Maynard stepped back away from them, as if he trembled suddenly with fresh fear. 'And if I tried, what price then for my life? One slice of a sword, or shot from his pistol, a missed footing on a cliff-top and he inherits all. The *quinta*, the land, and the precious wine company would be all his, and yours too, of course. Until he decides to rid himself of you also.'

'Stop it, stop it.' She had her hands to her ears, desperately trying to blot out the sounds of his voice, but she could not shut out the sight of his eyes, wild with awful horror, and Coriander felt the blood drain from her own face and neck at his next words.

'Oh, sweet Coriander, what have you done? You have signed my death warrant.'

Coriander slept late the next morning and woke feeling far from refreshed. It had taken a long time to relax sufficiently for sleep to come last night. Maynard's words had haunted her, and over and over again she had to recourse to almost spelling out Raul's reaction to them, so that she could keep it all in perspective. She recalled how he had laughed at Maynard, accusing him of over-dramatising, of allowing sibling mistrust to spoil Coriander's welcome.

'Not that old chestnut again,' Raul had said, as if he had heard the accusation a thousand times. 'Why will you not admit that you have no interest in the wine company and no real wish to run it? You want it only to thwart me. Shall I explain everything to Coriander? Is that what you want? To have all our wounds opened to public gaze?' The brutal words drove through the still air of that calm evening, but Maynard only drew back, as if unwilling to proceed further with the bitter quarrel.

Once Maynard had stridden away into the house, leaving them alone, Raul turned to console her. 'You must take no notice of his crazy accusations. Maynard gets carried away by his own anger and speaks before he thinks.' A shadow crossed his face. 'You have to understand that Maynard is not always entirely responsible for his emotions. The worst of it is that I promised my late father that I would keep a brotherly eye upon him, but I swear it grows ever more difficult.'

Coriander warmed to this new insight into her betrothed, pushing from her mind Maynard's outburst. 'I had hoped to reconcile you,' she told him in a quiet voice. 'But I can see the problems in such a task.'

Raul linked his arms around her waist and, pulling her close, rested his chin against her hair. 'You are too soft-hearted, sweet Coriander, and quite delicious. But you must realise from the outset that nothing you can do will bring my brother and myself together. The antipathy between us runs too deep and for too many years.'

'But you will not prevent me from trying?' she gently persisted, and noted how the smile vanished from his voice for a moment and the air grew suddenly chill as he answered that he would not.

But his mind dwelt not upon her words but upon his own thoughts. Should he warn her? Should he make her fully aware of Maynard's unstable nature? He had a reluctance to spoil her faith in humanity, and guessed that she was so in love with the idea of a family that she would not believe him in any case. He confined himself only to, 'Maynard is unpredictable. Remember how he loves to steal what is mine. Once you are my wife, you will be safe. Until then you must be on your

238

guard. But we must waste no time in making you so.'

She risked a teasing smile. 'Is that your only reason for wanting our wedding to be soon?'

An expression kindled in the green eyes which told her that this was definitely not the case, but, laughing, he refused to answer her question. Instead, he dropped a light kiss upon her forehead and said, 'Now, good wife-to-be, you must not worry your pretty head over it. Maynard and I are old adversaries and well used to bandying words. Put it from your mind and retire to your room for a well-earned rest, else you will be fit for nothing in the morning, which would not do at all.'

Laughing, and hugging the softness of his teasing close to her heart, she had scurried to her bedchamber. Now, with a night's sleep behind her, she must put all worries from her mind, for she was eager to explore her new world, and in no time at all was leaving her room with a healthy appetite to satisfy.

Later, having enjoyed her first experience of a custard-apple, ripe and tangy, together with fresh rolls and coffee, she almost fell over Ned, who was sitting on the white steps before the house, as she stepped out into the garden in search of her beloved Raul.

'What are you doing curled upon this step like a guard dog?' she teased, and saw the dull crimson hue stain his neck. 'So you were set to guard me? By whom?'

'The Capt'n asked me to wait on you, little miss, that's all.'

Coriander shook her head in mock despair. 'Did you imagine I would be carried off in the night by one of your fierce pirates? Everyone is far too solicitous of my well-being. I do assure you, Ned, that in the unlikely event of an invasion by sea bandits I shall put up a stalwart fight and am more than able to do so.' Her provoking wit brought not a shadow of a smile upon the square, robust features. Instead he continued stubbornly with his message.

'And Capt'n suggests that you may care to take a breath of fresh air and some exercise this morning.'

'Indeed I should,' she readily agreed.

'If you was to stroll by the wine company's offices, Capt'n said he would be right proud to show you about,' Ned finished with a satisfied nod.

'Is that what he said, that he would be right proud?' enquired Coriander with dry humour.

'Words to that effect,' Ned hedged, and was rewarded with a disbelieving but gentle smile.

'Then I think we might find ourselves in that vicinity, what say you, good friend?'

Ned's response was a wide grin as he set off down the cobbled streets at a spanking pace, with Coriander doing her best to keep pace with him.

They had reached the town and Ned was already leading her through the complex of narrow streets when a shout came from behind.

Coriander turned to find Maynard hurrying towards them, one arm waving to attract their attention. Catching sight of a flower girl, he thrust coins into the girl's hand in return for a huge orchid which he presented to Coriander. 'Good morning, sweet Corrie. How beautiful you look in your pale green gown and fair hair. Like this orchid glowing in the sun. Your petals all soft and silver-spun.'

Coriander pulled a wry face at him. 'What a dreadful rhyme. You have no need to spout poetry about me.'

Maynard looked faintly crestfallen and there was an awkward pause before he shrugged his shoulders, accepting her criticism with good grace. 'Nothing is more inspiring to an artist and poet than beauty, which you, like the orchid, have in abundance.'

Ned, who had been standing quietly by, judged it opportune to step forward, and, clearing his throat in a businesslike fashion, addressed Maynard with every appearance of respect but without a trace of servility. 'I was conducting Miss Coriander to the company offices, my lord, where we would have expected to find yourself on this bright morning, at work with Mr Raul.'

Maynard frowned slightly at the implied criticism, then, turning to Coriander, 'I wanted to walk along the front before I begin the daily grind. Have you heard the great excitement in town? Napoleon is in port.'

'So I believe,' Coriander said non-committally.

'Have you seen him?'

'No, but ...'

'But?'

Coriander felt herself flushing, aware that she had been about to divulge that Raul had visited with Napoleon, and instinctively felt it would be wrong to do so. 'Nothing,' she said.

Maynard grasped her hand and began to pull her along the cobbled street, which she noted was rapidly filling with people. 'He sails today for St Helena. We must watch him go. This is a historic moment not to be missed.'

'There'll be nought to see but a ship leaving port,' grumbled Ned. 'And Mr Raul said—'

'Oh, blow to what Mr Raul said,' scoffed Maynard. 'He is not our keeper. Raul takes enough time off without considering me.'

At the waterfront crowds of people were gathered, all eyes centred on the tall-masted ship making ready to sail in the harbour.

The sounds of the sailors' voices reached them on the breeze as sails lifted and billowed out, filling with the wind which would carry Napoleon Bonaparte to his miserable exile, a rainy stronghold in the Atlantic from which there would be no further escape, though he might try. Coriander, mesmerised by the beauty of its movement, was scarcely aware of Maynard's presence beside her until he spoke against her ear in that special intonation of voice which reminded her so much of Raul.

'I wished for this opportunity to apologise, Coriander, for my overly dramatic response to your news of yestereve.'

Coriander hastened to assure him that she had thought nothing of it. 'Raul should never have sprung it upon you in that fashion,' she conceded. 'It was bound to seem contrived.'

The ship was drawing away, leaning into the wind, and a cheer went up around them.

'Oh, I realise it was contrived. You cannot possibly truly care for him, any more than he cares for you. It would be a classic marriage of convenience, I understand that, for you are his passport to riches. But you need not risk your happiness in this way, dearest Corrie. You can do better than Raul. He is a selfish brute.'

Coriander felt as if all life-giving air were being squeezed from her body. 'Wh-what do you mean?' She turned to stare at him, the *Northumberland* forgotten.

'The wine company is Raul's god. Have you not yet realised? Why else do you think he crossed the seas to find you? He will do anything to protect his so-called heritage, for he is entirely single-minded and completely without scruples where the wine company is concerned.'

Ned, a pace behind, made a choking sound in his throat. But Maynard, his eyes narrowing with the intentness of his gaze upon Coriander, dropped his voice to a more circumspect level and continued as if he had not heard. 'Have you not noticed that he is often away on some secret business of his own, the truth of which he never discloses? Whatever mischief he is up to, you can be sure he is being well paid for it.'

'I know the company is important to

Raul, but I doubt he would do anything criminal for it.'

'Then you have greater faith in human nature than I,' murmured Maynard.

'I am sure you must be wrong,' Coriander stammered, recalling all too vividly the numerous occasions when Raul had absented himself without explanation, and of his immediate visit to Napoleon's ship the moment his own had docked. Could someone, the French themselves perhaps, be paying him to guard Napoleon, even to attempt a rescue? The thought made her heart contract painfully in her breast. Could she have been right, then, in her suspicions, for Maynard held them too? And what of herself and Raul's feelings for her? Was she no more than a pawn to be won in this game between brother and brother?

CHAPTER ELEVEN

The Beringer wine company, a solid stone building, its dark interior crowded with oak casks, was redolent of the tang of wine. Raul was only aware of this as he unlocked the great doors first thing each morning, when he would stand for a long moment to savour it. After that, its very familiarity pushed it out of existence for him.

None the less, one of his favourite tasks was to test the aroma and flavour of the individual wines in the sampling-room. He tried now the Boal, first holding a collection vessel over the wine to gather the full fragrance before putting it to his nose to draw in the bouquet. Next he rolled some of the wine over his tongue. Mellow, with a hint of aromatic sweetness, ideally suited to its colour of a rich smoky topaz. One of his favourite wines to enjoy with coffee and cheese, its richly elegant qualities, semi-sweet with a touch of spice, brought Coriander instantly to mind.

Her qualities, like the wine, were in perfect balance and harmony. A charming femininity linked with a strength of character which he could not help but admire. At times he experienced an almost irrational desire to go back to that evening in London at Funchal Place when she had taken him to task for his careless treatment of her. If it were possible to undo the hurt he had done her at the time and yet keep her in England, he would gladly return to that night. But if he did, would it enable him to trust her any more? Within moments of landing upon this island, despite his warnings, she had chosen to hurry into his brother's arms.

He wished that he could claim not to care what she did, but that would be a lie. His mind was becoming more and more obsessed by thoughts of her.

Cleansing his mouth, Raul proclaimed the wine perfect, ready in his opinion for shipping. 'But you try it, Fernando, I value your long experience.' He stood back and waited while his assistant went through the identical routine, but his mind slipped from the task in hand, returning to its earlier musing.

He could not dismiss his feelings as pure physical passion, or a natural protectiveness—not any longer. He felt bound to admit, at least to himself, that he found her an amusing and lively companion. The prospect of travelling through life with Coriander at his side was growing more and more appealing. If only he didn't have these other pressing matters to deal with he could give her his whole attention, try to discover her true feelings for him, for his pleasure in her was marred by two things. Her acquisitive nature, and his even greedier, cunning brother. He must guard his own feelings well, for it would be the easiest thing in the world for her to play off one brother against the other and have them both infatuated. The world was full of pretty women and if this one proved to be unworthy of his trust, for he did not yet acknowledge the word love, then he must be able to let her go, without sentiment. He sighed. His relationship with Isabella had been much less complicated.

A thought struck him. 'Has my brother arrived yet, Fernando?' he asked. Lie-a-bed Maynard never came in early, preferring to enjoy the fruits of success without the labour which provided it. 'Since the clock has already struck eleven, it is long past time for even he to be at his desk.'

'No, sir.' The assistant pursed his lips in disapproval as he shook his head. Mr Raul, he do not like the latecomers, Fernando often had need to tell his wife, who would have him linger at home in the mornings now that he was growing older. But he could not break the habit of a lifetime. Even when Mr Raul was not in Funchal, Fernando took care to maintain his own rigorous timekeeping while privately despising that of Mr Maynard. 'While you away, Mr Maynard says he has too much works,' finished Fernando with a tremor of a smile.

Raul echoed it with a sideways one of his own. 'I dare say you mean a lot, rather than too much, but even so, Fernando, I suspect you flatter him. Overwork will never kill my brother.' Raul set down the empty glass with a decisive click. 'Let us go to the *estufa*. I need to reassure myself that there are no further problems in that quarter.'

The *estufa* was the storage room where the wines were kept at a constant temperature, similar to that found in the hold of a ship sailing in the tropics, for about six months. Raul was proud of this new addition, for his father had refused to adopt the modern ways, preferring to transport every cask expensively and laboriously on the traditional long sea voyage. For some nonsensical reason Maynard had proved equally stubborn, and it had been a major victory for Raul when he, every bit as obstinate, gave orders for the central-heating pipes to be installed and put an end to the argument.

But one glance at Fernando's expressive face told him that all was not well. 'You wish to go now? At once?' Fernando hedged, and Raul raised a quizzical brow. 'Is there some reason why I should not? The heating system is now working efficiently, is it not?'

'Oh, yes, yes. No problem, no problem.' Fernando hastily reassured him, one bony hand slicing through the air as he sought the right words. 'Much wine has been moved, that is all. Not many *pipas* left.'

Raul glowered. He knew that Fernando was referring to the wine casks, but he could think of no reason why they should have been removed from the storage-room before the correct date. 'Where the deuce are they?' The words were clipped off short by sharp white teeth.

'The *pipas*, they go on the journey, yes?' He circled one finger in a tiny indicative gesture, his small face puckering in apology, for he knew how important it was to his hard-working master to modernise his beloved wine company and improve its productivity, as well as its profitability. Fernando held some affection for the traditional methods himself, but accepted the inevitability of progress.

'So that is how it is, eh?' Raul stood very still, well aware who was to blame for the change in routine. He curbed the natural human desire to inflict blame upon those close to hand, for there was nothing to be gained from it. The fault was not Fernando's. Nothing either to be gained from haranguing Maynard for deliberately flouting the agreement, for when had he ever kept his word? Raul should have known better than to expect him to keep this one. The wine would be safe enough, he knew that, and would return at the proper time. But the cost was excessive and unnecessary, and waste of any kind irked him.

'If we are to succeed in these modern

times, Fernando, we must leave the old ways behind.' Raul spoke with a sadness which touched the heart of the Madeiran, who nodded sympathetically.

'The wine cannot obey two masters,' Fernando said, and the two exchanged a long, silent look which said more than any words.

But Raul could not resist a sardonic smile at this cryptic comment. 'I too, at the moment, must obey two masters,' he said. His eyes glazed and it seemed to Fernando that his mind had drifted to other shores like flotsam on the tide. 'If Maynard is proving so obstinate over relinquishing the wine run, I feel sure there must be some other reason. Though he is a dreamer, his fondness for the traditions, unlike our father's, is nil. He is more concerned with the new styles in architecture, poetry and art than methods of wine-making. Why then is he so interested in this particular aspect?' The frown deepened, and Fernando held his tongue, reading well his master's need for quiet thought.

After a long moment, Raul spoke again. 'So much to be done. But which should have priority?' he asked, almost to himself.

'Whichever is closest to your heart,' said the Madeiran without hesitation, but Raul only gave a slow shake of his head.

'If only matters were as simple as that,'

he said. 'Which reminds me, Fernando, I wished to ask about your wife, Maria. She comes from Ribeira Brava, does she not?'

The older man frowned in puzzlement. What had his homely Maria to do with his master? 'She does, sir,' he began, but got no further as they both turned at the sound of the great doors opening to see Coriander hurrying towards Raul, her whole face alight with the warmth of her love.

Fernando looked in astonishment at the beautiful girl, and then at his master, and a knowing look came upon his face. If this was the matter which troubled him, he need worry no more, for here was his heart smiling up at him.

But Raul was not looking at Coriander, but over her head to accuse Maynard— 'You are late,'—who simply grinned with boyish indifference.

'I do not have your grumpy predilection to put work above all else. Coriander and I have been enjoying the sea air and the activities in the harbour. Someone must entertain our guest, so take away your forbidding dark looks, or rap my knuckles for being a naughty boy.' He held out a clenched fist, knuckles uppermost, which Raul pointedly ignored, showing not a trace of amusement.

Seeing his reaction, Coriander hurried

forward with fresh resolution, to take his arm in an affectionate squeeze. 'Do not scold, Raul. Maynard was only being kind. He showed me many of the different beautiful plants you have growing on the island. Now it is your turn to show me your wine company. I wish to learn all I can and promise to be an attentive pupil.'

He looked down at her bright face, hating the growth of suspicion curdling his heart. She had pandered to the one brother, now she seemed bent on doing likewise with the other. But was it fair to blame her entirely? Perhaps he had been unwise to announce their betrothal to Maynard. He had hoped to indicate to his brother that she was already beyond his reach, but he could merely have set him an irresistible challenge. The situation was growing ever more complex. Which of them, if either, could he trust?

Ignoring Coriander, he looked again at Maynard. 'No doubt you will be anxious to make up lost time by getting straight to your desk. There are new shipping orders to be made out. Fernando will advise you.' The crackle of frost in the tone was unmistakable and, after a long, hard, brooding look, Maynard stalked from the room with the small Madeiran hot on his heels.

'Is it necessary to be quite so hard on him?' Coriander asked, as soon as they were alone.

'Is it necessary to spend quite so much time with him?'

'Oh, for goodness' sake, he has only escorted me to the *quinta* yesterday and to your offices this morning. What of it?' Coriander gave a little half-mocking laugh, but Raul did not share her amusement.

'I thought I warned you not to spend too much time with Maynard. Are you determined to thwart me in everything I say?'

Coriander tried hard to conceal her despair at what she considered to be excessive, unnecessary lack of trust. A flame of fear burned her heart. Had Maynard been right? Did Raul merely look upon her as a bride of convenience, and he was afraid that she would offer her share of the fortune to his brother, instead of himself? Certainly if he lost her he would have difficulty retaining his hold upon the wine company.

'I did have Ned with me this morning, as you so carefully arranged. Why should you be concerned? It is surely much safer to walk through the streets of Funchal than London. What a fuss you do make.' She tightened her small fists with sudden and fierce anger. 'I refuse to be treated like an orphanage waif who must ask permission before she so much as sneezes. I have had enough of that. Now I wish to make my own way in the world.'

'Without guidance?'

'No, not without guidance, but at least with regard to my feelings on the issue in question. If you truly care for me, then you will also care about them.'

'And if you behave foolishly then I am not permitted to tell you so?' he retorted, with an icy calm.

Coriander had an almost irrepressible urge to stamp her foot; fortunately she managed to restrain it. It would do little for her case for independence if she behaved like a spoiled child. 'I simply think that you worry unduly over me, and over Maynard. He has shown nothing but kindness to me since I arrived.'

'Which is more than I have? Is that what you are saying?' sneered Raul, making Coriander flinch.

Exasperation flooded through her. 'Now you are putting words into my mouth. Stop it. What has come over you?'

'Perhaps, since you prefer to dally with my brother, I am wondering whether you would also prefer him as a husband,' Raul said with biting harshness.

Coriander's eyes widened with astonishment, then a giggle, born of nervous relief, rose inside her. 'You are jealous,' she said, her wide mouth curling instinctively upwards into a smile. 'Oh, Raul, how can you be so foolish? How can you think that I would prefer Maynard's company to yours?'

Raul looked into the velvet eyes and their loving innocence caused him yet again to taste the bitter gall of shame. However hard he may try to inure himself against her charms when he was alone, it was a different tale when she stood before him. 'Coriander,' he groaned, and he was pulling her into his arms, covering the warmth of her smile with the heat of his kisses, and her response was everything he could wish for. No sign now of the frozen child afraid to be touched. His laugh was shaky as they pulled apart.

'I think we'd best hasten with this wedding, don't you?'

'Oh, yes, please,' she said. 'But allow me at least to unpack my bags and settle into my new home. It is a little too soon yet, my love.' But even as she protested, her fingers were sliding about his neck, threading a sensual path through the thick curls, causing her own body to throb with the desire she could feel in his.

Setting her firmly away, he smiled down into her eyes, hazy with the depth of her love. 'Then I think we'd best confine our attention to more practical, everyday matters. I shall indeed show you around my wine company, and soon there will be the *vindima*.'

'What is that?' she laughed, leaning happily against him, all the niggling doubts and acrimony swept away by his closeness.

'The grape-picking, and yes, you can help. Though it is infinitely more tiring, there is not the same danger involved as in climbing a ship's rigging, so I can think of no reason to forbid you to try. So long as you do as you are told,' he scolded softly, tapping a fingertip upon her small nose, 'you will be perfectly safe to enjoy yourself.'

Settling in to life at the *quinta* was easier than Coriander had imagined. The first thing she did was to write a long letter to Pearl and Letty, describing her new home. She tried her best to paint a picture of the beautiful white house with its backdrop of blue-grey mountains and vistas of garden, sea and sky, by carefully chosen words. It required a good deal of concentration and she sat for long hours in the garden agonising over it. She wanted them to see it as clearly as she did, for she missed them both more than she had expected. Once the letter was safely dispatched via a friend of Raul's, whose ship was bound for

London, she felt that she could then relax and begin to enjoy her new surroundings.

The only disappointment was that she would have liked to see more of Raul, but he spent most days visiting various parts of the island where the Beringers held land, checking on the ripeness of the grapes, only returning late in the evening, and sometimes staying away for days at a time.

One night, as Coriander lay tossing and turning in her bed, longing for Raul, and wishing she had not been so foolish as to postpone the wedding he had proclaimed himself eager for, she thought she heard sounds below. Sitting bolt upright in her bed, she listened more keenly. Yes, it was he, talking with Ned no doubt, as he enjoyed his late supper. Without pausing to think she was out of bed in a trice and, pulling a lacy shawl over her nightgown, she ran down the steps on bare feet.

But as she came closer she discovered the second voice to be that of a woman. One of the servants perhaps. She could think of no one else who it might be. When she gave a light tap upon the door the voices stopped and there was a long pause before she heard the click of booted heels and the door was pulled open to reveal Raul in white shirt open to the waist of his dark trousers. The sight of him standing before her, the embodiment of her dreams, so strong and masculine, so undeniably attractive, made all of her planned little speech vanish so that she could do no more than gaze up at his surprised face with a small smile of apology upon her own.

'Coriander, what on earth ...?'

If she heard the rustle of skirts behind him in the room, she did not, at that moment, consciously acknowledge it. 'I'm sorry if I have disturbed your supper, but I would like a word, if that is possible.'

He half glanced over his shoulder before closing the door behind him as he edged her back into the hallway. The gesture registered somewhere in the back of Coriander's mind as odd. But at this precise moment she was more concerned with the plea she had devised and determined to put to him, on the long evenings she had spent alone waiting endlessly for his return. She had had enough of that in London. Madeira was meant to be different.

'I realise that you are busy, Raul, and have other matters which demand your time of far greater importance than myself, but ...' She felt herself flushing with embarrassment. She hated to be put in a position of having to almost beg for his favours. With an effort she tried to make her voice sound perfectly reasonable and rational, though her love for him was such that she was far from feeling that way. 'I wondered if I might accompany you on these treks. I am eager to see your island and meet its people.'

'The roads in Madeira are scarcely passable where they exist at all,' he informed her shortly. 'You would find it exceedingly uncomfortable.'

'But I don't mind that in the least,' she told him.

'I know you are most resourceful, Coriander, but in truth you would slow me down considerably. I can travel much faster alone.' She was forced to accept this indisputable truth, but time was growing heavy on her hands and so she tried a different approach.

'You did promise me an area of land for a garden,' she reminded him, but he only glanced at her vaguely as he began to pull his discarded coat back on and reached for his cravat, with apparently no plans for retiring for the night.

'Ask Maynard. The garden belongs to him,' Raul said, almost disparagingly. 'He always seems ready to oblige you with whatever you crave.' Sliding his arms into the sleeves of his coat, he came to take a hold of her shoulders and place a brief kiss upon her cheek which would have delighted her were it not for the inattentiveness with which it was accomplished. 'Now you must forgive me, Coriander—much as I enjoy talking with you, it is late, and I have to make ready to leave at first light to visit Porto Santo, which involves several hours at sea.'

'Porto Santo—isn't that where the pirate gold was sunk?'

Raul looked startled. 'How did you know that?'

'Ned told me. He seems certain we are about to experience a virulent attack from pirates.' She giggled and Raul seemed to relax, giving a sharp little laugh of his own.

'I hardly think that is likely. There has been no pirate activity in these parts for some time. I think we are safe enough.'

'Which is precisely what I told him.' Coriander put on her most persuasive smile. 'Since we are agreed then that the seas are benign, may I not be company for you?'

Raul pinched her small nose playfully between the stub of his finger and thumb. 'I suspect you are simply too inquisitive for your own good. The answer is still no. You must stay here and be a good girl and behave yourself for once.'

She was more than disappointed by his refusal; she was puzzled, and afraid that it signified more than mere concern for her safety. Wouldn't the *Northumberland* be likewise heading in that direction? If Raul had an assignation with Napoleon planned, she would be the last person he would want on board. And Ned's tales of sea pirates could be merely a ruse to keep her from interfering in his Captain's affairs. But Ned's beloved Captain was also her own love, and the thought that he was involved in traitorous adventures filled her with a sick terror. But what else could it be?

She watched him walk to the door, experiencing a prickle of jealousy for whatever it was which captured his interest more forcedly than herself. 'I believe Porto Santo has a beautiful long sandy beach? I should love to visit it.' She ran up to him, her violet eyes glowing with her love. 'Take me with you, Raul. I promise not to be a nuisance. I am a very good sailor, as you know.'

For the first time in days she saw a trace of the old warmth creep into his responsive smile. 'I think we can manage the rigging without you this time, Coriander.'

'But I miss you,' she persisted, slipping her arms up about his neck. 'I am not happy unless you are close by.'

'I miss you too, Coriander,' Raul said, and was surprised to realise that he actually meant it. 'But there are some instances when it would not be either suitable or advisable for you to accompany me.' Bending his head, he kissed her full upon the lips, a long, warm kiss which set a fire burning deep within her. But then he put her firmly from him, again with a preoccupied smile, and, turning upon his heel in that resolute fashion she had grown to know so well, he walked out into the still darkness of the night.

For a moment Coriander stayed exactly where she was, frozen to the spot, so bitter was her disappointment. It had all been going to be so perfect. She had planned to share his life totally, but he seemed scarcely interested in whether she was there or not. Had Maynard spoken the truth when he had said she was nothing more than Raul's passport to riches? The prospect frightened her so much she found herself running up the stairs to the solitary closeness of her room, where she was sure she would burst into instant tears. Instead she rushed to the window, her eyes seeking a last sight of her beloved as once again he abandoned her to her own devices. He was there, standing just below, but if she had meant to call out to him the words died on her lips unspoken.

Standing beside Raul in a pool of pale moonlight upon Maynard's carefully manicured lawns was Isabella. Coriander recognised her at once as the beautiful woman who had been curled like a crimson cat upon the white steps on the day she had arrived at the *quinta*. Once Raul's mistress, now here she was with one hand possessively upon his arm, gazing up into his face with an earnestness in her wistful face which cut Coriander's heart into painful ribbons. Unable to break away, Coriander stood and watched the two, who were oblivious to all else but the intimacy of their conversation. She saw Raul start to leave and knew a gush of relief as Isabella remained exactly where she was. Would the assignation end here? Then the young woman bent her face into her hands and burst into helpless tears, sinking to her knees upon the damp grass which, to Coriander's dismay, brought Raul hurrying back to her side. Kneeling beside her, he gathered her in his arms, rocking her back and forth as if comforting a babe. With a tenderness that stripped away the last of Coriander's hopes and dreams, leaving only pain and despair in their place, he helped Isabella to her feet and, with his arms still about her, led the girl away across the lawns to disappear in the enveloping darkness of night.

CHAPTER TWELVE

Maynard Beringer pushed the pieces of fish peevishly about upon his plate. A man of healthy appetites, he usually partook of his breakfast with relish, but not this morning and he was annoyed with himself for the apparent weakness. It was all Isabella's fault. She had not come to him last night, despite his sending for her, which had left him with disturbed sleep and put him in a sullen mood on waking.

Looking across the breakfast table, he took in Coriander's unusually pale appearance. She did not look well either. Probably mooning with Raul half the night. How he hated that man. Everything he wanted fell into his lap without difficulty, including the adulation of beautiful women and more riches than a second son had any right to expect. Was not he, Maynard Beringer, elder son and true heir, infinitely cleverer, and more deserving than his brother upon whom such things were wasted? While at times it had proved useful, he often cursed his father for his adoption of Madeiran traditional customs which had resulted in a very satisfactory portion of land being split into uneconomical pieces. Carl Beringer had even gone one step further by giving an equal share to this woman, succeeding, according to Raul, in making her young life a misery which was no doubt the old man's intention, owning as he did an unnaturally macabre sense of humour.

Maynard, however, had a different opinion on the matter. He saw his father's actions as a test. It was up to him, the gifted member of the family, to rise to the challenge. And if everything went according to plan he would make more than enough money this year to ensure he was the victor.

He looked at Coriander again, more speculatively this time. 'And are we soon to have a wedding in the family?' he asked, bringing her from her reverie with a start.

'Oh, not quite yet. Raul is fully occupied with the vines at the moment.' She flushed, embarrassingly in her own eyes, but Maynard thought it livened her pale face delightfully.

'Don't tell me Raul is losing interest? I assure you, my dearest Corrie, I would not dally were you mine.' He smiled at her, his pale eyes bright and probing.

'Not at all,' she said quickly, too quickly, as she tried not to show the unease she felt at recollection of last night's encounter.

Maynard felt a deepening of his depression. Their marriage must be prevented at all costs. 'So you have not changed your views on this alliance, despite my warnings?'

Coriander gave a brittle laugh, covering her nervousness by reaching for a slice of bread and butter which she did not want. 'Everyone seems bent on warning me against every conceivable happening—and some not so conceivable—since I set foot on this island,' she said with a valiant attempt at briskness. 'I vow it all seems somewhat excessive. I am perfectly well able to make my own decisions.'

Maynard twitched his fine brows upwards in a parody of polite interest, though his natural inclination was to glower at the woman for her obstinacy. 'I am sure I consider myself chastised for suggesting otherwise,' he said. 'I merely suspect you will find Raul a most neglectful and selfish husband.'

Coriander found this hard to dispute in the circumstances, yet was anxious to defend her love. 'Raul has mentioned the grape-picking, some festival or other. I believe we are to be married soon after that.'

Maynard's interest quickened. Time was shorter than he had hoped. 'I shall look forward to it,' he said. 'I too shall be at the *vindima*. And everyone enjoys a wedding.'

'Yes.' The stilted conversation was growing difficult and Coriander got to her feet, anxious to be gone. The empty day yawned before her, the picture of Raul and Isabella returning to haunt her with brutal clarity, and in desperation she turned to Maynard.

'I did hope to begin a garden of my own. I promised Pearl,' she began, and saw a cloud of brooding annoyance come down over his lean face.

'The garden is mine,' he said shortly, and she stepped back in surprise, alarmed by his reaction.

'I—I had no wish to interfere. I'm so sorry.' Turning, she made for the door, anxious to take herself away from yet another disappointment in what was meant to have been a magical new life. He reached her just as her hand was upon the knob, and she looked up into a face soft with remorse.

'I should be the one to apologise, Corrie. I slept badly last night and am in a grumpy mood this morning as a result. I shall find you a piece of land for your garden, I promise.' He took her hand and kissed it. 'Forgive me for my bad temper. You at least deserve one friend while you are here.'

Coriander smiled, her warm heart reaching out to him. Perhaps Maynard too had seen the two lovers together and suffered even as she did, knowing they were together somewhere on the high seas. That would certainly account for his touchy mood and poor sleep, as was the case with herself. 'You speak as if I shall not be here long,' she laughed. 'Yet I plan to spend my entire life upon this island.'

Maynard looked down at her, his eyes flickering over her innocent face. 'Yes, indeed, your entire life.' Lifting her hand, he kissed it once more, thinking how soft it was, how pretty, like the rest of her. As fragile as a butterfly. It would be a shameful waste, in a way. But some things were necessary. He was surprised that he had not thought of this answer before. 'I have a better idea,' he said.

Coriander discreetly withdrew her hand. 'What is that?'

'You know that I promised I would do my best to discover some information about your family?'

Coriander was instantly alert. 'Oh—oh, yes, I do remember,' she said, suddenly breathless with anticipation, and Maynard smiled at her eagerness.

'I have discovered that your poor mother came from a little village near Ribeira

Brava and some of her relatives, your family, still live there.'

'Oh, I do not believe it!' Coriander clapped her hands with delight. 'I should so love to meet them.'

'It is no sooner wished than granted, for I am your fairy godmother.' He bowed before her, chuckling teasingly, and she laughed with him. All recollection of having promised Raul never to be alone with his brother vanished in her overwhelming desire to find a place, a family, which she could truly claim to be all her own.

She was pulling the door open and was halfway down the hall in her excitement before he caught her.

'Where are you going?'

'I must inform Ned of our plan, for I agreed to meet him after breakfast.'

'Ned?' He put out a hand to stay her. 'You must not let that old fusspot dictate your life.'

'Raul likes Ned to keep close by me, in case—' She stopped, realising how very silly she sounded, worrying over whether one of Raul's old sailors would object to her taking an outing without his knowledge. It really was quite outrageous.

'In case?'

'I dare say he is still at breakfast himself and would be glad of a day free from entertaining me, but he still needs to be

270

told, so that he doesn't grow anxious if he finds me gone.'

'Then I shall inform him myself of our plans.' Maynard's narrow lips broke into a beatific smile. 'I shall also collect a picnic from Miguel, our most talented cook, and we shall enjoy a perfect day exploring the island together. What do you say?'

'I cannot thank you enough for your kindness,' Coriander said softly. 'I should enjoy that more than I can say.' The dull, lonely day filled only with sad thoughts of how Raul had deceived her, refusing to take her with him to Porto Santo but then happily taking his mistress instead, suddenly turned to gold. It would be wonderful to speak with someone who actually knew her mother, someone of her own family.

'Fetch a wrap or scarf while I speak with Ned, for you may well find it breezy as we climb higher. I shall show you such treasures of nature you would not believe possible.' He was as eager as a boy to be off on a treat. 'Ready in ten minutes?'

'I'll be ready,' Coriander assured him, and ran upstairs on winged feet.

It took no more than a moment to change into a pair of leather boots borrowed earlier from Ned himself, when she had still hoped to persuade Raul to take her with him. She decided on her

271

old red cloak and pulled this on over a sky-blue dress, daintily trimmed with satin bows all down the front. She was thankful that Maynard had relieved her of the task of explaining her decision to go on this outing to Ned, for she could not help but feel a little guilty. Though there was no reason why she should. Raul had shown none when he had left her last night, his arms about his mistress. A little jealousy would do him no harm; she was suffering enough on his account.

Minutes later she and Maynard were following the course of a *levada*, one of the man-made irrigation channels which came down from the mountains, supplying water to the myriad small fields. Trees and flowers grew over and along its brink, forming at times a silent green tunnel, as mysterious and beautiful as a fairy grotto. At others they came out into open places where Coriander was forced to balance precariously upon the narrow wall which supported the *levada*. It was a dizzying feat with the metre width of water sliding swiftly by on one side of her and, on the other, a vast emptiness as the ground sloped down into a crevasse below.

'It must have been quite a task to build these channels,' she commented as they stopped to catch their breath. 'Do they provide water for all the island?'

'Indeed they do. Some of them cut through hills, rocks and deep chasms and are many kilometres in length,' Maynard told her. 'Others are like small branches which reach every corner of the island. Supply of water is strictly regulated, of course, but it seems to work very well. The more land you have, the more water you are allowed to irrigate it. The *levadeiro* with his timetable and watch, decides how much water may flow in our *levadas* and we pay towards the upkeep. Though the Beringer responsibility is split now.'

'Does that matter?'

Maynard stopped, to whirl about so abruptly and face Coriander with such a look of feverish fury upon his face that she would have overbalanced had he not grasped her arm in a pincerlike hold. 'Of course it matters. The land should be kept in one single ownership. It is more efficient and economical that way.'

'Yes, of course,' Coriander shakily agreed, and after that kept conversation to polite appreciation of the flora and fauna, in particular a showy clump of tangerine and blue bird-of-paradise flowers, and a darting kingfisher that flew out right in front of her.

They ate their lunch sitting on a bridge which carried the *levada* over a tumbling waterfall that fell into the deep gulley below. The sun was warm upon her back, with very little breeze stirring the soft green leaves, and everywhere were bright patches of colour to attract the eye. Yet she felt slightly uneasy at the time it was taking them to toil uphill.

'Is it far to Ribeira Brava?' she asked. 'I love this walk, for it is very beautiful, but confess to tiring already with the steep climb.'

'We have not come so far. Look, you can still see the sea.' Maynard moved closer, pointing with an outstretched hand to the distant horizon. 'See, it is indigo-blue, like your eyes, Corrie.'

She gave an unconscious shiver, due, she supposed, to the damp spray which blew up from the waterfall which gushed beneath their feet. To avoid looking down, she willingly gazed out to sea, seeking a small blur or blot which might indicate Raul's ship. She saw nothing. 'My eyes are violet,' she corrected him, without thinking why she did so.

'Are they indeed?' Placing a finger beneath her chin, he turned her face towards him and looked deeply into them. She found his scrutiny faintly disturbing and was relieved when he relinquished the hold. 'So they are. How very unusual. But then you are an unusual person, Corrie.

I thought so from the first moment I met you.'

'What nonsense,' she laughed. 'I am a most plain, ordinary girl wishing only to find somewhere to settle and build a happy life.'

'With someone you love?'

She turned her face shyly from him. 'If that is possible.' She began to get to her feet and he put out a hand to stop her.

'What is wrong? Why do you go? Is it not pleasant sitting here?'

'Y-yes,' she agreed, but uncertainly. She felt oddly vulnerable seated upon the wooden spars of the bridge with the frothing water below. 'If we are to arrive at our destination and still have time to visit with my family, we should surely be on our way?'

She waited in breathless silence for a moment, then Maynard gave a smile which spread slowly across his face. 'You are probably right. Let us be on our way. We have no wish to find ourselves lost in the mountains with night coming on.'

It was something she had not even considered. Now she did and alarm was born in her. 'If there is any danger of that, perhaps we'd better turn back?'

Maynard only laughed, taking her arm to help her along the bridge which rocked alarmingly as they walked. 'It is but a few kilometres to our destination. Do not be concerned. I took you for a woman of spirit.'

Coriander was instantly annoyed with herself for the show of weakness. 'I hope I am that,' she said stoutly. 'It was necessary if I was to survive at Larken's Farm.'

'You have told me little of your life as an orphan. That must have been a most bleak existence,' Maynard said sympathetically, and as they continued their walk through the fragrant woodlands Coriander found herself relating the more amusing tales of how she and Pearl and the other children had used their wits to counter-balance Ezra Follett's greed.

But with each passing kilometre she regretted her madcap decision to accompany Maynard on this trek. She supposed it had been a result of pique on her own part because Raul had refused to take her with him. This journey would have been so much more pleasant with Raul. She could not help but think longingly of stolen kisses in the green woods, of lying in his arms cradled by the long grasses, of feeling the burn of his kisses upon her lips. Instead, these joys belonged to Isabella, and jealousy now soured the love she felt for him, an unpleasant emotion which shamed her.

As they walked Maynard showed her

small banana plantations, pumpkins ripening in the sun and, as they climbed higher, the sugar cane and cereal fields.

'In the topmost part of the island you will find the pines and chestnuts, and finally the barren places where only heather and the mountain goats can survive.'

'What a difference in one small island,' Coriander remarked and again looked about her. 'And where is Ribeira Brava? I am so looking forward to meeting with my family. Who will it be, do you know?'

For the briefest of seconds, Coriander thought he had not heard or even understood her question, but then he seemed to give himself a little shake.

'I want you to see my favourite place. I do not show it to everyone, but you are a special friend, Corrie, and I wish you to understand how much I value that friendship.'

They had been walking for some time along a rough track which served as a road, though it was no more than a wide ledge cut into the side of the mountain which rose dizzily to their right. Bringing their progress to a halt where the road turned at a sharp angle, its corner projecting far out to form a vantage-point, Coriander sank down thankfully upon a low stone wall and, shading her eyes against the bright sun, looked out over the network of fields that dropped like a crazy, tilting staircase below them. Beyond the land, the dark blue of the sea was still disappointingly empty.

'The eucalyptus and acacias are quite beautiful here in the spring,' he said. 'But come, there is something else you must see.'

Slipping over the low wall and dropping to the ground below, he urged Coriander to follow. With only a momentary hesitation she did so, allowing him to help her, trying not to look at the angle of the drop below, broken only by clumps of pink and white saxifrage and the stumpy growth of an occasional wind-blown tree. Maynard led her along a narrow, grassy path which wound its way round the hillside between huge rounded boulders. They were going slightly downhill now, much to her relief, though there was a slippiness underfoot and she held on tightly to Maynard's hand.

'Here we are,' he said excitedly, and pulled her out on to a rocky knoll where the view quite took her breath away. Before them lay a great canyon, its centre filled with a deep blue reservoir of water. And all around the perimeter stood the proud crags, their spiky hats twirled with pearly mists. 'Is it not beautiful?' he asked proudly, as if he had himself created it.

'Yes,' she laughed, almost in relief for

she had begun to feel uneasy over this impulsive outing. 'Oh, yes, it is very beautiful.' It was also the most vertiginous and she put out a hand to steady herself against a gnarled fig-tree which hung over the path. The scent of mimosa filled her nostrils and she felt foolish, and grateful, but at the same time a tinge of regret that it should be Maynard and not Raul who had taken the time to show her this special beauty. 'No wonder you love it here, Maynard.'

'Here you see the source of Madeira's water supply,' he said proudly. 'Come, look closer.' He urged her forward, and reluctantly she relinquished her hold upon the tree, clinging instead to Maynard's hand. She gazed down into the waters far below, dark and mysterious, its depth unknown, the reservoir cold and uninviting. A shudder rippled through her and she pulled back from the brink, breaking his hold.

Leaning against the fig-tree, her hands clammy with cold sweat, she tried to keep her voice steady as she spoke. 'Can we go now, to Ribeira Brava?' she asked, her mind snatching at the reason for their trek, wanting to be gone from this place.

'I will take you now. But I was anxious for you to see this place. It is one of the finest views on the island.'

'Thank you,' she said, her breathing rapid and shallow.

They traversed the return journey at a much quicker rate, so that the leather boots Coriander had borrowed for the walk slipped constantly upon the grassy path in her efforts to hurry.

Back at the wall, Maynard climbed over with practised ease and reached down to help Coriander. She was surprised by how high the wall was from this side, the top being on a level with her head, and how smooth. From the dirt road side she had found little difficulty in climbing it. From this position, with the cliffs dropping dizzily away below her, it was not so easy. But she was most anxious to reach the other side. Scouring the lichen-polished surface, she sought a toehold for her boot, found one and reached up as high as she could to take Maynard's offered hand. Putting much of her weight upon that hold, she sought for a second place for the toes of her other foot. She never found one. Perhaps it was the precipitous angle, or the encumbrance of her cloak, whipped about her legs by the fractious wind, which also carried away the words of instruction Maynard called to her. But one moment she was almost at the top, her only concern that of snagging her new blue dress upon the gritty stones, the next her hands were grasping at thin air as her body flailed backwards and downwards into the abyss.

If Raul had followed Fernando's creed he knew he would not now be faced with this dilemma. But he had not followed his heart. He had opted for duty.

Looking down upon the bent head of the snivelling girl, ebony waves stuck like seaweed to her pinched cheeks, he wondered what he'd ever seen in her. In comparison with Coriander she was an overblown rose against a delicate rosebud. He wondered too about this penchant of his for collecting lame ducks. He had accepted his responsibility to Coriander; now Isabella was the one to present him problems, dissolving constantly into weeping and wailing. And why? All because of his deuced brother.

'How many times did I tell you to keep away from him, Isabella? He will break your heart.'

Sorrowful black eyes, red-rimmed with the damp of tears, turned up to him. 'As you did.'

Crouching beside her, Raul took her firmly by the shoulders and gave her a little shake. 'You know that to be untrue. There was never love between us.'

She smiled at him through her tears.

'But it was fun, yes?'

He gave a soft laugh, acknowledging her remark with a twitch of his eyebrows. 'But Maynard is not the one for you either. He loves only himself, which you know well enough if you will only admit it.'

'And what am I to do when it is I who love him?' she persisted, a petulance in her voice.

Raul gave a small sigh, his patience beginning to wear thin. He had only agreed to take her on this voyage for the information she had promised to give him. Now he regretted that decision. She had done nothing but weep since they'd set sail, and he really had far more important matters to attend to than a lovesick woman.

'Isabella, please try to remember the question I asked you earlier. Whereabouts on Porto Santo did Maynard beach his boat on the occasions you came with him?'

Isabella stared at him, a pout blurring the lines of her shapely lips. 'Maynard will be much cross if I tell you,' she mourned.

'Maynard, if I am correct in my suspicions, is involved in criminal activities and could suffer grave consequences, as could you too, if you accompanied him.'

At last he saw fear dawn in the beautiful

eyes and knew that he had penetrated beyond the self-pity. 'Oh, but it was not I. I did nothing. I come with him, that is all. Many times have I tried to escape your brother, but always he makes me return to him. I am the lump of clay in his hands. I know it, I know it,' she babbled, fingers fluttering to cradle her cheeks in her anxiety to dissociate herself from trouble, and the wailing began again as she rocked herself backwards and forwards in despair.

'Isabella, stop that.'

Tiny whimpers still came from her throat. 'I should perhaps go home to my family.'

'Yes, Isabella, if that is what you want.'

She nodded fervently, but then shook her head in despair.

'Loving you both as I do, how can I betray the one to the other? It would be wrong, yes?'

'It might save lives,' he told her bluntly. 'If, as I believe, Maynard has discovered pirate gold and is selling it to enemies of the Portuguese there could be trouble ahead.' But she shook her head in denial.

'I know of no danger but that to my heart. I love both brothers, and both brothers wish to marry a young, untried English girl.' Isabella sank her head sadly against his shoulder. 'She can choose either of you, while I can have none.'

'You are growing morbid, Isabella. And what is all this talk of Maynard wishing to marry Coriander? Has he told you so?' Raul felt uneasy suddenly. Somehow, he had fooled himself into thinking that Maynard had accepted the situation as a *fait accompli*, that he would heed Raul's warning to leave her alone since they were already betrothed. Isabella seemed to be suggesting otherwise.

She shook her head. 'No, no. But I know him well. None better, yes? I see his eyes follow her. He does not see a pretty girl, as you do.' She smiled mischievously at him. 'He sees a third share of what should rightly be his. He wants everything for himself. He needs it, to prove that he is a man, like you.'

'Like me? What are you talking about?'

'Always he envies your assurance, your abilities, your talent to make the business hum with life, to make people respect you.' She smiled seductively at him. 'To make the women like you. He envies your strength. Maynard thinks this power and strength lies in the land, in money, in the buildings and paintings he will buy and create with it. He will let nothing stand in his way.'

'I know that.'

Isabella looked up at him, a new

frankness in her gaze. 'But you too are concerned for money, else you would not be here.'

'That is not true. I am here because Henry Veitch is convinced Maynard's activities could cause grave problems between the English and the Portuguese. You are here because you offered to help me put that right. Now, it seems, you have changed your mind.'

She stepped back from him, sweeping back her hair in a contemptuous gesture. 'You ask me to betray the man I love, not because you care about saving me from him, but because you care only for yourself,' she sneered. 'For the money you will be paid by this Henry Veitch or the gold itself if you find it. Men go mad for gold. Kill for it. I hate those pirates of long ago. I hate Maynard. I hate you.' She shook a fist in his astonished face.

'Ask yourself this, Raul Beringer. Do you love this girl you wish so much to marry? If you do not, then you are as callous and cold-heartedly greedy as Maynard. If you do, then why is it not she here beside you, instead of me? If you truly wish to save her from this brother you think so bad, why you not keep her safely by your side every hour of every day? Ask yourself that, Mr Clever Beringer, and live with your answer.' With a swirl of crimson skirts

285

she ran from him to the cabin below, and he stood alone on the deck of his ship with only the wind to soothe the agonising certainty that for once Isabella had said too much that was true.

CHAPTER THIRTEEN

Raul was disturbed. Isabella's stinging words had cut him more than he would have wished. Always his philosophy of life had been to put people before possessions. And Isabella was accusing him of exactly the opposite. Was he as guilty of the crime of selfish greed as Maynard? He was certainly guilty of lack of care, of thoughtlessness, perhaps an arrogance in thinking Maynard could be controlled by words rather than actions. He had been so anxious to complete these other duties which weighed upon him that he had given too little thought to Coriander, believing they would be together all the sooner if he could first clear these other matters away. He had not truly considered that it may then be too late.

Cold fear wrung his heart. Where was Coriander now? He remembered the brightness of her face as she had made her earnest, most beguiling plea for him to take her upon this trip. He had scarcely listened to her, so preoccupied had he been. To be fair to himself, he had believed that she would have been in greater danger upon this trip than back home with Maynard at the *quinta*. But Isabella's words had dispersed that frail confidence. She was right when she said that Maynard would stop at nothing to gain complete control, and he had blithely agreed with her, knowing it to be true.

'Turn the ship,' he called. 'Make for home.' If Isabella refused to co-operate he no longer had the time nor the inclination to search the island. It could take days, and he had the unnerving feeling that time was suddenly very precious, that Coriander was in need of him.

'Ship off the starboard bow,' came the cry, and Raul sprang to the side, cursing beneath his breath.

'Can you see who she is?' he asked.

'Aye, Capt'n. The *Northumberland.*'

'Damnation. Then we cannot return yet awhile. Keep a steady course, as we were.' He damped down his growing fears over Coriander's safety. Ned was with her, and with the end of his mission in sight he would soon be free to devote his entire life to caring for her, a prospect which filled him with supreme happiness.

Coriander lay stunned. Her body, curled about a boulder, neither moved nor seemed hardly able to breathe. Dizzying images whirled inside her head, as fickle as mountains glimpsed through the cloying mists. Faces, blinding flashes of colour, the sparkle of dark blue water, the slap of a hand and disembodied voices rose with a persistent regularity to torment her, but which reality and which fantasy she could not tell.

'Coriander, Coriander.'

The sound came from a great distance, too far for her to reach. Yet there was a familiarity to it which woke a need in her. She must reach it, whatever the effort, for she realised that it was Raul come for her, come to tell her that it was she alone he loved, not Isabella, not his traitorous spying activities, nothing but her.

'Raul.' From the depths of her being she found the strength to call out his name. A hand grasped hers, but the pain it caused to her shoulder made her cry out. What was he trying to do to her?

'Coriander, try to pull yourself up. Corrie, Corrie, are you awake? Are you all right?'

She opened her eyes. When the images vanished and the world stopped tilting she saw above her a familiar face. But it was not Raul's face. Maynard's hand was upon hers and it was he who urged her, in Raul's voice, to pull upon the boulder and try to ease herself upwards to safer ground. Disappointment and some other, unidentified emotion flooded through her. But she knew that she must obey, for she dared not look at what lay behind and below her. With a strength she did not know she possessed she pulled upon Maynard's hand, gradually edging herself further on to the boulder where she hung so perilously. When she was able, she brought up one foot, using that to push herself further up the hillside. Moments later the agony was over and she was somehow leaning against the stone wall which had proved her downfall. Beside her, Maynard hovered, anxiety creasing his lean face, his golden hair tousled from anxious fingers and from the effort to save her.

'I should not have brought you,' he kept repeating like a litany, and Coriander tried, and failed, to find the strength to reassure him that the fault was not his. She should have known better than to attempt it, particularly in borrowed boots several sizes too big. Raul had been quite right. She was an encumbrance, and after this she would stay safely at the *quinta*.

'Stay here,' Maynard was saying. 'Can you hear me, Coriander? You must stay here while I fetch help.'

She tried to speak but no sound came. She tried again. 'I-I'm all right. Help me up.'

But Maynard would not hear of it. 'No, no. You must take care. You may have broken a bone. You are most certainly too ill to walk all the way down the mountainside. Stay safely here in the lee of this wall, while I go and fetch a palanquin to carry you home.'

Before she was able to make any further protest, he had climbed the wall and was gone.

A wind sprang up from the sea and she pulled her cloak tightly about her, thankful now that she had thought to wear it. She could see clouds gathering and knew that night approached. Panic welled up inside her. Surely Maynard was wrong to leave her here? She must get home, somehow. Using the wall as support, she tried to push herself to her feet. Pain shot through her shoulders, slicing across her chest and down her arms with a ferociousness that brought instant tears to her eyes and a cry of agony despite her determination to the contrary. Very warily, she sank to the ground again, a wave of sickness washing over her.

'Dear God, what have I done?'

It was some hours before Maynard arrived back at the *quinta*. Ample time for him to remonstrate with himself over and over at his failure to complete the task. He should have finished it at the reservoir as he had intended. A body would never have been found there. But he had bungled it. For some reason he could not understand he had shrunk, not merely once, but twice from disposing of the damned girl. Even when he had let go of her hand so that she did finally fall, it had been apathetically done. He should have pushed her over the edge and made an end to her, relieving himself of the miserable prospect he now faced. One thing was certain: he could not allow the matter to rest. He had failed. Yet he had come close enough to success to know he must try again. And the third time he would be less squeamish. The third time he would make sure there was no handy boulder or fig-tree to cling to. The third time he would make absolutely certain that she was dead. A slow smile of pleasure spread across his face. And he would make equally certain that she did not die alone. For the moment he would have to go through the motions of trying to save her. It would not serve his purpose if she grew suspicious.

Two bearers, with palanquin, were soon dispatched and Maynard duly repaired to his bedchamber for a much-needed rest, having first issued instructions for food to be brought to him at once, and Isabella as soon as she could be found. He hated, more than anything, to be alone, and the *quinta* seemed eerily silent with no one in it but himself.

It was in fact late morning before footsteps rang across the mosaic floor of the hall and voices rose to disturb his slumber.

'Isabella?' he queried sleepily, raising himself on one elbow as he heard the door of his bedchamber open. But it was Raul who came towards him, not the sinuously beautiful figure of his mistress, and his face was black with anger.

In one swift movement he pulled Maynard from his bed and half dragged, half marched him across the room.

'Where is she? Tell me where she is or I'll slit your lying tongue from your mouth.'

Maynard began to shake. It was not often that Raul lost his temper, but when he did it was awesome to behold. 'It is none of my fault,' he cried, piteously trying to free himself. 'I have sent men to find her.'

With vile contempt, Raul slammed Maynard back against the wall, and almost spat his fury in his brother's face.

'If any harm has come to Coriander through you, intended or not, you'll live to regret it. Now tell me clearly. Where is she?'

'I—I cannot breathe while you hold me so,' Maynard squeaked, certain he was about to be strangled by his brother's grasp before he could utter a word.

Impatiently Raul released him, but retreated to hover threateningly as he waited for the explanation. As the story was told his expression grew darker. What a fool he had been. If he had not been so preoccupied with his own concerns, Coriander would be safe.

'Take me to her,' he ordered, and Maynard flinched.

'But I have told you. I sent men. They should be here soon.'

'When did you send them?'

'Last night.'

'Then they should have been back long since. Get up, you snivelling coward.' Pulling Maynard to his feet from where he had sunk down the wall into a crouched position, Raul flung him towards the door. 'Take me to where you left her. Since they are not back, there must be some further problem. Have you not the wit to see that? And when we find her, if Coriander lays the blame for this upon you, you can start trembling for your life in truth, my brother, make no mistake of that.'

'She will not. She will not,' he blabbered, desperate to escape Raul's tenacious hold but unable to do so. 'It was an accident, I swear it.'

'Let us hope you are right, and that we find her safe and well.' Raul's voice was softly menacing and Maynard made a silent prayer that that would be the case.

A mist had come first and then the darkness. Coriander slept for a while and woke feeling much better. Her heart had stopped its mad racing and the pains in her shoulders and ribs seemed less severe. Droplets of mist turned to cold moisture upon her skin and the prospect of remaining here all night grew less and less appealing. It could be hours before Maynard was able to bring help from the *quinta,* and even then how would they find her in the darkness? With fresh resolution she gathered her strength. She knew what she must do. She would follow the path on this side of the wall in the hope of finding a place with footholds or low enough for her to climb. So long as she kept a hold upon it, she could not see any great risk to her safety.

Taking a deep breath, she drew herself to her feet. The first flush of pain took her breath away, but when it eased she began to make progress. With steady, careful steps she edged her way along the path, carefully testing each step in the darkness before she put her full weight upon it.

To her surprise, and relief, the path led downwards and before long widened into a track as it entered woodland. She knew then that she was safe, and sat down upon the root of a tree to still her quivering muscles and shattered nerves. Relief made her tired and she laid her head back against the bark, closing her eyes against the anonymous blackness of night. Exhaustion overcame her and the next thing she found was that her body had slid down into the cradle of the tree's roots and the brightness of day was warming her closed lids. Opening them wide, she heard the voices. Lifting her head, she listened with all the intentness of a wild creature. The sound came from high above. Someone was calling her name.

Wincing from the pain of her protesting muscles and the soreness of bruises, she got silently to her feet and began to walk slowly back up the track, listening all the while. Then she was running towards the voice, silver-fair hair streaming in the wind behind her like rippling ribbons of light.

'I am here,' she cried.

'Coriander.' It came again, and she

knew that she was not mistaken this time. Picking up her skirts, she ran as fast as she could go back through the woodland. Before she reached the path by the wall, she saw him running towards her, and knew supreme joy as his arms gathered her up in a crushing embrace.

Coriander was not allowed out of her bed for three days. Three achingly wonderful days when scarcely an hour passed without Raul calling in to bring some titbit or drink from the kitchens, a morsel of gossip or simply to sit by her bed and hold her hand.

'When we reached the precipice and you were nowhere in sight my heart died within me,' he told her for the umpteenth time and a glow of joy burst afresh within her. 'I found a blue satin bow from your dress so knew it to be the right place, but you were gone and my world was as empty as the skyline.'

'I could never leave you,' Coriander whispered softly, and curled her small fingers about the solid strength of his hand.

At her touch he leaned forward to gather her in his arms and rain tiny, caressing kisses over her cheeks and hair. 'My darling Coriander, you will never know the relief and joy I felt at sight of your familiar red cloak which will forever be a favourite of mine.'

Coriander chuckled delightedly deep in her throat. 'And I thought you found it so outmoded, as you once did my dresses.'

He laughed too, cradling her in his arms, wanting to feel her close against him but ever conscious of the discomfort he might cause to her bruises. 'You may wear it forever to remind me of this day when I thought you lost but found you again.'

She laid a hand upon the broad planes of his cheek, her eyes taking in every beloved feature of his face. 'We shall only ever be separated again, my love, at your wish, never by mine.'

The smile he gave her was all the answer she could have wished, but he added, 'Then we will ever be together, for I shall never choose it. The sooner we are wed, the better. I swear I cannot bear even a moment apart. Every day, every long night, every hour I am not beside you is too long. We will pick the grapes, enjoy the festival and then, my sweet darling, you and I will pledge our troth in very truth.'

'Raul, there is just one thing,' Coriander said with gentle hesitation.

'Ask anything, my darling,' he murmured, thinking she required some feminine frippery, 'and it is yours.'

Coriander cleared her throat of sudden

nervousness, wondering how she should begin. 'It concerns Napoleon.'

It was the last thing Raul had expected and his eyebrows shot up in crooked surprise. 'Napoleon Bonaparte?'

'Yes.' Coriander risked a glance at his face and, apparently finding it reasonably benevolent, deemed it judicious for her to continue. 'From the first moment I boarded your ship ...'

'You mean when you stowed away,' he could not resist teasing her, and Coriander had the grace to blush at proof of her forwardness at that time.

'I first saw Bonaparte's ship in Torbay and you went aboard. We saw it frequently as we travelled to Madeira, and once again as soon as we docked you went aboard with the British Consul. And I suspect your apparent visit to Porto Santo was actually connected with the *Northumberland* for it had so recently sailed before you.' Her breath ran out and so she stopped speaking.

Raul was looking quizzically at her. 'You are most observant. But what exactly are you suggesting?'

A long silence stretched out and Coriander fervently wished that she had never brought the subject up, but having done so she had no option but to persist. 'I did wonder if you could have any connection with Bonaparte,' she said with some haste, as if to get an unpleasant task over and done. Raul stared at her in astonishment for half a minute, and then to her complete surprise burst out laughing.

'You think I'm a spy for the French?'

She gave a small nod, her expression bleak.

A softness came into his green eyes as he curbed his laughter. 'That must have caused you some pain, my darling, yet you still loved me?'

'Nothing can prevent that.'

'Then let me at least put your mind at rest on that score.' Taking her hands in his, he kissed them softly upon each palm before gathering them close within his own. 'My allegiance is not to the French as your vivid imagination supposed, but to the Prince Regent who is, incidentally, one of my very best customers. For him I promised to watch Napoleon and see that he reached St Helena safely and that no attempts were made to rescue him. Even now I suppose I should still be following him, but he is well on his way and for no reason beyond my instincts I felt you to be in greater danger. I was proved to be right in that.'

'Then you are not a spy?' Coriander asked in a small, breathless voice.

'Nothing so romantic,' he told her

teasingly. 'I have performed similar tasks for the Prince in the past. But I am no more than an honest citizen doing his duty for no reward whatsoever. Even if one had the temerity to send an account to his Royal Highness I doubt he would settle it. On the contrary, I shall probably feel bound to make him a gift of a case of vintage malmsey along with my report.'

'I see.' She gave a sheepish smile and was relieved to see amusement in his eyes and not anger.

'For someone who has made a career for herself as a highwayman, seeing spies everywhere seemed perfectly normal, did it?'

'I'm sorry. Please don't tease me any more,' she pleaded. 'I am suffering embarrassment enough.'

And, with explanations completed to Coriander's satisfaction, she slid her arms about his neck and, uncaring of hurt to her bruised ribs, pressed herself close against him. His lips upon hers filled her with such a sweet yearning she wondered if she could wait even a week. Her whole being cried out to become a part of him. Raul was no longer a separate person in her mind, but another dimension of her own self, and only together did they create a whole.

On the fourth day Coriander was allowed

to sit in the garden for a little while and enjoy the warmth of the sun. There was no sign of Maynard and for that she felt oddly grateful. She had seen little of him since the accident beyond an initial visit from him to confirm she was well and beg her forgiveness. Though she knew it had been simply that, an accident, a part of her mind felt troubled by the events of that day. Maynard had at times behaved oddly, and she could still remember the eerie apprehension she had felt at his unexpected bursts of laughter at what to her had seemed far from amusing. She began to understand Raul's disquiet over his brother's behaviour. There was something unstable in his nature, yet it was hard to define.

But most of her mind was occupied with the more delightful prospect of her coming wedding. It would be a quiet affair, taking place as soon as the grapes were safely gathered. Not even Raul's own wedding could be allowed to risk a bountiful harvest upon which a year's work and their future livelihood was invested. She was content to sit in the sun and dream of which dress she would choose to wear as his bride, the cruise he had promised her as a wedding journey, and afterwards a life to be enjoyed together here in Madeira. Raul was planning a new home to be built for them while they were away, and when it was completed Coriander intended to invite Pearl and Letty to come and visit or share it with her if they wished. Her heart was so full of happiness she wondered how she could bear it. All her troubles were over, all the doubts banished. She could give herself to Raul in love and complete trust to be his forever, and nothing now could spoil that.

The grapes hung plump and ripe upon the vines, the leaves having been plucked back to expose them to the warmth of the sun. Many of the vines grew over *latadas* which were structures comprised of posts strung across with cord, reminding Coriander of the rose trellis walk at Lady Wilchester's house. Everywhere there was sunshine and laughter, the brightly dressed figures of the harvesters moving rhythmically along the rows, dropping luscious bunches into cone shaped baskets. They sang as they worked, each group vying with the other for the wittiest, merriest song, known as the *desgarradas*. Coriander had never heard such enthusiasm and joy in a place of work before and could not resist joining in as best she could by humming along with them.

She loved working contentedly beside Raul, a large apron covering her print dress, asking from time to time for a translation of the jokes which were bandied about. Sometimes he obliged, but sometimes he only pursed his lips and shook his head and Coriander returned, giggling, to her task, no longer finding his protectiveness at all irksome.

It was hot, tiring work and every hour or so they would break to refresh themselves with fruit juice and fresh food, Raul always managing to find a quiet place where they could be alone for a few moments.

'Where will you take me on our voyage?' she asked, before digging her teeth into the ripe flesh of a melon and squealing as the juice ran down her chin.

'What a child you are,' laughed Raul, mopping her face with a napkin. 'Where would you like to go?'

Her eyes slanted vivaciously at him and she gave a little sigh. 'I declare it would be lovely to see Pearl and Letty again, but perhaps that is too much to ask.'

'When did that ever stop you?' he chortled. 'Do not play the coquette with me, for I know you to be a determined miss who will have her way if she wills it.'

Violet eyes stretched wide. 'What a calumnious statement that is, Raul Beringer. Have I not been a dutiful and obedient companion to you?'

He twisted one brow in mocking despair. 'Dutiful? To a degree. Companion, yes, I think you have. But obedient? Oh, Coriander, you will never be that.' He burst out laughing and she playfully slapped at him to make him stop, but instead he caught her hand and they rolled over and over in the sweet-smelling grass, tumbling together like children, like lovers.

'If obedience is what you want, then you shall have it,' she declared, catching her breath.

'How boring that would be. I think men who require dutiful, obedient wives must be as dull as those wives inevitably become. I shall ask only that you be yourself, sweet Coriander.' Whereupon he robbed her of the last breath in her body and covered her with embarrassment by kissing her with fulsome enjoyment upon the lips. Blushing furiously at the sound of distant chuckling, she pushed him away and pulled herself to a more decorous sitting position. Her print dress had ricked up, revealing shapely legs left bare on this warm day, and a flounce of white petticoat. Looking up, she caught sight of Maynard a few yards off, and he looked at her unsmiling as if he had been watching for a long time. The warmth of the sun turned to ice upon her skin and hastily she flicked down the hem of her dress, offering a tremulous smile of friendship to him. A slow grin spread across his face and then, getting to his feet, he stood up and leisurely walked away. For some reason the encounter spoiled her day, and she no longer felt any inclination to share in Raul's playful teasing.

'Let us eat, I am starving,' she said by way of an excuse, and, having worked hard all morning, he readily agreed.

'On the last evening we have such a feast your eyes will pop,' he told her. 'We build fires and cook our food in the open. You will love it.'

She smiled lovingly at him. 'I love everything about this life. Even you.'

'What more can I ask?' he returned, and reached for a wedge of cheese, a contented man.

As the baskets were filled they were carried to the *lagares* where the grapes were crushed to pulp. This, to Coriander, was the most entertaining, if exhausting part of the whole operation. Men, women and children in cut-off trousers or tucked-up skirts, bare legs half buried in the fruit, slowly pulped the grapes, keeping a steady rhythm in pace with their joyous songs. The heady aroma of fruit was almost overwhelming. Coriander watched with delight and interest, but declined their offer to take part, though she thanked them for it.

The resulting *mosto* or pulp was next placed in the press and given two thorough squeezings. Raul told her that the local people would add water to the remaining skin and seeds and crush it for a third time. This would provide them with *água pe*, a weak wine with a low alcoholic content but which they enjoyed in celebration of a good *vindima*.

'All that remains now,' said Raul some days later when all the baskets of grapes had been pulped and pressed, 'is to transport the *mosto* back to Funchal and make wine.'

'You make it sound simple.'

'To a degree it is. Much of the hard work is done, for the moment at least, until the next batch of grapes is ready for harvest.'

Coriander, flopped against a fig-tree, allowed her jaw to sag in open dismay. 'You mean this is only the beginning?'

Raul laughed as he swung himself down beside her. 'Grapes ripen at different times. The white grapes grown in the north part of the island will be the last to be ready. But don't worry. I shall not insist, this year, on taking a hand in every one myself. I have other, more important plans for the next few weeks.' The expression in his eyes sent a tingle right down to her toes, which curled of their own volition within her kid slippers.

'I am glad to hear it,' she whispered, and for a moment they were content to gaze upon each other, words being quite irrelevant.

Later they watched together as the *borracheiros* carried the kid skins of pulped grapes slung across their shoulders, hats pulled well down to keep off the sun, long staff in hand, a swinging procession along the road to Funchal.

'And while the fermentation process gets under way, you and I, Coriander, will liven the festival still further with our wedding.'

She turned to him, eyes shining. 'I can hardly wait.'

His arms coming once more about her waist, he murmured softly against her ear, 'I can see no reason why we should, can you? And I certainly have no inclination to do so.'

He gathered her close, and readily she gave herself up to the joy of a lingering kiss which soon lit with the passion both of them could scarcely repress. She had believed themselves alone now that the workers had all departed, and so responded with a freedom and abandonment which stirred them both to greater heights. As his hands moved down to caress her breasts she made no protest, only arching her body seductively, wanting him as desperately

307

as he needed her. But as he lifted his head to trail fiery kisses along the line of her sensitive throat, and sought the fastenings of her gown with urgent fingers, she opened eyes dazed with her longing to see a flicker of movement in the bushes behind his head. A figure moved stealthily away and, as it crossed a sun-filled patch, he turned his face towards her and she saw quite clearly that it was Maynard.

CHAPTER FOURTEEN

They were married in the small white-walled church at Monte. Ned stood in proudly to give the bride away, telling her, as did the groom once he saw her, how beautiful she looked. Coriander chose to wear a simple white dress embroidered in the Madeiran tradition, and upon her hair, which hung as a silken cape down her back, she wore a circlet of mimosa flowers. Her young rosy face glowed with happiness and, if Raul had not already discovered his love for her, the moment she came towards him in that little church would alone have captivated him for life.

'I do wish Pearl and Letty could have been here,' she said as they walked in a joyful procession, their friends and estate workers scattering rose petals to lead them to the *quinta*. 'Letitia would have enjoyed a good cry.'

'There must be no tears this day,' Raul insisted, popping a kiss lightly upon her flushed cheek. 'Let Letitia save her tears for when you see her.'

Coriander stopped in her tracks. 'Will I?'

'What?'

'See her?'

'But of course. Do you think we would travel all the way to England and not call in for a cup of tea and one of Letitia's delicious home-made scones?'

Coriander squealed her delight, flinging her arms around Raul's neck so that he swung her laughing off the ground.

'That is the best wedding present you could have given me,' she told him, but his eyes twinkled wickedly as he replied.

'Oh, I think we can do even better than that.'

Hot-cheeked, she abruptly released him. 'You are quite incorrigible, Raul Beringer,' she muttered beneath her breath, but he only laughed all the more.

'And you would have me no other way, Coriander Beringer,' he whispered back, and she cast a look of surprise at him for it was the first time she had heard her new name.

'I rather like the sound of that,' she said, smiling.

Tucking her arm within his, he leaned over to nibble her ear. 'I shall whisper it to you in your sleep.'

'Have done with your teasing,' she said hastily as Ned drew near, a glass of Madeira wine held out for each of them.

As they gratefully drank the delicious nectar, Ned raised his own glass in salute to them. 'I wish you both every happiness and hope as how you'll forgive me for my neglect, though I never meant it,' he finished rather quickly, wagging his head from side to side in his agitation.

Smiling, Coriander surprised and pleased the old man by presenting him with a light kiss which brought a glow of colour to the weathered face. 'If Maynard never informed you of our outing that day, how can you be responsible? It was not your fault, Ned, and you must put it from your mind once and for all.'

Ever since that fateful day, Ned had constantly gone over and over how he could have prevented the accident, but every time he came back to the point where he remembered sitting in the kitchen enjoying his breakfast and Maynard calling in and sending him to look for Isabella, saying only that Coriander would not be requiring him as she intended to relax in the garden. He was sure that was what the Viscount had said. Maynard had made no mention of any outing. And, since Ned was obliged to search for Isabella, with negative results as it turned out, he was unaware of the preparation of a picnic. Whether Maynard was Viscount or not, Ned was ready to speak a piece of his mind on the subject when he saw him again. He rather expected him to be at his brother's wedding. 'I've been keeping a look-out for Mr Maynard, but have seen no sign of him this day.'

There was the smallest of silences before Raul spoke, and Coriander, listening wide-eyed, hated the harshness of his tone for all she understood it.

'I know not where he is. Nor do I care.'

Ned, clearly embarrassed for having brought the subject up, hastened to refill their glasses. 'Drink up, drink up, for 'tis a day to celebrate.'

'I shall be quite merry soon,' protested Coriander.

'Then give her more,' teased Raul, much to her disapproval, but when Ned made to refill her glass Raul shook his head and, smiling, Ned withdrew.

Once in the gardens of the *quinta*, everyone was more than ready to relax and celebrate after the long days of hard labour, and, as the sky blushed pink with the fall of the sun, cooking fires were lighted and the feast prepared. And such a feast.

There was a choice of pumpkin or watercress soup with *bolo do caco*, a tasty round bread made from wheat and potato flours which the women cooked over a hot flat stone. To follow were thick white steaks of the deep-sea fish, black scabbard. Then there was the *espetada*, which was juicy chunks of beef and pork speared on to laurel sticks and barbecued to perfection. This latter was served with a delicious Madeira sauce made from a secret recipe the talented Miguel was not prepared to divulge. In addition there were tomatoes as big as apples, grilled till their skins crinkled, crisp salads and *atum com milho frito* which were tuna steaks with fried corn. Just when Coriander felt sure she could eat no more along came the fresh fruits of banana, mango, melon and pear, wine jellies, and of course the *bolo de mel*, the ever popular and delectable honey cake.

'No more,' she protested, laughing. 'I shall grow so fat I will sink the ship.'

'Never,' Raul murmured, sliding his hands about her slender waist, and the feel of his body against hers sent her senses reeling in ecstasy. Everything was quite perfect. She felt herself the luckiest woman alive to have such a wonderful man who so clearly loved her. It seemed odd now that she had ever worried about his motives for wishing to marry her. Reaching up, she kissed him softly upon the lips and she heard a low groan, almost of agony, deep in his throat.

'Do not touch me so, Coriander, until we are alone or I'll not answer for my actions. Will this day never end?'

She chuckled happily. 'It is my wedding day and I intend it to last as long as possible,' she declared, lifting her chin in stubborn resistance. 'Come along, the dancing has begun, and you must teach me the steps.'

Pretending resistance, Raul allowed himself to be tugged and enticed into action.

It was in fact almost dawn before the last of the revellers left and Coriander and Raul were free to make their way, sleepy but happy, to their bedchamber.

'Are you very tired, little one?' he asked softly as, closing the door, they were at last alone.

Coriander turned shyly towards him. 'Less than I expected. But it was a wonderful party.'

He murmured her name just once before taking her into his arms, and, holding her close, kissed her softly, exploring the sensitivity of their emotions. As the kiss became deeper, more possessive, the fire of passion was born in them both. Coriander helped him with the fastenings, bows and buttons till the white dress lay in a forgotten crumple upon the tiled floor and the underslip soon followed. As his hands gently cupped her firm young breasts she felt a rosy flush creep over her skin and she looked away in blushing confusion. Then Raul was swinging her up in his arms to lay her down gently upon the bed.

But all shyness was swept away as their bodies met as man and wife. Raul caressed her with a love and tenderness which set her body trembling with need. And in that moment of fulfilment when she felt him move deep within her, she cried out his name with love and passion and afterwards wept upon his shoulder. She had dreamt of this moment many times but never had she envisaged such wonder, such a glorious merging of the senses. The release of tension from her young body brought in its wake a flood of joy and sweet sensation of security, unexpectedly delicious in its intensity. And as she lay within the circle of his arm, her cheek resting against the warmth of his bare skin, she knew at last that completeness of love she had looked for all her life. It mattered no longer that she had been abandoned by her family as a babe, that her unknown mother and father had died. The years as an orphan at Larken's Farm were wiped clean and she knew that this was a new beginning, a rebirth, and the source of her life and future happiness rested in this one man who lay so close beside her, stroking her hair and murmuring her name with tender devotion.

The sun was hot upon her sprawled body when she at last woke from a deep, dreamless sleep. Her first thought was for Raul, and she stretched out a hand only to find the place beside her empty and the sheets cool to her touch.

'Raul?' She sat up, pushing her hair back from her face, tense suddenly that it might all have been a figment of her imagination or that he had abandoned her with a return of that callous neglect she had hated so much.

'My love?'

She sighed her relief as he came towards her, the sunshine bathing his golden skin with an iridescent glow. Smiling, he lay down beside her and, gently pulling away the single sheet, looked upon the slender lines of her body as if he could never have enough of her.

'You are embarrassing me again,' Coriander whispered, curling herself protectively against him, and, laughing softly, he nuzzled his lips against her ear.

'How can there be any embarrassment left between us after last night?' He kissed her and felt again the surge of desire rise instantly within him as their bodies touched, and with a shiver of desire he pulled her closer, trailing fevered kisses down her throat to the curve of one breast. Never had he felt such passion and need for a woman before. And for all her seeming innocence she had astonished and delighted him with her response to his lovemaking. She was twining her eager limbs about him and once more he took her, glorying in the sensations awakened by her love, the almost ethereal power she gave to him.

If food was brought to them that day they ate with little awareness. Not once did they venture out into the warmth of the sun. Their world comprised only of the bedchamber and, more importantly, each other. They talked as they had never done before, exchanging confidences, teasing, playing, laughing, and then there was the loving. Each time Raul made love to her, and it was many during that blissful twenty-four hours, the ecstasy of their passion grew ever more profound. As day turned into the second night they lay together in the sweet-scented darkness and slept the deep sleep of the truly contented.

But the idyll, as far as Coriander was concerned, came to an end the next morning. It began pleasantly enough with the two of them enjoying breakfast together, but this time when the dishes were cleared away and Raul had finished his bath he did not return to her side; instead he reached for his clothes, though with a smile crinkling the corners of his eyes.

'Enough of this lazing. If we are to set sail on the evening tide I must make some preparations and so, my love, must you.'

Coriander bounced in childlike glee up on to her knees upon the bed. 'I can be ready in no time,' she promised.

Pulling on his coat, he pecked a brief kiss upon her nose before striding to the door. 'Good. Nevertheless, I know what you females are like so I will send Isabella to assist you.'

It was as if he had douched her skin with ice. 'I-I can manage well enough on my own,' she faltered.

'Nonsense. Isabella can easily act as maid for you and will be more than willing to do so. In fact she has already said as much.'

'As my maid?'

'A lady usually has one, you know.'

'But must it be Isabella?'

'Whyever not? Oh, I see.' Returning to her side for an instant to lift her chin with one finger, he looked deeply into her eyes. 'I hope this attitude of yours does not indicate a loss of that trust I have so carefully nurtured. You must not be afraid of Isabella. She belongs to my past and whatever existed between us, which was very little, is over and done with.'

Coriander, gazing earnestly into his eyes, wanted desperately to believe him. Yet the uneasiness was still there when some time later that morning Isabella herself slid into the room with that strange, catlike movement she had, and, leaning against the door-jamb, regarded Coriander through slitted dark eyes.

For a long moment neither of them spoke. Then Coriander, mindful of her new position as Raul's wife, decided that the first move must come from her.

She cleared her throat. 'It is very good of you to offer to assist me,' she began, careful not to offend the other girl's dignity by mentioning the difference in their new status. Coriander waited for a reply but was disappointed, for Isabella only pushed out her lower lip into a pout, beguiling, attractive, but none the less indicating a resentment in her new role of which Raul had given no sign.

Coriander tried to offer an encouraging smile but felt the corners of her own mouth only tremble unconvincingly. Isabella had not moved. Determined not to be unnerved by the girl's silence, Coriander turned smartly away and began pulling dresses from a cupboard and laying them out upon the bed. 'I should be glad of your opinion as to what and how much I should take with me. Naturally a wedding journey is new to me and I wish always to look good for Raul. Besides which, we are to conclude our trip by a visit to London and so I must present a suitable impression when I meet with my old friends again, don't you think?'

Glancing across at Isabella, she was pleased to see a spark of interest at last take shape upon the girl's face.

'You go to England?'

'I believe so,' Coriander agreed.

'Soon?'

'Very soon.'

'With Raul?'

'Yes, of course.'

'And you stay in London? You not come back?'

'That is for Raul to decide,' said Coriander, and made a sudden decision to make matters very plain between them, in case Isabella should be considering a continuation of her relationship with Raul. 'Wherever my husband goes, in future I shall accompany him,' she said with unequivocal firmness, and then thinking

319

perhaps she had been a trifle too brusque added more gently, 'But I shall be most glad of your help until we sail.'

'Oh, but I too am to sail with you,' Isabella burst out, nodding eagerly. 'I ask Raul and he promise.'

Stunned by this new information that Raul's mistress was to accompany them on their wedding journey, Coriander could think of nothing to say for a whole half-minute.

'But what of Maynard?' she said at length. 'Will he not want you to stay with him?'

Isabella wrapped thin arms about her own slender waist and rocked herself from side to side as once again the lower lip jutted pettishly. 'Maynard, he has gone from me.'

'Oh, I am so sorry.' There was an awkward pause.

'I try not to blame you.'

'Me?'

'But yes. He want much to marry you,' Isabella cried out, her voice heart-rending as if she were about to cry. Coriander found herself feeling suddenly dreadfully sorry for the poor girl.

'I am sure you are wrong in that. Maynard never said anything on the subject to me. We were simply friends, like a brother and sister, you understand.'

Coriander was at pains to make this clear, particularly if they were to spend much time together on board ship. Should Isabella believe that she had stolen both the men in her life, Coriander's position would be untenable.

'I do not speak of love,' the girl scoffed with a sneering curl to her full lips. 'Neither brother loves anything but themselves and their precious wine company, or land, or property. Things, things, things,' she cried out in a shrill voice. 'They only use people for their own purposes. Always.'

'Oh, no,' Coriander protested, appalled by this condemnation of the man she had just married. 'I cannot believe so.'

Isabella narrowed the smouldering eyes, shading them with thick dark lashes. 'This business will not end until one of them is dead.'

Coriander gasped, horror-struck. 'Oh, I cannot believe it will come to that.'

Isabella curled her lip in derision. 'Then you have much to learn, English miss.'

'I am no longer that. As Raul's wife and Maynard's sister-in-law I hope to be in a stronger position to reconcile the two brothers. And I do assure you that you and Maynard are free to pursue your—um—er—relationship as you think fit. I fear Maynard suffers guilt because of the accident but will soon return to you,

I am certain of it. Do you not think it would be safer if you stayed on the island and waited for him?'

'Maynard will find me,' she said incomprehensibly, though so obviously believing it that Coriander dared not disagree.

'Then I think we should at least try to be friends, should we not?'

Isabella's dark brows rose a fraction in surprise. 'In England you do not mind the mistress, no? That is good.' She shrugged her shoulders. 'Then for Raul's sake, we will be friends, yes.' She moved towards the dresses to begin tossing them in various directions according to status.

Watching her, Coriander felt a dark shadow cross her heart. It seemed that her marriage with Raul would have no effect whatsoever upon his relationship with his mistress.

Amazingly everything was prepared in time and the ship sailed with the evening tide. That first night, as she lay cradled in the arms of her husband and rocked by the gentle swell of the ocean, all Coriander's fears were swept away. No mention was made of Maynard, nor Isabella, as they took their fill of the love each could offer the other. Coriander was determined to make a good wife to Raul, so had no wish to reveal her jealousy. On the contrary, over the next few days she went out of her way to be especially friendly towards the Madeiran girl, keeping her by her side as often as possible. She tried not to admit to herself a dual purpose in this exercise, though it did occur to her that while Isabella was with her she could not be with her husband. Yet Coriander hated herself for every thread of suspicion she felt, for she knew it would ultimately spoil that fragile flowering of love between herself and her husband.

But as the days passed, Isabella's behaviour grew ever more odd. She was easily startled, jumping at the slightest sound, sometimes not hearing what had been said to her. She would constantly be glancing worriedly over her shoulder as if she waited for something, or someone, or feared that her strange behaviour had been noted. As indeed it had. Coriander often held the distinct impression that Isabella had deliberately contrived to slip from her company, for the next time she saw her she would be with Raul, talking with a strange earnestness or clinging to his arm as if she begged something of him. The sickness which washed over Coriander during these moments had nothing to do with the suck and swell of the waves.

She made up her mind there was only one way to deal with the puzzle, and that was to watch her with a persistent closeness. If Isabella meant to steal Coriander's husband from before her nose, then she would make quite certain she knew of it. Coriander could not help but give a deep sigh of near depression for having believed all her fears to be over with Raul's assurances about his relationship with Napoleon, for she still had to contend with those he had with his brother and, it seemed, his mistress.

'Are you feeling quite well?' Coriander asked Isabella one day. 'You do look unusually pale.'

If she had been pale she now turned even whiter. 'Why you think so? I am very well, thank you. Only perhaps a little tired, maybe. I not sleep so well on the ship.'

'Then you must take a longer nap in the afternoons, as I do, if that is the case,' insisted Coriander with a brightness she was far from feeling. Could Isabella's tiredness stem from more lively afternoons than her own? She dared not believe that was so. Nevertheless her own sleep was disturbed by the thought and she vowed to do something about it.

'What can you and Isabella have to talk about so often and so earnestly?' she asked Raul with a false brightness. 'I do declare you gossip together like a pair of old fishwives.'

'Can this be jealousy, sweet wife?' chortled Raul, his glee only too apparent, and he pulled her down on top of him on their narrow cabin bed.

'Indeed no. Whyever should you think so?' Coriander hotly protested, which made him laugh all the more.

'Let me show you how I feel about Isabella,' he growled, pretending to bite her ear and making her squeal. And as he made love to her all thoughts of her jealousy vanished in her eagerness to become a part of him, to taste the warmth of his skin, the urgency of his love, the touch of his caress. It was later, as she listened to the steadiness of his breathing beside her, that the dual meaning in his statement began to plague her over-sensitive mind. Had he meant that undoubted show of love for her alone, or was it in truth a demonstration of the feelings he still held for Isabella? Could Raul be so cruel? She liked to think not, but in the darkness of the night it was hard to be entirely sure.

Her anxieties were made worse the next day by a subtle change in Isabella's manner. Her dark eyes were no longer coyly hidden beneath lowered lids but wide open, bright with expectancy. Coriander could not decide whether it was suppressed excitement or nervous anticipation. Covertly she watched her as they took their usual turn about the decks, and saw there was even the hint of a smile upon the brooding lips. That alone intensified the growing fear in Coriander's heart.

That night Raul did not come to her. She tossed and turned endlessly, sure he would come soon. But the hours passed and he did not. Desperately she tried to close out the agony of her thoughts, but all the while she held a picture of Isabella and Raul together as lovers.

At length she got up and, reaching for her gown, quickly dressed herself. On bare feet she slipped soundlessly from the room and stole along the passage, keeping hold of the rail in case the ship should lurch. She came to the mahogany door which led into the room Raul used to conduct his business and was reminded of another door, another time, in her own country. On that occasion she had made a complete fool of herself. Anxious not to repeat the experience, she did not lean upon this door, nor its polished brass handle, though she put her ear as close to it as she dared. She could hear the murmur of voices within. They grew louder, followed by footsteps and hastily she withdrew into the shadows of a second doorway as she heard the door-handle turn.

'I suggest you are worrying unduly,

as ever, Isabella.' It was Raul's voice and he sounded kindly, the familiar voice softly caressing even to Coriander's frayed nerves.

'But you do not understand how serious I am,' Isabella said, and there was no doubt about her agitation.

'I know you are very serious,' said Raul and he laughed. 'You were ever so.'

'But you not listen,' she cried insistently. 'You go ahead and marry her when I tell you not to do it. Why you not listen to Isabella? Am I such a fool?'

'No, Isabella, you were never that,' said Raul gently, and Coriander's heart contracted with fresh pain. 'But I had to take the risk, don't you see? It wasn't safe not to. Maynard would have won, then, wouldn't he?'

'Argh. Men.' Coriander heard the stamp of a foot and then Isabella's voice deep with anger. 'One day you will live to regret your action. You will see that I was right.'

'I trust not. Now go. Watch her. And if you should see anything which concerns you, then report at once to me. Otherwise we will meet again at the usual time. Say nothing to Coriander, do you understand?'

A grim silence followed, and then the click of heels and swish of skirt as Isabella flew by, her feet hardly seeming to touch the ground.

Coriander stood frozen in her shadowed shelter long after the mahogany door had closed and the tap of heels had died. She would not believe that Raul had married her only to win the contest over Maynard. The thought was too terrible to be endured, and she would never accept it. Yet Isabella and Raul shared a secret, they had said as much, which she, his wife, was not to know of. And they had made an assignation to meet again. Heart pounding painfully against her breast, she ran on silent feet back to her cabin and, dragging off her dress, flung herself upon the bed. She had to press her hands into her mouth and bite her teeth down hard upon them in order to prevent herself from breaking down and crying.

CHAPTER FIFTEEN

It was two days later when Coriander first saw the ship. It appeared on the horizon, glimpsed briefly through the sea mists like a ghost vessel. She was so astonished that she rubbed her eyes to look again, to find only emptiness. She thought she had imagined it, but later in the day it appeared again and she was certain that it did indeed exist.

'Did you see the ship?' she asked Isabella, who stood beside her at the rail.

'What ship? I see nothing.'

'But you must have. It was there, on the horizon. Who do you think she was? It cannot be Napoleon this time; he is long gone. I must go and tell Raul.'

Isabella put out a hand to stop her. 'Do not bother him. There was no ship. Sometimes, at sea, it is easy to have the imaginings.'

But Coriander thrust her hand aside. She knew that what she had seen was real. She ran to Raul, who was working in his cabin on his navigation charts. He lifted his head in surprise when she burst in upon him, but was instantly alert to what she had to tell him.

'A ship, you say? Are you sure?'

'Absolutely. Isabella would not believe me but I saw one, through the mists.'

There was the slightest change in his expression, so small that had she not been so finely tuned to his every movement she might not have noticed it. But there it was. Doubt. He confirmed it with his next words. 'Only you saw this ship?'

Bleakly Coriander nodded.

'Then perhaps it was simply a kind of mirage. It can happen at sea.' He turned back to his charts. 'I should forget it if I were you.'

'But I did not imagine it, I did not. I know my imagination ran amok taking you for a French spy, but this is different, Raul. I saw the ship with my own eyes and again later in the day. Perhaps it is following us.'

He looked slightly askance at her and, setting aside his maps, came to peer down into her upturned face. 'And scurrying to hide in the mist whenever she thinks herself observed? Why not go and lie down, my love? You are probably suffering from lack of sleep, for which I am largely to blame.' He smiled at her as he led her to the door. 'Perhaps I should leave you in peace for a while until you are yourself again.'

'I am perfectly well,' she told him, but the crack in her voice belied her words and he shook his head at her.

'Sleep, little one. That is what you need. I shall insist that you stay in your cabin until you are well.'

Coriander gasped. 'Stay in my cabin?' She felt like a small child who was to be punished for a misdemeanour.

'It would be for the best. After two or three days you will be thoroughly refreshed.'

She was desolate. 'But I have no wish to spend two or three days alone in my cabin, and not even see you.'

'Allow me to know what is best for you,'

he said in a tone of voice which brooked no denial. He frowned at her. 'On numerous occasions I have suggested that to be the case and so far you have always ignored my requests. Perhaps on my own ship my own wife will allow me to make the rules, for once.' He kissed her so delightfully upon her lips, and he sounded so firm and yet solicitous of her comfort, that she could find no words with which to argue.

And so Coriander was banished from her husband's sight, confined to the claustrophobic quarters of her cabin with only the torment of her suspicions for company. Tears misted her eyes with the certain knowledge that he chose to believe his mistress and not she. As she paced back and forth in the tiny room she kept repeating over and over, 'I did not imagine it. I did not.' But as no one came to her, no one heard but herself.

But despair and exhaustion finally caused her to wonder if perhaps Raul and Isabella were right and she had indeed made a mistake. The ardour of her new husband and her own great love for him had left little time for sleep at night. And in the afternoons when she should have been resting she had chosen to follow Isabella in her restless pacing, spying on her, watching her every move. And on several further occasions had been rewarded, if that was the word, by seeing her leave Raul's cabin. Sick with misery, Coriander lay down upon her bed. Perhaps she was reading problems where there were none. Perhaps indeed it was this vexing inability of hers to trust anyone, even her own beloved husband. Lids heavy with sleep drooped over violet eyes. She must take Raul's advice and try to rest. Once she was refreshed she would be better able to review the situation.

Sleep must have come almost instantly despite the whirlings of her thoughts for the next thing she was aware of was a great noise. Voices shouted and there were loud bangs ominously like the sound of guns. Then the whole ship shook with a terrifying loud vibration which brought Coriander bolt upright in her bed, eyes starting in horror from a sleep-softened face framed by the silver halo of tousled hair.

She was out of bed in an instant, all promises to stay in her cabin fled from her head. Her one thought was to find Raul, assure herself that he was safe.

It took no more than a moment to reach the deck, for she did not pause even for a dressing-gown. The wind struck chill through her thin night slip, but she scarcely noticed as she took in the mêlée on deck. Men were fighting with fist and dagger and some flourished pistols, a thread of evil black smoke indicating they had been fired. The wooden planking of the deck seemed to be awash with bodies and blood and, transfixed with horror, Coriander had not even the strength to call out Raul's name.

And then suddenly before her stood the roughest-looking rogue she had ever set eyes on. She heard the scream but had no idea that it was her own. Even as she tried to escape she knew it was too late. The man grasped her, tucking her in the crook of a muscled arm as if she were no more than a bag of salt. She kicked with her heels against his great shins, but the sound of his rasping laugh told her of the uselessness of her efforts. He smelt of the sea, of strong tobacco, and of wine. He shook her with a laughing violence before flinging her with her back against the rail of the ship.

'Here's a pretty prize.' A slick of spittle flecked the corner of his mouth and Coriander thought she would vomit at his feet if he laid a finger on her, which it seemed he had every intention of doing. 'And what will you give me for not throwing you to the fishes, eh?'

'I wouldn't do that if I were you.'

'Raul.' The sight of him made her go weak at the knees, but then came a resurgence of energy and, ducking neatly beneath one hairy arm, she fled to his side.

The point of Raul's sword held beneath the chin of her captor might have had something to do with his willingness to be rid of her.

'Leave this to me, Coriander. Stay back. Damnation, girl, will you never do as you are told?'

She heard a rustle of movement from behind and, half turning, screamed his name out loud to warn him as a second ruffian lunged on to Raul's back, felling him to the ground. They fought like tigers, each one desperate to reach his dagger first. Coriander, frustrated by her helplessness, looked about for some means to offer assistance. She found a lump of wood and flung it at the man, but the giant's fist caught it in mid-air, then caught her to him in an iron grip. Raul was on his feet, reaching for his sword which had fallen some distance away.

'I'll get you, you scum,' he yelled and thrust his sword at his swarthy opponent, who expertly parried it. Raul cut free and struck again, and for many moments the clash and clank of steel filled the night air.

But when a third of the vagabonds appeared, Coriander saw that the fight was lost. One knocked the sword from Raul's hand while another cuffed him across the back of his head with the butt of his pistol.

Raul slumped forward into the arms of the second, and before Coriander had time to appreciate what they were about they had tossed him over the side of the ship. She heard the splash of his body falling into the black water with incredulous horror.

Then she too was lifted by a pair of great hairy arms, and for a second she looked straight into the mocking eyes of her abductor and breathed the alcoholic vapours from his wide, laughing mouth as he opened up his arms and let her fall.

She was caught in a second pair of arms and did not, after all, hit the water. But she found little comfort in this fact as she was flung down into a longboat, the stench of rotting fish hitting her nostrils.

She cowered shivering on the wooden seat, avoiding all contact with the rough-looking fellows who took the oars and started to pull out, presumably to a waiting ship.

'Where is Raul?' she cried. 'You cannot leave him to drown.'

The men said something in a language she did not understand, but it was only too clear they cared not a whit for Raul's fate. It was impossible in the half-light of encroaching night to make out any figures aboard Raul's ship. To Coriander, it looked eerily deserted, as if no persons were left aboard. The *Bella Regia* was a ghost ship.

Turning to her abductors, any query as to the whereabouts of the crew, of Ned, of Isabella, died on her lips as she took in the nature of their appearance. Ned's words came rushing back to her. Here indeed were the sea bandits he mentioned, his warnings which had so amused her. She was not laughing now. Trying not to let them see her scrutiny, she noted their evil-smelling clothes, the glint of daggers in their belts, the shaggy beards upon pock-marked faces. One even had a long scar which crossed one half-closed eye and slit one sagging cheek. She felt a sick panic at the sight and smell of them, yet even in her terror resolved to hold calm.

She saw the approach of the neighbouring ship with mixed emotion. If Raul had been taken safely aboard then nothing else mattered. And if he had not? She put that frightening prospect from her mind as with surprising courtesy they helped her climb the rope-ladder.

Coriander was taken to a small but clean cabin where a bowl of warm water and a change of clothes had been set ready for her. With a heavy-beating heart she made use of the water to freshen her face and hands, and tried her best to tidy her hair by pushing damp fingers through the tangled curls. Grateful for any garment to cover her thin nightgown, she pulled on the cotton shirt and breeches, which did at least seem freshly laundered. There was nothing to be done now but sit upon the narrow bunk bed and wait, heart pounding fearfully in her breast.

She did not have to wait long before the door opened and a small, wiry man, his narrow egg-shaped head wrapped in a dirty scarf, shuffled into the cabin. A dark growth of hair lined his upper lip, which was pulled back in a sneer, and in his hand he carried a dagger. With this he indicated that she should go before him along the passage.

'Where do you take me?' she asked, but at the furious jerk of his head knew she had no option but to obey. Her knees were weak with fear and her whole body trembled.

He led her to a much larger cabin where, having tucked the knife back into his belt, a grin of wry amusement upon his face, he left her. Coriander heard the key turn in the lock, but made no move to run to it and call for help, for she was past such instincts now. She merely stood, stiff with pride, sick with foreboding, in the centre of the room staring at the black port-hole, thinking only of Raul. Was he out there in the cold seas, his mouth and eyes and

337

lungs filling with black water?

She did not turn when she heard the sound of the key once more in the lock, nor even when the door creaked open.

'And so, my dear Corrie, here you are at last.'

At the sound of the familiar voice she whirled about, the smile of joy and relief half forming upon her face almost instantly freezing at sight of her visitor. Once again she had been deceived by the likeness in the tone. But this was not her darling Raul who stood before her, but his brother. And she could see at once that here was a very different Maynard from the one who had offered to show her his beautiful island, This face was twisted with loathing. This voice was sharp with cruelty. Coriander saw that it would take every ounce of her own agile wit to contrive a way out of this trap. For she was certain now that that was what it was.

There came a return of all her old courage. The girl who had faced up to Ezra Follett, had risked dishonour or transportation rather than see her young friends starve, was not going to give in easily to such as Maynard Beringer. 'Where is Raul?' she demanded, lifting her chin to face him and unconsciously causing her eyes to glisten with defiant anger.

'You are a fine woman, Coriander,'

Maynard said appreciatively. 'Marriage with you would have been a fascinating experience, but I was not good enough, was I? It had to be your darling Raul.'

'Where is he?' she persisted, but Maynard only strode over to the large mahogany desk and poured two glasses from a flask of wine. Coriander shook her head when he offered her one.

'Why should you imagine I know or care where my brother is?'

'Your men, at least I assume they were your men, threw him overboard.'

Maynard chuckled. 'How very careless of them to drop him. Do not fret too much, my dear. These are not shark-infested waters—not often, anyway.'

This new danger brought a prickle of ice down her spine. Desperately trying to hide her fear, she pulled her lips up into a tremulous smile. 'I had hoped that you and Raul would drop this petty rivalry and become friends.'

Maynard gave a mocking smile. 'Petty rivalry, is that what you call it? We can never be friends, not while there is breath in my body. He robs me of my just heritage and thinks I will not protest.'

'He has robbed you of nothing. Your father chose to make it this way.'

Maynard slammed down his glass so hard that the stem broke and a red pool of wine spread over the polished desk-top. He leaned forward, pushing his face so close to hers she could tell it was not his first glass this day.

'But I intend to rectify his error. I have made certain that I will win this foolish contest.'

'In what way?'

His hand reached out and she tried not to show how she cringed from his touch as, grasping her elbow, he marched her towards the door. 'There is something I wish to show you.'

He led her along several passageways and then urged her to go down a wooden ladder which led deep into the hold of the ship. After a moment's hesitation as Coriander looked down into the inky blackness, she took hold of the ladder and did as she was bid. It seemed to go endlessly downward and it was with some relief that she felt solid floor beneath her feet and stood watching the swing of Maynard's lantern as it descended above her. Soon he stood beside her and, holding his lantern high, led her forward.

They were evidently in the hold of the ship, for all about them were huge wooden casks and a familiar aroma.

'These are the *pipas* of wine,' he told her, and she nodded her understanding. This, then, was the wine run. These casks

340

were being shipped around the tropics in the traditional method. But they were not the only items in the hold. All around the walls were huge leather trunks and boxes. Seeing her eyes upon them, Maynard led her over to one.

'I see you are interested in what I have here.' Reaching down, he lifted the lid of one of the trunks. It was heavy and he had to set down the lantern in order to do so. As he slowly raised it, the shaft of light from the lantern burst into a thousand shards as it bounced and reflected off the tumble of gold and silver within.

Never had she seen anything like it in her life before. Before her eyes was a treasure trove in very truth, and she sank down beside the trunk, her knees too weak to support her.

'Impressive, eh?'

'Am I dreaming?'

'Dreams, aye. And reality. It exists all right. Sunk off Porto Santo more than a century ago by Captain Kidd himself.' Maynard picked up a silver goblet, ran his tapering fingers through what must have been a hundred or more golden coins. Somewhere at the back of her mind she thought she had seen the like before, but then it was gone in the wonder of the astonishing scene before her.

'Who do they belong to? The Government?'

Maynard flung a shower of coins into the box with a loud cackle of laughter. 'The Government? No, indeed they do not. These little lovelies belong to me, and only me. Finder's keepers. These boxes of recovered treasure are my security for the future. I fooled everyone into thinking I preferred the old ways of maturing wine by taking the casks round the tropics, but that was merely a cover up to give me the excuse to be often sailing in open waters.'

'And all the time you were merely at Porto Santo digging for gold?'

'Diving, my dear Coriander, off Porto Santo and Madeira. Filling in the rest of the time with a little privateering of my own. Hence the need for the stalwart if colourful band of men who greeted your arrival. Most of the *pipas* are in fact empty, until we fill them with a different kind of treasure.'

She was on her feet again, trying to take in the full import of this tale. 'But what do you do with it all?'

Maynard beamed at her like a small boy pleased with his own cleverness. 'Sell it, of course. There are many willing to buy who do not ask awkward questions. Some of the artefacts bring a great deal of money, particularly from the French who enjoy the thought of winning one over the Portuguese.'

'The French?'

'I realise they are our enemy, but that is a political matter and politics is no concern of mine.'

'You care only about money.' It was not a question and she spoke with open contempt.

'About wealth, Corrie dear, and possessions which are rightly mine, such as my home, my land and the wine company.'

A wave of hot anger washed over her. 'What need have you of the wine company if you own such a fortune as this?'

'Because it is my right. I am the eldest. Why should Raul have it?' He ground his teeth together and the sound went through her like a knife. 'What is mine stays mine. All of it. This gold ensures that I win this stupid contest my misguided late father set us. You could have shared it with me, my dear. Together, you and I could have been the most powerful people on the island. Like a King and Queen in fact. But now, sadly, it must end here.'

'What do you mean?' Her blood chilled. His expression was mild, a smile curving the sensuous lips, and there was pleasurable anticipation in the pale grey-blue eyes. It terrified her.

'You have expressed a desire to learn more about our trade. Well, this is your opportunity. You can experience for yourself what happens to the wine on the run through the tropics. By the end of the six months I doubt you'll have matured as sweetly as the Madeiran nectar.' He took a step back, away from her. 'Fasten her up.'

Any further query died on her lips as hands grasped her on each side. She found herself carried backwards then dropped into a large empty cask, still resonant with the aroma of wine. Rough hands forced her down so that she was crouched within it. Even as she reached up her hands in protest the circular lid was hammered into place above her head.

Time ceased to have any meaning for her. Every second was an aching agony. It was hot in the cask and the strong smell of the wine made her head spin. Remembering the stories of Kings and adventurers Letitia used to tell them in the schoolroom, she supposed she should be thankful for not being dropped into a vat of malmsey as the Duke of Clarence had been long ago. But how was she to escape? And where was Raul? If he was dead, did she truly wish to live without him? She must not think such thoughts. He was a good swimmer.

He had told her so. She must hold fast to that. It came to her then that Raul must have known Maynard's ship would come. That was the reason he had ordered her to remain in her cabin. He had meant only to protect her and, as so often in the past, she had defied him. And with terrible consequences.

Her head began to nod and she jerked it upright. For some reason she was sure sleep would be fatal. She began to run her hands over the rough wood. Perhaps there was a hole somewhere. Dear God, she must not suffocate. She must get out and find Raul. But how?

'Did I do well? I not tell her you come.' Isabella pouted provocatively at Maynard. 'And Raul almost he refuse to meet with you.'

Maynard smiled angelically at his mistress, smoothing the silky skin with cool fingers. 'Raul can never resist a confrontation, particularly if he imagines he can win it.'

Isabella rolled over in the bed, curling herself against his side. 'And what you do with him? Did he drown?' She was more than a little curious to find out. Raul had ever been important to her. Maynard, however, only laughed, refusing to answer her probing question.

'I note that you do not ask about Coriander's safety.' He plucked a grape from the bowl on his locker and popped it into her mouth. 'We shall soon be richer than our wildest dreams. This shipment must be the last for a while. The Government has finally grown suspicious. We must take care. Later, when they have grown careless again, we can return.'

Isabella's dark eyes gleamed. 'There is still more gold?'

He pinched her chin, not unkindly, nor gently for she squealed. 'Enough, my greedy puss-cat. More than enough even for you.'

'Then if there is so much why not let them go?' she suggested casually. 'What harm can they do to so rich and clever a man?'

A puzzled expression came into his eyes. 'Let them go? Should I?'

Isabella wriggled closer, running her hands over his smooth, lean chest. He had a beautiful body, there was no denying it. 'If you have all this gold, and more when you sell the treasures to the Frenchies, why soil your hands with problems? Let them live. Let them see you enjoy the fruits of your father's labour, and of your own cunning. While they get nothing.'

He looked at her blankly for a long moment, his fine brows raised in mild surprise. 'I had not considered.'

Isabella watched with interest, hardly daring to breathe, as Maynard thought deeply on her suggestion. She cared nothing for the English miss. But Raul, he was special and should not be wasted as shark meat. But it was Maynard who truly troubled her. If the two brothers did meet in a final confrontation, she guessed which one would win. He always had, except that one time, and bore the scar to prove it. For all Maynard's strange ways, he was her man and she loved him. She desperately wanted to keep him alive. For his own sake, not simply for the gold, she told herself, so convincingly that she came to believe it.

'You will let Raul go?' she queried again, but it was once too often. She saw her mistake in the drawing together of the eyebrows, the tight curl of the upper lip, the flare of aquiline nostril. His tapering fingers were closing about her neck and she was clawing at his hand, the want of air burning her chest.

'That is all I hear from dawn to dusk. Raul. Raul. Raul. Perhaps I will kill Raul and keep her. She would be less trouble than you with your endless questions. Never speak his name again to me. Do you understand?'

She was nodding, as far as she was able, face puce with her desperate lack of oxygen.

Already her head was spinning. Soon it would be too late. She tried to gasp his name and something seemed to penetrate the screwed-up tightness of Maynard's face and he took his hand away. Contrarily, he was all contrition, smoothing and kissing the purple fingerprints upon her neck with soft, reassuring kisses.

'I cannot think what came over me,' he purred. 'As you know, I am not a violent man.' He swung his long legs out of the bed. 'Perhaps I should go and speak with Coriander. We may be able to come to terms, after all.'

CHAPTER SIXTEEN

Ned crouched behind a rock as the pirates rolled the casks of wine across the cave. What he wouldn't give right now for a drop. His mouth was parched and his head ached from all the battering it had taken. His old mother had been right. He did have a thick skull. It had been put to the test these last hours. But he was concerned about the Capt'n, not to mention his good lady. Since the ship had docked he'd watched the villains unload the casks, rolling them one by one down the ramp into the cave, but he'd seen no sign of them.

The three ruffians, or sea bandits as he preferred to call them, pushed the last cask into place and took themselves off. For a twist of baccy and a tot of rum, thought Ned with a twinge of envy. As their laughing voices faded there was nothing but the echoing drip of water in the hollow caves. The light was poor now that they had removed their lanterns, but sufficient to see by, and Ned crept from his hide-away.

'By, but this is no place for rheumatism,' he groaned, flexing his stiff knees. Mebbe Capt'n Raul was fastened up somewhere in these caves hereabouts. The only way to find out was to look and hope he had as thick a skull as Ned and had likewise been left for a dead man.

Ned crept stealthily in and out of the casks, peering short-sightedly behind each one. No sign of the Capt'n. He thought he heard the pirates returning and hastily flung himself behind a large cask, bumping his knee against it as he did so.

'Drat it.' He winced as the pain shot up his leg. Maybe it was time he hung up his sea boots. He was getting too old for these capers. And senile too, for he was hearing whispering voices in his head now. 'Wake up, old man,' he admonished himself, and then he heard the whispers again and his blood froze.

'Ned.'

Could the smell of wine make you puddle-headed? He'd thought he heard his own name. Wide-eyed, he gazed all around but could see no one. When the cask beside him actually moved of its own volition he expected to die of a heart attack on the spot.

'Ned!' This time the voice was more persistent and a tapping accompanied it.

'By jove, can it be?' He was scrabbling to his feet, grasping hold of the cask, running his weathered hands over it. 'Mistress Beringer?' he whispered in as loud a voice as he dared.

'Ned. Oh, Ned.'

He heard the unmistakable catch of relief in her voice. 'Hold on, little miss, while I find something to prise this lid off,' he hissed against the sides of the barrel.

'Hurry, before someone comes,' she cried, and he had to beg her to keep quiet while he frantically searched the dark cave. At length he found a piece of flint and a large stone which served as hammer and chisel and brought the lid off in no time. Seconds later he held the sobbing Coriander in his arms, patting her awkwardly upon her shoulder, making soothing noises and several 'there

there's' until she had herself sufficiently under control. Her first question did not surprise him and he told her with a sad shake of his head that no, he did not know where Capt'n Raul was. He only wished he did.

'Then we must search for him,' Coriander said urgently. 'I refuse to believe that he is dead, despite seeing them throw him in the ocean.'

Ned stared at her. 'You saw them throw him? He be drownded, then, for sure.'

'No, Ned, he is not. I'm sure I would feel it if he were. He is alive.' Old Ned looked at her with a pitying expression and Coriander turned her face away so that she did not see it. 'If we both look for him ...'

Hardly had Ned opened his mouth to point out the uselessness of this exercise, and shouldn't she consider her own safety as the Capt'n would've wished, when he heard footsteps returning. Pulling Coriander with him, he dived behind a stack of wine casks, muttering a silent prayer for help to his maker in whom he had absolute faith.

'You doltish fools.' The voice was undoubtedly Maynard's and the two sank deeper into the shadows. 'How could you be so stupid as to mix them all up in this way?' Maynard struck one of the casks with a stick. 'Which one holds the girl. Tell me that.'

The three pirates muttered a stumbling reply and Coriander dared scarcely breathe. If they had mixed up all the wine casks then they would never find her nor realise she was missing. But her hopes were soon quashed.

'What is this?' Maynard had found the open cask. 'She has escaped, you dolts, while you were swilling your rum.'

Coriander and Ned flinched at the loud crash, rightly guessing it to be the empty cask being hurled across the stone floor. The lid followed, bowling noisily after it like a child's hoop. 'Find them!' Maynard bellowed. 'And you, Antonio, check on our other prisoner. We don't want him escaping.'

Coriander, recklessly risking exposure, peeped over the top of the casks to watch the direction in which Antonio went, then quickly ducked down again as she saw Maynard turn towards her.

She squeezed Ned's hand in the tension of the moment as they listened to the click of retreating footsteps. After it had been silent in the cave for some moments, Coriander once more peered over the casks. This time they were alone. Crouching next to Ned, she started to whisper her plan.

'Raul must be confined in one of these

caves and I intend to find him. Do you think you can find a boat?'

Ned looked blank for a moment, not sure what she was asking of him. 'A boat?'

'To sail us safely back to Madeira. It need not be a big boat. We'll have to row if necessary.'

Ned gulped as he considered rowing all the way from Porto Santo to Madeira, a distance which would take five or six hours by ship, due to treacherous currents. 'We stay together, little miss. First we find the Capt'n. Then we find a boat.'

Nothing she could say would persuade him otherwise, and so it was agreed. They left the sanctuary of the casks with reluctance, making stealthy progress around the walls. Coming to a narrow opening, no more than a fissure in the rock, Coriander urged a doubting Ned to follow her down it.

'The air grows more fetid,' Ned hissed. ' 'Tis further from the sea.'

Coriander squeezed the old man's hand reassuringly. 'We must be brave, for Raul's sake.'

Ned puffed out his chest. If the little miss could be brave, then he most certainly could. He had never believed all those tales of dragons in underground caverns in any case. Wasn't he an Englishman?

The way through to the inner caves was not so easy as Coriander had expected. The tunnels were narrow, and so low that for much of the time they had to walk bent almost double. All the while Coriander was afraid of meeting the pirate named Antonio on his way back. Since they were forced to walk single file and she had optimistically taken the lead, she wondered what she would do if she came face to face with him.

The light increased to a dull greenish glow and she heard the hum of voices ahead. Flapping her hand at Ned behind her to slow down, she sank on to hands and knees for the last few yards. Before them lay a huge cavern, as high-roofed as a cathedral. But it was not empty. Several of the pirates were stacking boxes and trunks similar to those she had been shown on board ship. Once more she and Ned were forced to take hiding while they watched the men at their nefarious activities.

'This must be where they hide the loot,' Coriander whispered, and then realising that Ned knew nothing of Maynard's activities, quickly outlined what he had told her.

'Don't surprise me one bit,' he said curtly. 'He always was a wrong 'un as a boy. But where be Capt'n?'

Coriander's gaze roved desperately around

the cavern. 'There he is.' She almost shouted in her excitement and Ned grabbed hold of her in case she should leap out to him, which she instinctively wanted to do. Raul was slumped against a post, feet and hands apparently fastened to prevent him from escaping. 'However shall we get to him?' There was little hope of all the pirates conveniently vacating the cavern so that they could walk across and untie him.

'You wait here while I see if I can reach him,' said Ned valiantly. 'They'll most likely think I'm one o' them.'

'I shall come with you,' she whispered, and grinned cheekily at the look of shock on Ned's face. 'If you can pass yourself off as a pirate, so can I. See, I am already dressed in shirt and breeches.'

Ned's jaw dropped open for half a second and then he closed it with a snap and Coriander saw how the chin jutted obstinately. 'Capt'n wouldn't want you risking your life for him, little miss. Besides, the brightness of your hair would give you away.'

'Then I'll wear your hat.' Without asking permission, she removed the Madeiran woollen cap with its long ear flaps from Ned, leaving the old man's head baldly shining in the soft green light. She smiled apologetically as she pulled it well down over her own head, tucking her curls inside it. 'Sorry, Ned. But my need is greater. Now if I rub a little dirt into my cheeks. There we are. Who would guess?' she asked, remembering another occasion when she had undertaken disguise.

'Just about everyone if you wear that pretty smile, mistress.'

Coriander, her face suitably glum and fierce, kept closely behind Ned as he edged his way into the main body of the cavern. Busy with their tasks, the pirates paid them no attention and, to make it look more convincing, Coriander and Ned picked up one of the boxes and carried it over to the rest of the stack.

'Ajude-me, por favor.'

Coriander froze, horrified, and pointed a finger to herself in query. To her dismay the pirate nodded.

'He wants you to help him,' Ned hissed in her ear.

Coriander, considering it wise not to disobey, obligingly and ineffectually offered her brawn in the transportation of a particularly large box. Losing patience with her feeble efforts, the pirate finally cuffed her ear and pushed her away, lifting it in his great arms with apparent ease. Coriander hastened back to Ned's side, heart pounding like a drum. He was by now hiding behind a barrel, within a few feet of where Raul stood, head drooped forward, arms pulled around a post and tied at the wrists behind. Coriander's heart went out to him. She could not even tell whether he was alive. Surely he must be or they would not trouble to secure him.

'We'd best take care,' Ned whispered, uncertainty setting in.

'We cannot give up now that we are so close.' The man she loved was no more than a dozen feet from her, but in order to reach him she must cross the open floor, right past at least two of the pirates. Her mind was working furiously. There must be some way. 'Do you speak Portuguese?' she asked Ned, and he pulled a wry face.

'Some.'

'Is it morning or evening?' she asked, and he told her that as far as he knew it must now be morning and gave her the Portuguese. She told him what she wanted him to say and saw him struck dumb with shock. Determined to carry through her plan, she could only hope he would soon come out of it.

Taking a deep breath, she looked once again at the open space she had to cross which seemed to have grown in size. This was infinitely more terrifying than waiting for Ezra Follett in the dead of night. She wished fervently that she had dear Pye with her. With the reassuring pressure of Ned's dagger tucked into her belt, she stepped out on to the open floor and boldly walked towards the pirates. She prayed that Ned was following her.

'*Bom dia,*' she said brightly, nodding to them and continuing her progress across the floor, trying to lengthen her stride to a suitable swagger. One or two stopped to stare at her, but she remembered to glower fiercely as she asked them how they did. '*Como está?*'

She had reached Raul and her fingers were touching his, grasping his hands. She was hoping and praying he would not recognise her when he woke and spoil their chances by making a fuss. A *frisson* of hope and joy sparked off by her love for him ran through her to find his hands warm and very much alive. But still the pirates stared and she was certain that they would hear her heart thumping. She began to struggle with the knots.

'*Não.*' One of the pirates had stepped forward and was gesticulating at her, then he gave out a torrent of Portuguese which Coriander did not understand. Where was Ned? A cold sweat broke out down her spine and between her breasts. Slowly she drew the dagger from her belt. And then she heard him.

Ned came storming across the cavern, a

358

small tornado driven by such a fury that the pirates drew back in astonishment at the sight of this little man shouting loudly in fluent Portuguese.

'You stupid boy!' he bawled. 'Did I not tell you to bring the prisoner right away? All you do is dawdle and the master is calling for him. He is very angry, do you hear?' Stepping up to Coriander, he cuffed her briskly across the back of her head and she shrank snivelling to the ground, shielding herself from further blows, much to the amusement of the pirates. Swiftly she slit the ropes that held Raul with the point of Ned's knife, and as he slumped unconscious to the ground she knew a moment of complete panic. How on earth would she and Ned manage him between them? At over six feet and a powerful man, he was rather more than one old man and a girl, albeit one dressed as a boy, could manage.

But she had reckoned without the pirates, who were fascinated by Ned's rough treatment of this dolt of a boy and anxious not to enrage their unstable master. Two hastened forward, and together the four of them managed to carry Raul out of the cavern and more than halfway down the tunnel. All along the way Ned kept up his ill treatment of 'the fool boy' and Coriander snivelled and whined and played her part to perfection, while making sure she spoke not a word. To their intense relief Raul finally woke and angrily insisted upon being set down upon his own feet. Laughing, the pirates dropped him, and returned back up the passage to the gold, which was to them far more interesting.

'What in damnation is going on?' yelled Raul, his furious green eyes lighting upon Ned's innocent face. But that was nothing to his astonishment when a young pirate boy flung himself into his arms calling him 'my darling' and smelling strongly of wine. It was only when the small, delighted face turned itself up to his that he recognised her and his heart gave a painful lurch. 'Coriander.' Neither of them could speak for a long moment after that, and Ned was left to shuffle his feet and glance anxiously to left and right expecting any moment to be recaptured.

'I do think as how we ought to be a-going,' put in Ned, gruffly clearing his throat.

'You are right, Ned. Lead on, good fellow.'

Ned did so, unsure exactly where he was leading.

'How did you come to be here, and how did you find me?' Raul asked Coriander.

'No time for explanations now. We must find a boat and get away from

360

here,' she said, but saw the lines of grim determination set on Raul's face.

'I have a score to settle with my brother.'

'Not now,' she urged, pulling him through the maze of wine casks. 'We must find our way out. Deal with Maynard later, if you must, when he does not have the support of a dozen ruffians at his side.'

Raul pulled his arm free. 'Do you take me for a coward? He captured you, slung me over the side before fishing me out like flotsam and tying me up.'

'But he did save you,' Coriander said urgently. 'He could easily have let you drown.'

Raul snorted with derision. 'One of his men saved me. Besides, that is not the way Maynard plays the game. He does not care for accidents. He prefers a more titillating spectacle.'

Coriander shuddered. 'How can you say such a thing about your own brother? You are obsessed by this—game—as you call it.' They were conducting this ill-timed argument, much to Ned's dismay, in the open cave.

'And what fate befell you? Did he simply allow you to escape?'

Coriander hesitated as she recalled how Maynard had been willing to fasten her in a wine cask and leave her there to perish. 'He did return,' she said, stubborn to the last.

'You seek the ideal family. Unfortunately the Beringers do not fit the bill, for though I know Maynard has undoubted charm he is sadistically cruel. He once killed my dog by—' Raul stopped as if he could not say the words. 'But there, I'll not burden you with tales of our boyhood. Now he steals from his country as well as his own brother.'

Coriander looked at him in open dismay. 'You knew then, about ... all this?' She waved a hand at the rows of casks.

'Yes, I knew,' said Raul grimly. 'And I knew too he meant to have this confrontation at sea because he was aware I was on to him.'

The memory of gold coins came to her, fifty of them, of unknown origin, and her blood chilled. 'You knew all along, didn't you? Right from the start. You had some ... some of these pieces of ...' Her voice choked on the words. She could not go on. It had taken her long to learn to trust Raul and now she found he was unworthy of that trust.

He looked uncomprehending for a moment, and then he smiled as if it were of no significance. 'Oh, those pieces of gold. The ones you—' He glanced quickly at Ned, who was listening

362

intently. 'Ah, but I never intended to use them. When Maynard gave them to me to use in bringing you to Madeira, I knew my suspicions were correct. I realised they were all the proof I needed.' He looked at her in sudden concern. 'Why are you shivering? Are you ill?'

'The little miss is cold,' put in Ned, growing agitated. He had known better moments for a quarrel. 'We must get her home.'

'Ned is right. I am the dolt not to be thinking of your safety.'

They hurried along passages slippy with green slime and dripping with icy water. Much of the time they were in darkness, with nothing but each other's hands and the wall to guide them. Coriander allowed herself to be squeezed through narrow tunnels without protest, but her mind screamed within. He had known his brother had all these riches. He had known from the start he could never win his father's contest—unless he married Coriander and took control of her share in addition to his own. When the darkness finally softened and a chink of light showed ahead they all instinctively increased their pace.

Fresh air was bliss on her face. Coriander drew in great, thankful breaths of the salted sea breezes. Out on the cliff face they all three looked about them, stretching their limbs with relief.

'This isn't Porto Santo,' said Raul. 'This is Madeira. I recognise this cove.' Grasping Coriander's hand, he started pulling her along a path which climbed the precipitous cliff-side. 'Come on. Let's get you home.'

Halfway up they heard the shout of fury. Below in the cove stood Maynard, one fist waving furiously at them, a grim band of his pirates gathered around him. Coriander needed no urging to go faster, and, glancing back over her shoulder, saw that Maynard came in pursuit. She stumbled over a rock and fell headlong, dizzily scrambling for a hold on the lip of the path. If Raul had not been so close behind to help her to her feet she would have fallen to certain death. Ned too was experiencing difficulties, his scarlet face lined with the efforts of exertion.

'Don't wait for me,' he croaked. 'Go ahead, get little miss home.'

But neither of them could leave the old man to the uncaring hands of the dreaded sea bandits. With one before and one after him, they propelled him the last yards up the cliff path. But the incidents had badly delayed them and the younger, fitter crew behind had gained.

On reaching comparative security on one of the tilting terraces, a small square of verdant growth lovingly tilled and nurtured for generations by agile, resilient farmers, Raul stopped and turned to look back at his pursuers. 'We cannot escape them, Coriander, and I will run no more. I must face my brother and have done with this dispute. Ned, take Coriander.'

But she ran to grasp his arm. 'Have done with this battling, I beg of you.'

The face he turned towards her was harsh as he experienced the desperation of his responsibility. He'd been a fool not to have this confrontation years ago, and a greater one to bring this girl into the midst of the conflict. He should have stood up to Maynard instead of merely resenting his selfish greed. If he hadn't turned a blind eye to the more twisted workings of his macabre mind which took equal and unnatural pleasure in pinning out live butterflies and casually slaughtering a much-loved dog as he did in stealing his brother's favourite bow, Coriander would not now be in such danger. He pushed her roughly from him, almost shouting at her. 'You do not understand. Go. Do as I say this one time.'

'No, Raul. I love you.'

For a second he looked stunned. Then, snatching hold of her, he thrust her fiercely into Ned's arms, a snarl almost of loathing souring the generous mouth which had

365

once offered the sweetness of his kisses. 'Do you think I want to be hounded by a foolish girl who never will do as she is bid? What do you know of love when you give it so freely to either brother?'

Coriander felt the hot blood of her anger run beneath her skin. 'And what of you and your mistress?' she taunted him. 'You seem to prefer her charms while supposedly taking your wife on a wedding journey. And do not say it was all on her part. You agreed to take her with us.'

Raul flushed with fury, made worse by the guilt of knowing there was some truth in the accusation. It had been Isabella who had told him of Maynard's intentions to accost him at sea, and he had believed her presence might be useful. But a part of him had also sought to protect himself from the depths of this new emotion he felt, for Isabella's presence would remind him of his former self. He saw now the cruelty as well as the futility of such an exercise. He could not run from commitment forever. 'She offered to help watch over you while I took a small detour to search out Maynard's cache of gold, that is all.'

'Gold.' Coriander flung the words at him with loathing. 'And you dare accuse me of love of it. I would say that Isabella is right, that it is all you ever think of, except that I know she spent a good deal of time with you, so you must have had other things on your mind for a part of the time.'

'Are you saying you spied on me?' Raul's voice was dangerously low, but Coriander flung back her head, her ire such that not even an encroaching crew of pirates could stop her having her say.

'I saw her on more than one occasion leave your cabin. I heard you laughing and talking together, both at the house and on your ship. She told me why you married me and I believe her. You care for nothing, Raul Beringer, but your own selfish ambitions. Have your mistress, and your wine company, and much good may they do you. I care not a toss what you do.'

Whirling upon her heel, she stamped away from him, boiling anger in each telling step.

'She be a fine woman when stirred,' said Ned at Raul's elbow, open admiration in his tone.

'Indeed she is,' conceded Raul thoughtfully, recalling other occasions when Coriander had been stirred by more interesting emotions. 'Go after her, Ned, there's a good chap.'

'Aye, aye, Capt'n,' said Ned, and despite the exertions of the past twenty-four hours the aged sailor set off at a brisk pace in her wake.

It was at this point that Raul felt the prick of cold steel against the back of his neck.

It was Isabella who came to her with the news. Coriander was in the garden, venting her frustration and misery by attacking the soil with fierce stabs of her trowel. Ned had begged her to lie down, to rest and recover from her ordeal.

'You rest,' she had told him, not unkindly. 'I cannot, not until this matter is brought to an end.' The garden acted as a therapy and she dug her fingers in the warm soil, sieving the weeds, crumbling the rich brown once volcanic earth, then forgetting what she was doing and carefully planting the weeds back again.

'He is dead.' Coriander had not heard Isabella's approach, and now she dropped her trowel at these words, every vestige of colour leaving her face as she crumpled into a faint at Isabella's feet.

Moments, a lifetime later, when she opened her eyes the pain made her long again for oblivion. No one was ministering to her and so she was forced to sit up unaided. Isabella was crouched upon the grass, her arms wrapped about her knees as she rocked herself to and fro, making small crooning noises of wailing misery to herself.

However painful it might be to learn of it, Coriander had to know how Raul had met his end. Slowly, not wishing to alarm the distraught girl, she edged over to Isabella and asked the fateful question.

'Tell me what happened, Isabella, I beg you.'

The girl clasped both hands over her mouth, and the dark eyes were a picture of anguish. Gently Coriander took the hands away and, swallowing the last remnants of her pride, put her arms about her husband's mistress in shared comfort.

'They fight. Oh, such a fight. Like the dogs they will not let go.'

'You were there?' Coriander asked in surprise, feeling a stab of sharp jealousy that it had been Isabella with him at the end and not herself. If only they had not had that last fierce quarrel she might have been able to help him. At the very least they would have parted on good terms. Tears blinded her eyes. She would live with the agony of it for the rest of her life.

Isabella nodded in answer to her question. 'They fire accusations at each other. Always it had to come to this.' She shook her head in despair. 'They hang over the cliff edge and I scream at them, but they not listen, they only scrabble at each other's throats. It look so much Maynard will win this last battle for he on top of Raul, straddling him like he ride a mad bull, only he have the bull by the throat and he will not let go.' A shudder rippled through her. 'He have fierce clench in those hands. I know,' she said with a meaning Coriander could not mistake. 'But then it is all over and he fall like feather in the breeze.' The red mouth opened wide and again she began to wail.

Struck dumb by this story, Coriander waited spellbound. When no more came she shook Isabella, who was in any case growing near to hysteria. 'Stop it. Tell me properly. Who was tossed like a feather? Raul?'

Wide black eyes looked into hers in astonishment. 'No, no, Maynard. Raul is alive. He murder his brother as I always said he would.'

CHAPTER SEVENTEEN

It was time to leave. Coriander stood on the waterfront, her bags at her feet. A chill breeze blew in from the north. Winter was coming, but she would not benefit from its milder nature on Madeira's shores. She would meet its full ferocity in England. Coriander tried to concentrate on the brighter aspects of her return. Seeing Pearl again, and Letty with her fussing ways, hot, buttered crumpets by the fire and frosty walks in the snow. Yet even these delights failed to incite any great enthusiasm in her. Many matters would need to be settled, of course. Not least where they would live. And she would have some explaining to do as to why she had not fulfilled her promises.

Ned stood beside her, a morose expression on his homely face. 'You could change your mind,' he said, 'and stay.'

She smiled ruefully at him. 'There is nothing I would like better, Ned, but it is not to be.'

'You've spoken with the Capt'n, then?'

Coriander hesitated as she recalled that last painful conversation with Raul. 'Yes, I've spoken with the Captain.' She had told him that she meant to return to England, leave him free to enjoy Isabella, the fortune which would have gone to Maynard, and his precious wine company. She had almost relinquished all claim on her own share, but common sense had prevailed. It would be reckless to throw away one's security and return to Pearl and Letty empty-handed. Raul had

371

accepted her decision without argument and had offered to find a suitable man of business in London to handle her affairs. An annuity would be paid through him, thus seeing her nicely placed for life. She took this information quite matter-of-factly. It didn't seem greatly important at the time, and she had constantly to remind herself that she did need a roof over her head, food to eat. And a man to love? Some things, it seemed, were beyond her reach. The magic of Madeira had not fulfilled its promise.

'Here he is, the Capt'n's coming.' Ned was beside himself with excitement and Coriander's heart gave a painful leap of hope as she saw the familiar figure stride towards her. Had he come for her? But as soon as he spoke she could tell that relations between them were as strained as ever.

'Good morning, Coriander. I trust you are quite recovered.'

It was as if he were addressing a stranger, not his own wife.

'Thank you, yes,' she told him with a chill inclination of her head. But Raul Beringer was not a stranger. He was the man who had married her for money, an incredible notion to one who had been raised an orphan. He was the man who had devised a meeting at sea to murder his own brother for the same reason. He had pretended ignorance over Maynard's treasure-seeking activities and yet had in his possession on that first fateful night they met fifty gold coins of foreign extraction. This was the man she loved. How could she ever recover?

'I have asked the Captain of the *Mercury* to delay sailing till tomorrow.'

She was instantly alert. 'Why?'

'No need to look so wary,' he said coldly. 'I shall not prevent your leaving.' Hope died in her like a fragile orchid left without nourishment.

'Then why the delay?' she asked in a toneless little voice.

'There is someone I think you should meet.' He sounded faintly irritated. 'I had been saving it as a surprise, but ...' He paused and looked thoughtfully at the toes of his boots. 'Anyway, it seems it must be now or never, and the latter would be a pity, for I know how eager you are to find your family.'

'You have found them?' For a second the light in her eyes made him feel it was meant especially for him and he responded with the flicker of a smile.

'Yes, Coriander. I have known for some time. As I said, I sought a suitable occasion.' Again he looked down at his boots. 'But none presented itself.'

Raul took her to Ribeira Brava and, since neither of them were in the mood to enjoy the magnificent mountain scenery or marvel at the pools, poplars or sugar cane groves, they cut through the green valley and headed directly for a small group of peaked houses high on the hillside beyond. Coriander could not help but feel the enchantment of the place. They were like pixie houses, their straw thatched roofs reaching right down to the ground. There was a central green-painted door in the triangle of white wall at the front of the house, with a green shuttered window at either side and one above. In the doorway sat an old woman, her face as brown and wrinkled as a walnut. She was sewing on a tablecloth, but set this to one side as soon as she became aware of her visitors. Smiling with delight, she ushered them inside.

'May I get you some refreshments?' she asked.

'You speak English.' Coriander was surprised.

'I learned it many years ago when I worked at the *quinta*.' She glanced at Raul. 'Good morning, Viscount.'

Coriander was taken aback on hearing Raul so addressed, and then embarrassed at her own foolishness. Raul only smiled.

'I would recommend, Maria, that you

continue to call me what you always have.'

The old woman grinned, showing still white teeth. 'I did not always call you good names,' she chided, and he laughed again, a merry sound that somehow warmed Coriander. Turning to her, he explained.

'Maria looked after me when I was a small boy. She often had need to reprimand me and call me a rascal.'

'Ah, but you were not a bad boy. Not like ...' There was a small silence in which Coriander expected Raul to explain or Maria to offer her condolences. Neither did. At length the old woman invited Coriander to be seated before the wood-burning fire and offered her fruit and wine, which she felt obliged to accept though had little appetite for either.

While Maria fetched them, Coriander looked about her. The house was sparsely furnished. Besides the wicker chair upon which Coriander now sat there was a wooden table and some three-legged stools, a wide stone oven where Coriander could see a freshly baked batch of bread and a door which led off into a bedroom. Coriander glimpsed a carved pine bed covered by a delicately embroidered coverlet. Despite the smallness of the house, the whole place seemed light and airy and bright as a new pin.

'I came here as a bride,' Maria explained, taking the seat opposite. 'I have had four children in this house and seen them all married. Now I welcome my grandchildren here.'

'You must be very proud of them,' Coriander said, wondering where this was all leading.

'They are important to me, and to my husband Fernando.' The dark eyes in the high-cheekboned face seemed to look beyond Coriander, as if they saw a different time, a different place. The silence lasted for a long time as they sipped at the delectable wine. 'You are very like Cassandra. You have her smile.'

Coriander edged forward in her seat. 'You knew my mother?'

'She was my niece.' Maria nodded sadly. 'She was ever the odd one out. Not content with life as it was. I hope you are not that way.'

Coriander flushed prettily. 'I hope I am not.'

'Her mother, my sister Rosa, your grandmother—you understand?—' Coriander indicated that she did '—sometimes despaired of this beautiful, wilful daughter who would not accept her station in life and then met with such a tragic end.'

Coriander set her glass aside and with half her attention noted that Raul must have quietly withdrawn, for the two of them sat alone in the circle of firelight.

'Rosa and I always worked at the *quinta*. It was good work, well paid and the Beringer family were kind. Mostly we were blessed with sons who went to work in the fields, but Rosa produced this beautiful girl child and when she was old enough we took her with us to the *quinta*. Everyone fell in love with her. She was not dark like the other children, but fair, unusual but not unknown on Madeira.' The old woman smiled coyly, looking oddly young for a moment. 'English soldiers have visited Madeira in the past also. The colouring comes out from time to time. Because of her beauty Cassandra was spoiled and allowed to play with the two brothers, though she was a little older than them. When she was sixteen she was given a job and money of her own. But it was not enough. She wanted more. When Carl Beringer's wife died, Cassandra set out to ensnare him. She had no shame.'

Coriander lost her appetite for the tale. Perhaps she had idealised her mother, and to find that like others she had feet of clay was more than she could take. Please tell me no more, she wanted to say, but could not find the words.

'She did not care about love, not until she met Josiah Leite. He too was a wine merchant of English extraction, but not so wealthy as the Beringers. But Cassandra found that she loved him.' Maria paused. 'I know you have heard all this from Raul. But what you do not know is why she did not marry her beloved Jos and what happened after Cassandra sailed for England. It was all very simple. The two lovers had been meeting in secret and Josiah begged her to call off the arranged marriage with Carl Beringer. Cassandra could not bring herself to do so, unwilling to admit that what she felt for Jos was truly love and more important than any riches. When she did finally break the betrothal, it was too late. Jos had already left for America, his heart broken. Carl Beringer would have proceeded with the marriage but, knowing she was with child, to her credit, Cassandra declined, not wishing to sully the Beringer name. She married a young, besotted admirer who would have been a good husband to her, if the good Lord had allowed it.'

Coriander was staring at the knotted fingers in her lap. 'And when you heard they had died?'

'Rosa said it was God's punishment and we thought that was the end of the matter. And then we got word about you.' Maria looked at Coriander boldly. 'I dare say you thought us cruel not to bring you home

378

to your family. At first Rosa could not bear the scandal and decided it was better you stay in England. Then later, after her husband died, she might have done something. I believe she wrote to you.'

'Yes,' Coriander burst in.

Again the faraway look in the dark eyes. 'But Rosa had never recovered from the loss of her lovely child, and now her beloved husband had gone and with him her will to live.' Maria fell silent and Coriander did not interrupt her thoughts. After a moment she lifted her head and smiled at Coriander. 'My husband works at the wine company. When he saw you there, he said it was as if the clock had turned back the years and it was Cassandra standing before him. And when Raul asked him for my help in searching for your lost family in Ribeira Brava we knew it was you. We welcome you at last back into your family, Coriander, and hope you will not think too harshly on those long gone who did only what they felt able to do.'

Coriander fell to her knees before the old woman, tears starring her eyes. 'I shall never do so. I am glad to have found you, whatever the circumstances.' The two women embraced, but it was the older one to break away first. 'There is something else, Coriander. Your father, Josiah Leite, did make a fortune in America and, like many other émigrés, returned to his homeland of Madeira. He too is dead, but left for you all his land and his money. We have kept it in good faith for you, but now it is yours.'

The old woman stood up and went to a cupboard set in the wall, from which she drew a small box. In the box were documents which gave all the details of a private income and the land which was hers on Madeira, including a house. Coriander was a woman of means in her own right, left her by her own father. More importantly, to her, it meant he had cared enough about her and Cassandra to bestow it upon her. She looked instinctively for Raul to share this revelation with him, but he was not there and the pleasure in her news turned to ashes in her mouth. Blinking back the tears, she grasped the old woman's hands firmly between both her own.

'I have no use for land on Madeira. Give it to your sons. One day I too shall return and they can show me what they have grown on it.'

'You are generous,' said Maria, and now the tears were in her own eyes. 'We are poor people. This land is good land and we have tilled it. But always knowing one day you may come to claim it.'

'Now it is yours, for all time.' Once

more they embraced, and when Coriander left it was with promises to write and keep in touch, and one day not too far distant to return. Privately she wondered if that was a promise she could keep.

'That was a kindness you did in there,' Raul said.

She did not look up at him, so failed to see the softening flicker of emotion which momentarily crossed his face.

'It seemed sensible.'

His face tightened. 'And you are well satisfied, since at last you are a woman of fortune?'

Coriander turned to him in cold fury. 'You will never understand, will you? I wished only for modest security and to know where I belonged, that is all.'

'And to have your independence.'

'What is wrong with that?'

'Sometimes it comes at a high price.'

'At least I am honest about my wish for it. You pretend to need me, your wife, then ignore me or reject me for another. You do not need me, Raul Beringer, only the share in the wine company I hold. Well, it is yours, you can have it. For I have that which my own father left me. I have no more use for you or your money.' Coriander was close to tears, but was fiercely determined not to show it.

Raul eyed her with a thoughtful scowl.

'You have got what you came for. Do you now intend to stay and enjoy it?'

She turned her eyes to his and looked into their cold green depths, thinking for a moment of what might have been, but then turned away, unable to bear it. 'I see no reason to stay.'

As the *Mercury* sailed out of the harbour, Raul watched it go with deep sadness in his heart. So many mistakes. If he only had the power to undo them. But what was the use of that, for even as she accused him of selfish obsessions over the wine company she spoke of how important the income left to her by an unknown father was. Far more, it seemed, than him. The evil of money. How he hated it. The Beringer family had squabbled over it throughout his entire lifetime and now his unstable brother was dead because of it. And even in death Maynard had succeeded in despoiling all hope of happiness with Coriander. Hunching his shoulders against the coolness of the wind, Raul turned and set off on the long, lonely walk home back to an empty *quinta*.

'I think you are the most cross-grained nincompoop I ever did see.' Letitia Larken scowled at Coriander, making her feel the recalcitrant schoolgirl once again. 'How could you be so foolish as to leave him?'

'He did not want me.'

'What arrant nonsense. Did he say that he did not?'

'N-no.'

'Well, then?'

Coriander sighed. They had been over this ground so many times in the weeks since she had returned home, she had long grown weary of the constant castigations. 'Sometimes it is not necessary to hear the words,' she explained for the umpteenth time. 'I feel he had only one love in his life, his wine company, and there was Isabella to satisfy—other needs.'

Letitia clicked her tongue in irritated disapproval. 'A wife does not win her place by handing it over to the mistress. I despair of you, Coriander, for this is most unlike you. Where has your spirit gone, girl? Is he not worth fighting for?'

Coriander set aside the lace she was mending with a weary sigh; the stitches were all wrong in any case and would have to come out. She did not feel up to Letty's cross-patch scolding this morning. Indeed she felt decidedly under the weather. 'As I have already told you, Letty. Since Raul plainly showed his preference for Isabella had not diminished and his interest in his business was all-consuming, even to the point of murder, not to mention breaking our wedding journey for a little light treasure-seeking, I saw no possibility of continuing to live with such a man. The marriage was a sham. And now I would be obliged if we can put the matter behind us and not mention it again.'

'You are both of you stubborn children, each refusing to admit mistakes and come together.'

'We can never come together,' said Coriander with bitter certainty.

'Are we never to go to Madeira, then?' asked Pearl in the smallest of voices. 'It is not that I am unhappy here, Coriander. This is a fine house Ned found for us to rent, and near enough for me to still call upon Tom and Edward at Lady Wilchester's, but I was looking forward to seeing Madeira. You wrote such magical letters about it.' Her young eyes shone and Coriander knew again the pain of guilt. 'And I would so have enjoyed making my own garden.'

'You shall have a garden, Pearl,' cried Coriander jumping to her feet. 'An English one. We will return to Larken's Farm and make it beautiful again. We will work the land and create our own little world.' Her eyes were glassy with unshed tears.

'Oh, I forgot to tell you. I sold Larken's Farm and have invested the proceeds for a small income for myself. I am not getting any younger,' confessed Letitia when she saw the expression in Coriander's eyes. 'The farm was too much for me.'

Coriander's shoulders sagged. 'I know,' she said, popping a kiss on the elderly woman's still smooth brow. 'Then we could find another little house in the country if you prefer.'

'Pearl, you must not complain about matters which are quite irrelevant,' said Letitia sternly, then, turning her forget-me-not eyes to Coriander with bland innocence, added, 'It is not the place which is important but the people in it. Except to decide where your baby will be born.'

There was a small stunned silence in which Coriander sank weak-kneed back into the chair she had just vacated. 'B-baby?' she said at last. 'What baby?'

Letitia smiled benignly. 'Do not think I have not noticed how you have chosen to take tea in bed in the mornings and have quite gone off fish for luncheon. You look decidedly peaky at this very moment. I venture to suggest, though I confess I know little of such matters, that it will prove to be a girl. Lady Wilchester certainly thinks so.'

Coriander was aghast. 'You have discussed me with Lady Wilchester?'

Letitia looked vaguely affronted, as if she had been accused of some dreadful crime. 'Christina is my dearest friend. Why should I not? Is it something to be ashamed of?'

Coriander felt quite unequal to combating this argument. At length she said, 'I would have preferred the opportunity to spread the news myself. And I must ask you to make it clear to Christina that on no account must Raul be told of it.'

'Pshaw! What nonsense.'

Coriander was on her feet again and there was no mistaking the light of battle in her eyes. 'I mean it, Letty. If you go against me on this, I shall not be responsible for the consequences, particularly with regard to our friendship. I have no desire to appear to beg for Raul's consideration or care. I am perfectly well able to care for the baby myself.' One tear rolled untidily from the corner of an eye and slipped traitorously down her cheek. 'I can at least save my pride.' With this parting shot she made for the door. But Letitia had not done.

'What place has pride where love is concerned?'

Coriander stumbled momentarily before fleeing from the room, her will-power almost in shreds.

And so the days passed in comparative peace and idle, if mundane pursuits. Since the news was out in the open, Coriander took to sewing baby clothes. She looked forward to the birth of her baby and meant it to have every advantage which love and motherly care could bring. Everything of which she had been deprived. She tried not to think of her child's need for a father.

One day as she was thus employed in the small blue drawing-room there came a tap upon the door.

'What is it, Ned?' she called, recognising the sound.

The door opened and the old man bustled in, somewhat flustered. Ned had opted to return with her to England and she had been glad of his company. Invaluable in helping her deal with affairs, he had now undertaken the duties of butler, which she confessed did not entirely suit him, but he seemed content enough.

'There be someone to see you, ma'am.'

'Who is it?'

'He would not give his name.'

Coriander frowned. 'Then show him in so that I can discover it. Oh, and hold the tea until Letitia and Pearl return from their walk, will you? I dare say this is only a message from Mr Brownlow wishing me to sign yet another document or other.'

'Very good, ma'am.' Ned withdrew, stiff with the grandeur of his new appointment, and Coriander smiled. She could not imagine life without him now. But just as quickly the smile faded for she had said that before, about another, of far greater importance to her than dear Ned.

'Well, then, Coriander May, you'm come a long way, eh?'

The tiny matinee coat she had been stitching slid to the floor as Coriander stared in startled dismay at her visitor. He stood, needle-sharp upon her rug, a figment of her past sprung to life.

'Ezra Follett.' She said his name on a hoarse whisper and he grinned, showing the familiar yellow teeth sloping inwards, the rasps of his breath coming in uneven little gasps.

'Glad to see you've not forgotten me.'

'How could I ever?'

His bright weasel eyes raked the fashionable drawing-room. 'You've done all right for yourself, that's for sure. Ain't ye going to ask me to sit down, then?'

She was tempted to say no, but thought better of it. The only way to deal with Ezra Follett was to have the patience to hear him out. He must be here for a reason, and the sooner he said his piece, the sooner she could be rid of him. It took little effort to guess the line he would take. 'Be seated if you must,' she said, elegantly reclaiming her sewing, 'but whatever it is you want I very much doubt you'll get it.' She met his pale gaze with determination in her own and was relieved to find she could do so without qualm.

'Well, then, if that's the way it is, let's to business.' Tweaking the knees of his grubby breeches, he sat down, his skinny frame looking incongruous upon the embroidered seat of the fashionable Regency chair. 'You remember we had some once that was left unfinished.'

Coriander raised surprised brows. 'I think you must be mistaken.'

He shook his head. 'Oh, no, I'm never that. Make it my policy in life not to be. Those fifty sovereigns we once shared—'

'Shared?' Coriander gasped, unable to prevent herself from butting in once more.

'Oh, I know I promised to keep an eye on your share for ye, but you'll not be a-wanting it now you'm so well off. Problem is, things are more expensive nowadays and I find myself, to be frank, a bit embarrassed for funds.'

'That is your problem,' said Coriander icily. 'You and I had no agreement about money, as you well know, Ezra Follett. It was from you I meant to steal that night. You owed it to me, to us all, not least Letty for your petty thieving over the years.' She realised as she spoke that all fear of Ezra Follett had quite gone. She could look upon him now with equanimity and see him for what he was, a grubby little worm of a man who should be kept as far away from civilised humanity as possible. 'I think you'd best leave. We have nothing to say to each other.'

'Oh, but I've something to say to you.' His eyes narrowed and the smile died. 'You left me without a roof over my head, which I consider to be most inconsiderate, most inconsiderate indeed. How would you like it? I feel I deserve some recompense for that inconvenience.'

'Oh? And what do you suggest?'

'Five hundred guineas would do for a start.'

Coriander gasped. 'Five hundred—'

'Guineas. Later we can discuss a more settled figure. For now that will establish me in a place as pleasant o' this one of yourn.' He flicked a glance casually over the elegant furnishings. 'T'ain't a bad place this at all. Mebbe I can find a like one nearby.'

Coriander's voice dripped with icy contempt as she answered him. 'I can imagine no circumstances in which I would be persuaded to give you a farthing.'

'Oh, I reckon that's not the case. After all, you wouldn't want these fancy neighbours o' yours learning of how you spent your youth, now would you? Shouldn't think they'd care to share their pretty tea tables with a felon.'

Coriander felt as if she were about to

choke, but, getting to her feet, she stood rocklike before him, not a tremor in any muscle. 'Get out of my house, Ezra Follett, and never come back if you know what's good for you. Think yourself lucky that my husband is not present.'

'Husband?' He paled visibly.

'That is what I said. My husband, Raul Beringer, the Viscount. He would stand no nonsense from your scurvy dealings. Feel free to tell anyone whatever you choose. I doubt you will tell them anything I have not already told them myself, certainly those people who matter to me. As for the rest, I do not care a jot what they think. I refuse to be blackmailed by you. Take your miserable scum of a body and deposit it outside my house.'

Ezra Follett leaped to his feet and advanced a step towards her. For a second she experienced a flicker of the old fear, but then it was gone and she met his gaze with a detached hauteur.

'Were you requiring any help, m'lady?' The door had softly opened and Ned stood within the room, small, solid and four square, the years of sea-faring showing in every toughened muscle and sinew.

'I believe Mr Follett is just leaving,' said Coriander. 'I doubt he'll be troubling us again.' She did not let out the held breath until Ezra Follett had indeed shuffled from the room, every step showing him for a defeated man. Coriander sank shakily back into her chair.

'Follett have gone, and I can vouch for it that he'll not return,' confirmed Ned some moments later. He had disliked the man on sight and had taken great pleasure in throwing him bodily into the street so that he'd had to scurry out of the way of a passing carriage, even grubbier as a result, with Ned's words of what would befall him if he returned ringing in his boxed ears. 'And Mistress Letty and Pearl be returned.'

Coriander drew a relaxing breath. 'Thank you, Ned. Please bring in the tea, will you?'

As the old sailor withdrew, Coriander felt a surge of satisfaction that she had managed to stand up to Ezra Follett so well. Never again would she fear him. He was gone from her life and she felt cleansed. She had everything that she had ever wanted. Freedom from Ezra Follett's tyranny, security in the shape of a home and modest income, friends in Letty and Pearl. And even a baby of her own on the way. Why then did she feel so utterly miserable? Did she need to ask? But there was nothing she could do about it. Even if she took Letty's advice to return to Madeira, she could not do so yet because of the baby. The pain in her breast at this thought was almost unendurable, and now her body did begin to shake, though not in reaction to Follett's threats. But because by the time her baby was born she guessed it would be too late for any hope of reconciliation, if it was not so already.

Raul glanced up from his desk in irritation as Fernando entered the office. 'What is it?' he barked.

'Last season's wine is ready for tasting,' ventured the Madeiran.

'Can't you manage it yourself?' came the stinging reply, and Fernando sighed. Mr Raul is not the man he was, he told his beloved Maria constantly. Always now he is hot-tempered and unpredictable as a volcano. If only his Maria had tried to keep the girl on the island instead of letting her go. Mr Raul had not been the same patient gentleman since that day.

'You usually enjoy the tasting and the sniffing. I not like to deprive you,' he said.

Raul slammed shut the ledger he was working on and, pushing back his chair so ferociously it overturned, he strode unheeding to the door. 'I dare say for once you can manage it by yourself. I'm sure I shall survive the deprivation. I grow used to it.' Slamming the door on these parting words, he did what he had never done before in his life, and that was to leave unfinished business on his desk and stride out through the town and out on to the headlands where he stopped to stare bleakly out to sea.

It was as if he had the power to see across the miles which divided them. He saw Coriander as she had been on that day so long ago, young and fresh in her skinny, ill-fitting gown, fetching water for his horses in that dingy stable. His heart ached at the memory. Many times he had thought of provisioning a ship and setting sail for England. But what could he say to her?

He picked up a stone and threw it far out to sea. He did not hear the splash, only a silence, an empty void like his own life. How could he endure it without her? He had recognised the growing attraction he felt for her long since, but knew now it was more, much more. He loved her. It was as simple and as complicated as that. Closing his eyes, he brought her picture once more to mind as he did every day for fear he might forget the mischievous beauty of her smile, the glow of her hair, the artless passion of her lovemaking. They had become as one person on that first magical night as man and wife, a spiritual gift one to the other. She had given herself totally and generously in her love to him, and he had rewarded her by taking his mistress on their wedding journey. Could he ever forgive himself for such crass tactlessness? Could she? Could she ever believe that Maynard's death had been unintentional, if not exactly surprising? Their bitter fights had ever ended with himself as the victor. Unfortunately the consequences this time had been more final.

He had diligently carried out his duties to the British Consul and recovered the treasure Maynard had stolen from Portuguese waters, just as he had carried out the Regent's duties. Raul smiled bitterly to himself. A man of duty and loyalty, indeed, but at what cost to his own happiness? And what do you intend to do about it? How many times that small voice had asked that innocuous question over the last months. How many times he had got so far as striding down to the harbour, even on one occasion calling a crew together. What had stopped him? The answer came sharp and chilling. Pride. After years spent with an uncaring father and warring brother he had lost the art of showing his feelings.

Raul stared once more out to sea, which was empty but for a single ship making its way into port. A wind sprang up and

Raul shivered, his brow furrowed in deep thought. Then he was whirling on his heel and running, stumbling in his eagerness to reach the harbour. He would call his crew once again, only this time there would be no change of mind. He would sail to England, find Coriander and make her believe him. He would prove his love for her if it took the rest of his life.

His booted heels rang loud on the harbour stone as he galloped along it, calling as he went. 'Pedro. Joel. Find the men. Prepare the ship for sailing.'

But he got no further, for there before him was a miracle. The answer to his prayers and night-time dreams. But this was no orphan child in an ill-fitting dress. This was an elegant, assured woman in an organza dress, her shining crown of silver curls threaded with pink satin ribbon.

'*Obrigada,* Raul,' said Coriander, smiling shyly, and then every breath was vanquished from her body as he swept her up in a crushing embrace.

'My darling, darling, Coriander,' he murmured, as he took her lips in a deeply rapturous kiss. It was Coriander who finally insisted on extricating herself from his embrace, and for a long moment they were content only to look into each other's eyes and absorb all the unspoken desires.

'Do I take it that you are pleased to see me?'

His answer was a growl of despair and she laughed softly, tracing with her eyes every beloved feature of his face. Then she looked about her with the faintest hint of anxiety.

'Isabella is not with you?'

For a moment she thought Raul would explode, so tense was he, but he merely tightened his lips and said that no, she had returned to her family as she had often wished to do. 'Isabella was nothing to me,' he said with a humble sincerity. 'Nothing happened between us on the ship.'

'I believe you.' Reaching out a hand, she stroked his cheek, and he grasped it and pressed his lips into the palm. There would be explanations, and apologies, of course. But nothing could spoil the magic of this homecoming, and she knew with a wondrous certainty that she had done the right thing. Independence was a hollow victory without love to temper it. Cassandra had left it too late to return to her lover. Her daughter had no intention of making the same mistake. As if this thought had reminded her of something, she turned from him and walked back to Pearl and Letty who stood with Ned at a polite distance. Letty handed the bundle to her with a smile upon her good-natured face, and Coriander took it gently from her and, walking back, placed it in her husband's wondering arms.

'I fear she has my stupidly colourless hair, but your beautiful green eyes. I think one day she may break a few hearts.'

Raul pulled back the soft blanket and gazed with astonishment and the awe of new-found love upon his daughter. A nerve flickered at the corner of his mouth as if the emotion of the moment was too much for him. Then his tender gaze met Coriander's and they both smiled.

'Isn't there something you should tell me?' Coriander probed. 'Something you have never yet said.'

Raul's eyes looked faintly bewildered for a half-second, and then he smiled. 'I'm not very good with words. I suggest we take our new family home, for I have matters which need urgent attention with her mother, feelings of ... which require ... demonstration.'

'I shall not quarrel with that,' Coriander agreed, tilting her face for a kiss.

'Then that will make a pleasant change,' murmured Raul with a return of his roguish wit, and he slipped an arm about her shoulders, the other proudly cradling his daughter close. And together, the Beringer family and friends made their way home.

This Large Print Book for the Partially sighted, who cannot read normal print, is published under the auspices of

THE ULVERSCROFT FOUNDATION

THE ULVERSCROFT FOUNDATION

. . . we hope that you have enjoyed this Large Print Book. Please think for a moment about those people who have worse eyesight problems than you . . . and are unable to even read or enjoy Large Print, without great difficulty.

You can help them by sending a donation, large or small to:

**The Ulverscroft Foundation,
1, The Green, Bradgate Road,
Anstey, Leicestershire, LE7 7FU,
England.**
or request a copy of our brochure for more details.

The Foundation will use all your help to assist those people who are handicapped by various sight problems and need special attention.

Thank you very much for your help.